MY JOURNEY THROUGH TIME
First Stop

T.W. O'Dell

ISBN: 0991190009
ISBN-13: 978-0-9911900-0-3

DEDICATION

This book is dedicated to my boys along with the rest of my family, and my friends who have always been there for me.

More importantly I dedicate this book to my angel, she's my light in the window, and my heart's only desire, without whom I wouldn't know how wonderful someone can truly be (she even occasionally makes me sound like a greeting card), my beautiful wife.

CONTENTS

ACKNOWLEDGMENTS

Melissa Ravelli My Wonderful Editor without whom this book would probably still be in development and not half as good as it is now.
Carolyn Gill My Exquisite Graphic Designer who made the front and back covers come to life, and tell you a little of what you can expect to read about.

PROLOGUE

Fourth of July 2215: I was woken at zero-one-hundred by the voice of the base alarm. 'SECURITY BREECH ON LEVEL TWENTY' the voice echoed through my head. Checking the base hologram next to my rack shows the security breech is located in the Time Lab.

"Oye, not again," I grumble.

As a security officer I'm required to check out every alarm, but having connections in that particular lab, I already know there have been several false alarms there over the past few months; the research they are conducting is messing with the security sensors.

"At least this should be quick," I say to myself while jumping up and grabbing my shirt, pants, belt and 'Ballistic Armor-Piercing Rounds Blaster' or BARB from under my pillow. Quickly stumbling out of the room still stepping into my left boot I make my way down the corridor toward the elevators.

In an effort to be efficient all of the security Officer's quarters and offices are on level ten, the middle of the underground facility, which happily for me means less travel time to check this "emergency" out and return to my nice warm bed.

Entering the elevator, I consider my misfortune in pulling emergency response duty for tonight. Knowing the answer gave little comfort of course; the base had been running a skeleton crew for the last week, due to some maintenance that needed to be performed on the ventilation system, apparently people suffocating is a bad thing. Anyway being the senior security officer I would normally have the time off, but seeing as most of the other military detail had permanent off base accommodations, and my little get away conveniently fell through at the last minute, well you get the picture.

The descending elevator begins to shake, then seems to fall the last ten feet dropping me flat on my ass before it stops at the bottom level.

"What the hell was that?" I exclaim, as the elevator doors open to blaring fire alarm sirens.

Immediately smelling what could be mistaken for warm chocolate chip cookies. I realize with the amount of particulates in the air it must be that new form of Research Department Explosive (RDX) plastic RD-12 they're working on, a few levels up. Only knowing this as I was able to attend one of the other researchers' tests on the stuff last month. I remember thinking 'That was one hell of a fireball, wonder if it comes in peanut butter'.

Approaching the lab I notice, the four foot thick carbon steel security door is missing. Not open, not ajar like my car would have you believe, but gone, like a cat burglar had a taste for four foot carbon steel doors, and chocolate chip cookies. Drawing my BARB, and peering into the room cautiously I remark, "This is definitely *not* a false alarm."

Realizing there's now no chance for sleep tonight, my adrenal glands have kicked in and my heart is doing its best to pound itself out of my chest. I peak around the corner, nothing seems out of place in the immediate entry to the lab; well other than that vaporized two ton door, and what is now starting to smell more like burnt cookie dough than chocolate chip. At which point I figure I'm going to be doing paperwork until I'm sixty four. Which is a lot of paperwork when you consider I'm only thirty two now.

The lab is set up as most offices would be, a traditional entry with a reception and seating area. Followed by offices for the Scientists that work the lab, and finally in the very back, the actual lab itself, usually sealed by another form of security measure.

In this case we're talking about the most secured lab on base, so it is equipped with all the toys, a second massive door, a series of biometric locks including a retinal scanner with hand print analyzer, and voice recognition.

Smacking the base alarm on the wall just outside the lab, the loud emergency siren begins ringing throughout the base. Overpowering the fire alarm for this floor; not only is the emergency alarm much louder it's an almost disorienting sound, this also causes the yellow warning lights to turn red.

We have all of twenty or so people on site due to the ventilation system maintenance, but I'm hoping that the siren will keep whoever is in there from hearing me creep in on them, and perhaps disorient them enough to make my job a little easier.

Now entering the reception area it still appears clear although the hairs on the back of my neck are now standing on end. I see that the door to the offices is slightly open. As I sneak up and peer through the narrow opening I can see two men yelling back and forth to one another. One is a stocky bald man with a beard, and mustache. He kind of looks like Gimli from the 'Lord of the Rings' books actually. The second is a tall muscular man, with what looks like a Special Forces military tattoo on his forearm.

They appear to be guarding the lab entry. Which has wires hanging out of the retinal scanner and the handprint reader. The stocky one looks startled by the new screeching alarm.

"At least something is going my way," muttering to myself.

The taller man yells at him, "Just relax the whole base is on leave for the ventilation system maintenance, remember?"

"Not all of them," I mock, kicking open the door BARB in hand. "Now drop your weapons!"

They both look startled, and not at all like they're going to drop their weapons. The taller one quickly elevates the front of his automatic rifle toward me the stocky one follows suit, I open fire. Two shots and it's all over, with a BARB the explosive round setting will completely incapacitate if not kill in one shot, no matter where it hits. Thanks to my own Special Forces training these two jokers were hit, square in the forehead, they obviously suffered the latter.

"So much for questioning them I suppose…"

I cautiously approach the lab door they were guarding, with all its extra security precautions that seem to not have helped out at all, and immediately recognize the greatest fear of this facility, the audible sound of an open time portal. A sound only known to me because my older sister Dane, the lead Scientist in this lab.

Dane is the one that introduced me to this facility, and helped me get this job, once I returned from my tour in the Antarctic. I mean sure my Special Forces background and Intelligence community experience and connections made me a shoe in, but she made the initial introductions. She, and I were even roommates in an off base residence for a while, where she shared many of her latest advances, and lab secrets. That is until she decided to marry a creepy scientist from the 'Viper' lab on level thirteen, which of course forced me to seek other off base housing or move on to the base permanently. Of course moving onto the base was all I could afford by myself.

Entering the lab it's already too late, the bright blue light from the glowing incandescent time portal is an ominous foreshadowing of events to come. Unfortunately, the mastermind behind this little escapade has already made their jump. The read out on the console to the left of the portal says August first nineteen thirty four. The walls start to change around me almost instantly, paint disappearing to bare cement. Glancing over my shoulder, the hallway I've just come from now appears to be dilapidated and collapsing in on itself as if it had been heavily bombarded from above. The two bodies I just dropped are now gone.

To the left of the control console is a large standing safe digitally controlled and state of the art. This is where Dane keeps her top, top secret project the 'Relativistic Prototype'. This is the device that can do what all these fancy gizmos that take up an entire warehouse of a room can, but fits on your forearm almost like one of those carpel tunnel wrist braces. So far due to the limitation of equipment size time travel has been a one way trip, and limited to passing notes to five minutes ago in the lab environment. Unfortunately that means the *'Relativistic Prototype'* has never been field tested, or even listed as semi-operational, but it's the only thing that can return me home once I deal with this idiot.

Quickly examining the keypad I punch in the only set of numbers that pop into my head, my own birthday zero-seven-one-zero-two-one-eight-six it opens.

"Wow that was kind of narcissistic, but thanks big sister…" I remark.

Grabbing the *'RP'*, I start to remember all the long conversations with Dane about the space time continuum, and "what it meant to me". The first thing that came to mind was this portal was due to collapse in on itself at any second, and looking around at the walls they are definitely starting to age what appears to be faster and faster, stress fractures appear out of thin air, like spider webs up the now bare cement walls.

Now realizing the only reason this room and I haven't completely transformed, or worse ceased to exist entirely is because of our relative proximity to the still open time portal.

To the right of the portal platform, is a rack of "Expedition packs", they are labeled according to time period and meant to be filled with things one might need on a sightseeing trip, pure water, medical supplies, flashlights or torches, period clothing, temporal emergency beacons, but be invisible to the naked eye. In fact the only reason you can see the bags now is due to the special light the rack sits under. I grab one labeled 'Johnny' hanging near the portal, and jump in.

T.W. O'Dell

1 A NEW WORLD

Regaining consciousness, my forehead is bleeding all over the rock it landed on, feeling the blood drip off my brow is almost sobering, you know, if it didn't hurt so bad.

Of course my life could actually be in danger from a massive concussion or blood loss, as there is quite a bit of blood. I'm reminded of what it feels like to be hit in the head with a golf club. Which seems like I've always imagined having your head backed over with a truck would, but that's a story for another day.

With blurred vision I can only guess that exiting the other side of the then unstable portal rematerialized me backwards launching me into a tree, and smacking me right in the occipital lobe or visual cortex.

Something they taught us in basic training for Special Ops, in order to disorient your opponent hit them in the back of the head, leaving them unable to focus, possibly knocking them out all together or potentially blinding them for a time, you know what they say "it's all fun and games until someone loses an eye", or in this case "can't see because their neural pathways are scrambled."

Lying flat on my stomach, it takes some time to collect myself. Listening to the new surroundings there are birds all around, it lacks the sounds of modern civilization, no car horns, no people, and the ground feels like it's covered in leaves, well, other than the bloody rock part.

Turning my head to the right, I start to blink the world back into focus from my limited, fuzzy view, it appears I'm in a forest. The weather seems pleasant at least, feels like the mid-seventies if I had to guess. It occurs to me I don't know where, or even *when* I am, so I guess if I'm going to die at least it'll be a mystery.

Recalling some of our late night conversations there was a particular instance when Dane had informed me that the longer a time portal stays open the closer to the creation time and place it becomes, until it finally syncs with the original portal and collapses in on itself entirely. So the only information that's certain at the moment is, it's very unlikely I made it all the way back to nineteen thirty four, and that my exit point is nowhere near the portals' original destination longitude and latitude. A fact which completely missed my attention in the rush to get through the portal in the first place.

"ahhh, Damnit…" I mutter.

"Huh, Well, at least my mouth still works," remarking as I rotate my jaw and roll over onto my back to sit up, blood now sliding towards my ears, and getting all over the back of my head.

Propping myself onto my elbows and attempting to survey the land as my vision finally begins returning to normal. I notice the expedition pack with my name on it had landed next to me.

Finally managing to make it into a sitting position is dizzying but opening the pack, I find a small medical kit at the top. "Odd coincidence." Thinking out loud again, and looking around like I'm on one of those gag television shows.

Inside I find a mirror that shows a fair amount of blood on my face, basically everywhere. As anyone who's ever had a head wound will tell you, they bleed like crazy. Tearing open a presoaked alcohol wipe, I attempt to clean what appears to be a decent gash, and wipe the rest of the blood from my forehead, and face. Then apply a '*Regenerative Tissue Stimulator*'. I know they say the alcohol is a useless step now, but I'm old fashioned when it comes to germs, plus I needed to wipe off my face anyway. My sister always called me a 'Germaphobe', but hey a little extra caution never hurt anyone right?

Once the Regenerative Tissue Stimulator has completed its cycle I check the readout which reports:

Laceration… *Sealed*

Surrounding Abrasion… *Repaired*

Concussion Sustained… *Steroid & NSAID Administered*

I put the Regenerative Tissue Stimulator back in the medical kit setting it to the side, and remove a small MRE from the Expedition pack. I'm not sure how long I was knocked out, but it seems like I haven't eaten in a day, so even the MRE tastes gourmet. That could just be the concussion talking though.

After finishing off my 'meal', my head is still pounding, but it's time to get up and get my bearings. Using a tree to steady myself, and looking around I start to take a blurry inventory of what made it through the portal with me.

Seeing the '*Relativistic Prototype*' a few feet from where I had been laid out, under a fallen tree branch causes a sigh of relief. Its outer casing appears to be okay, but it doesn't turn on.

"Oh for cry'n out loud!" I comment through gritted teeth. Then slumping back down to a seated position on a nearby downed tree branch.

Starting to smile I recall a conversation with Dane, "the outer shell is constructed of a newly developed, insulated Titanium Molybdenum composite, which allows for extreme light weight and copious amounts of protection, the thing's nearly impregnable," she told me. Laughing at the time I remarked that seemed like "overkill". She just smiled and said "Well I've got to make it tough enough to deal with you, don't I?"

"Well, nothing I can do about that now…," talking to myself again.

Looking at it I also remember her saying that this unit is designed to be worn on your wrist up to your elbow, and have control over the "entire space time continuum at the touch of a button", or a thought, or something like that. Dane never did get around to explaining all the intricacies, but she did tell me that touching it should turn it on, or at least illicit some reaction.

"Suppose I'll have to figure that out as I go too…" reaching back to feel the knot on the back of my head.

"So; Now I have to repair a device that was still in the 'prototype' stage? This thing may or may not have ever even worked in the first place. SERIOUSLY?!" I shout, my head pounding from my own loud mouth.

"Dane should be here, this is her thing, not mine." Clutching my head and whispering, as if to appease my own pain.

Sitting there and trying to critically assess the situation is almost a joke at this point. Dusk is setting in rapidly and the day was well on its way to sunset.

With no interest in wandering around an unknown forest in the dark, I conclude that it's probably best to start setting up camp for the evening. There's clearly no point in getting lost any more than I already am.

The pain in my head is starting to dull a bit, but it is still throbbing. The one clear thought I'm able to muster is that I have to get a fire going or risk freezing tonight. The temperature has already dropped considerably and the sun isn't even all the way down yet.

Rising from my seat, I drop the 'RP' and begin to collect some closely situated rocks arranging them in a circle for a hearth, before gathering a few small branches and some dried leaves. My head throbs every time I bend over, but I know I can't stop collecting materials to start the fire.

Luckily my BARB is the latest design, thanks to Dane bumping me to the front of the beta list. So the advanced hand cannon can switch from using a traditional forty five caliber round, to my personal favorite the forty five caliber 'explosive rounds'.

These have a very high phosphorous content and are much like what used to be called "tracers" a few hundred years ago, they cut through metal like a hot knife through melted butter, and then they explode. Really allows you to "reach out and touch someone" if you catch my meaning. I've "heard" they're especially useful for hunting a target with infrared goggles and being on the other side of a wall.

The trick is setting the charge timer, which is done on the BARB itself so that the projectile knows when to detonate. Too long and you may go through the next wall, too short and you may not penetrate the first wall. Luckily modern tactical infrared goggles provide the numbers for you. Otherwise by the time you did all the math, the target would have moved, and or shot you. Which according to the latest Special Forces handbook is not the optimal outcome.

Those have been the two standards for almost forty years in my time. Now there are the two new design implementations; a mode I could only refer to as a 'lightning gun'. Which basically will either stun your opponent or fry them, depending on your mood, or settings. Of course if they have a pacemaker or an artificial organ of some kind, they're in real trouble either way, apparently there's an electromagnetic pulse aspect to this setting they have yet to work out, or the fact that it's so much current that it's basically frying any electronics you shoot with it. I don't know the specifics but I've been warned that it's still in 'beta' testing for a reason.

The other new mode is what Dane called a particle beam, which just looks like a high powered laser to me. Apparently it sucks particles in from the air around it, and then fires them in a continuous stream at near the speed of light.

So far I'm finding this mode very useful for cutting tree limbs. In fact a fallen tree proved to be an excellent test of this mode, using my BARB to sever off some of the larger limbs worked better than I could have imagined.

Regarding the BARB it all boils down to, running out of bullets, once this happens you're left with the latter two options to either put holes in people, or well, cook them. I'm not complaining mind you, it's always nice to have options, but I still wish they'd come up with a version that has a never ending supply of bullets, like in the movies. Maybe I'm just a traditionalist that way.

According to Dane, both of these new modes were old Tesla designs that they finally figured out how to implement, and miniaturize. Which tells me that she was also consulting with this lab and why I was moved to the top of the beta list so easily.

The default setting on the BARB's particle beam is five, this is strong enough to go through a human skull without any noticeable recoil, kind of like turning on a flash light really. Dialed back to two seemed to make short work of my tree limbs for firewood, but I was noticing some scoring of the ground on the other side of the tree limb itself.

Once I have enough logs to get me through the evening I set up a nice pyramid in my newly constructed hearth with dry leaves surrounding and all through the base. Rolling the particle beam dial all the way down to zero for "power output", I soon discover is perfect for starting a camp fire.

"Have to remember to mention that to the boys in R&D, if I can ever get this whole thing sorted out." I mutter, while rubbing my still throbbing head, and easing back down into a sitting position.

There I began contemplating my situation, strolling between the conscious and unconscious realms of my mind like they're battling for time to speak, I finally realize that I'm all alone. It also occurs to me that during my "spook" training at Quantico we learn that agents have gone mad from far less a system shock.

I can now tell you that realizing you are alone in the world, that's one thing; but realizing that your world no longer exists and that you are beyond truly alone, not just in place, but in time, well that's not a feeling I would wish on my worst enemy. Add a concussion, and the feeling that the fate of the world may very well rest on your shoulders alone, and you might want to shoot something. A lot…

"I could really use a drink…" Muttering to myself again.

I begin to look around and remember on top of all that, I really don't know what the world outside of this forest looks like anymore.

I just keep picturing those bare cement walls cracking around me. They had layers of thick enameled paint applied over years, and years of maintenance on them only seconds before…

Really I can only assume that I will never even be born if I don't do what it takes to correct this time-line. Hell my last conversation with my sister was to argue about her new wife Liz. Guess I was just jealous that I didn't get to hang out with her much anymore.

We were always close, ever since we were kids, and she was always brilliant. Made most of my college professors look like amateur night at any night club by the time she was twelve.

I remember a group of neighborhood kids that used to pick on me, and somehow she mixed up something that made them think I was six feet tall and ripped, I don't know what it was but they were convinced of it until I was actually six feet tall and ripped, and now she's just gone?

"Blinked out of existence by some psychopath that wanted to rewrite history to meet their own maniacal delusions?" I whisper, staring into the flames of my campfire.

Rolling up my belt to use it as a pillow, I lie down next to the fire and drift off to sleep. Dreaming of something Dane had said to me last month...

"Look Johnny, you have to hear this. There is something going on at the lab, and I'm not sure I can trust this information with anyone else. Over the past few months we've had several recorded 'false alarms'. The thing is they're not exactly 'false'; I believe that someone is actually entering the lab, disabling the security system, and then checking up on our progress, possibly doing their own testing or even stealing our research.

I'm telling you this because I think something is coming, something big, and I need you to keep an eye out for it. I'm not sure exactly what is going on yet, but it's got to be either someone at the 'Director' level, someone internal to the lab itself, or a higher ranking Security Officer. Those are the only people that have access to the lab when I'm not there.

We have the maintenance shutdown coming up in a few weeks for the Fourth of July, and I know that you were looking forward to taking some time off, and staying with Liz and me for a while, but I need you to stay on base. You are the only one I trust, you are the only one who can fix this."

Waking up and remembering when we had that conversation all I took from it was "Blah blah... You're not getting any time off, blah blah... we're not hanging out like the old days. Blah blah... It's the me and Liz show now, deal with it. Blah blah..."

Rubbing my head and muttering "Fix this? What the hell did she know, and when? Perhaps I over simplified?" finding the bruise on my head, and quickly finding out it still hurts like crazy.

I open my eyes, and roll over to sit up. Again easing myself up to my elbows, and then up into a full sitting position I find myself facing the biggest ugliest hairiest pig I've ever seen. The tusks on this thing had to be twelve inches long. "Where the hell am I?" Wondering still groggy and in pain.

Knowing pigs have very limited vision I fumble slowly and carefully trying to grab the BARB from the belt holster behind me where I had slept on it that night. The 'pig' for lack of a better word, eventually catches the movement, and starts to charge. Yanking the whole belt around me, I fire my BARB through the holster hitting the pig right in the snout; of course the BARB is still set on the lowest setting from lighting the fire, the pig looking surprised stops for a moment letting out a blood curdling squeal while I roll the particle beam dial all the way forward, it starts to charge again this time with a fire in its eyes.

My second shot is not as accurate and its squeal has definitely reminded me how much pain my head is in. However I do manage to catch him across the top of his head, blasting a hole straight through him and the fairly large tree behind him. A hair more and I would have missed him completely and been gored by his massive tusks.

He falls dead only inches in front of me. So far I'm not too impressed with the past, but at least I've gone from a burnt cookie dough smell to the smell of fresh crispy bacon.

Now collecting my thoughts and remembering the dream in more detail. It doesn't take long to recall why my own simplified version was all I remembered. That was the last night we had actually hung out together, a "siblings night" Dane called it, Liz had left us to our own devices to go do "family bonding stuff".

We had gone to this little pub around the corner from Dane's house, a place we used to frequent before Liz moved in. They didn't all know our name or anything like that, but that waitress she knew us well, and was definitely interested in one of us, although we never did figure out which.

"Wait let me guess, a bottle of McClelland's Highland Single Malt Scotch and two glasses". She'd say batting her eyelashes, as we sat down at our usual booth in the back corner.

Which in our time they had to special order for us, since McClelland's had gone out of business roughly two hundred years prior. Drinking with Liz was always her treat though, she was an egghead from a very young age, but she always appreciated the finer things in life, and being the head of the "Time Lab" meant she had the salary to enjoy whatever she wanted. A single bottle would run her around twenty five thousand dollars, if memory serves, but she's got the deep lab coat pockets, and a discretionary fund that would make most scientists choke on their cheap ties.

Sitting in the back corner like that was my own preference. In the intelligence community you're taught to get in the habit of always picking out a spot where keeping everyone and the door in your visual range is just second nature. According to my training agent this rule dated back to the old west, something about too many law men being shot in the back while drinking or playing cards, or so she said.

That night however I recall both of us being extremely intoxicated, or so I thought. We had gotten more than half way through our lovely bottle of single malt, when she laid that story on me.

The more I focus on remembering that night, brings to mind the tag on the expedition pack. It had my name on it, and a version that only Dane would use too.

"What the hell is going on here?"

Reopening the expedition pack, it seems Dane had known much more than she let on. Just under the Regenerative Tissue Stimulator is a field manual, written in her own handwriting, but it looks weird, like she was shaking when she wrote it. She even used a code that we used as kids, when we didn't want our teachers or parents to know what we were talking about.

Trying to remember the code I quickly decipher her opening note to me "Johnny, this field manual explains exactly what's wrong with the '*Relativistic Prototype*', and how to fix it." It continued "Yes I got it to work! It's the biggest breakthrough since; well I'll explain that later. I had to sabotage it though as I told you; well what I guess would be only a short time ago for you, I didn't want someone else using my technology much less knowing that I had it working, so I never even reported it worked."

"Wait she had it working then sabotaged it so that only I could use it? NOW?!?" talking to myself.

As I continue reading, I find that it details what I need to fix it, and lists a tool kit also included in the pack, and how exactly to make the repairs once the material is acquired.

I quickly search for any other personal note from Dane that might be included, but find none. There is a change of clothes that look kind of odd to me, and what looks like an old key with the number twenty one twelve on it.

"I'll have to look into that when I reach some sort of civilization I guess." Again talking to myself.

Also inside at the very bottom of the expedition pack I find the prototype for the new 'Viper' suit, complete with hood. This is a skin tight "Smart Suit" that is virtually impenetrable, regulates body temperature, can withstand massive amounts of heat or cold, and comes in a stylish metallic blue color. It is of course being developed for military applications around the globe, and off world. This was Liz's project, she had mentioned it in passing at dinner one night a few months ago, but was quickly quieted by Dane. To my "water cooler" knowledge they were supposed to be years away from a working prototype. Could I have been wrong about her? Dane has pull, but I'm pretty sure only a lab head could have managed something like this.

Liz had to have been working with her this whole time; she was in on it. Looking out for me? I thought she couldn't stand me. Normally I would consider this "the surprise of the century", but in this case I was literally in another century, and god knows where, so that slot had been filled. This however would definitely fall into second place without any current competition.

With that, I don my new impenetrable, state of the art underwear, which seems to adjust to the size of the wearer, tightly.

11

The suit has what looks like a small data port for the Relativistic Prototype on the left forearm just below the elbow.

"Well at least this explains the connection between them, a direct interface for another project? This had to be a custom side job."

Connecting the Prototype to its port, and the rest of the device then dangles down to my wrist. As this happens something in the Relativistic Prototype finally activates, a sort of metallic band extends out from either side of the Prototype like a bracelet around my wrist, and then interlocks itself into place.

Further examination reveals that the suit also comes with a belt, gloves, and booties which all appear to be made from the same material; these also seem to cinch up while pulling them on, and then magnetically lock to the main body of the suit itself. The belt is designed much like my current belt, and has a holster for my BARB, with pockets that utilize magnetic flaps for a number of things, including both the Regenerative Tissue Stimulator, and the tool kit Dane left for me.

After situating the belt, I'm overcome with the sensation that even though I'm in excellent physical shape, this suit is still not exactly something to make you feel comfortable about running around out in the open, at least not when it's this form fitting anyway.

"Talk about leaving nothing to the imagination, sheeesh!"

Putting on the change of clothes from the bag to hide my new 'super' outfit helped my state of mind a bit.

"Boy… these accessories are something else. Wonder why Liz left out the purse?" I remark gathering all my worldly belongings and shoving them in the expedition pack.

Walking what seemed to be east, based solely on the time of day and direction of the sun. It's been hours since I started out from camp, and I'm beginning to realize how thirsty I've become.

With my training I quickly spot my own signs of dehydration, dry mouth, dizziness, and being lightheaded have all started to set in.

And now increasingly aware that it has been at least eighteen hours since arriving in this time, and a good six hours before that I went to bed which would have been approximately my last glass of water. That puts my last fluid intake at roughly twenty four to twenty eight hours ago. Now normally this is when people start to panic, but normal people haven't had my training. So taking a deep breath I proceed forward making the best of what could be a very bad situation.

Examining the landscape around me for what may be a stream or river I spot a clearing just ahead, and it appears there is a pretty substantial size city, just through some trees on the other side. Steadily approaching the area, my thoughts of water fade as the ground begins to shake under my feet.

Looking left over the horizon appears a line of tanks which start rolling right up through the clearing. I instinctively recoil back into the tree line to avoid detection, it's time to contemplate my next move.

Sirens start blaring from the city, and a booming voice telling people; "Please proceed in an orderly fashion to your designated shelters. I repeat, you need to get off the streets, and into your designated shelters."

Tanks rolling in front of me for what seems like forever, and they even appear to be an advanced model, more closely related to those of my own time. It occurs to me that I may not have traveled back through time very far at all. On top of that; this has to be the largest tank force I've ever seen or heard of anywhere, they just keep coming, and coming with no end in sight.

"Where the hell am I?" muttering to myself again.

About this time I hear a much more sinister sound; jets appear to be dropping bombs on what looks like the North side of the city. This is also the direction the tanks are headed. As the rain of fire begins, everything around me seems to pause as I wonder if this is real, or just some nightmare I can't awaken from. Could this all be from the concussion? May be some side effect of the Time portal?

I reach into the Expedition pack and put on my hood, "No point in getting another head injury I guess." Then something crazy happens.

The hood seems to magnetically lock into place like the rest of the pieces but much more intense, as it locks down the open face is lit up by what appears to be a force field of some kind, and then a Heads Up Display (HUD) appears in front of my eyes that seems to wrap all the way around my head, even showing me a rear view on the far sides of my vision. Distance vectors, speed, trajectory, power, cloak status.

"Cloak status?" I say, finally all that talking to myself pays off.

The suit answers, "Cloak ready, Johnny!"

It's Dane! The only person in history to get away with calling me 'Johnny', and I'm damn glad to hear it.

"Dane is that you?" I ask.

"Well it's not Elvis moron."

"What the hell is going on? Where are you?" I demand.

"I can't give up all my secrets little brother. Well, at least not yet, but by now you've probably figured out that you are the only one of our time-line that can do anything, not only because you are more than one hundred years in the past, but also because our time-line has been completely eradicated," Dane responds.

"I was afraid you were going to say that."

"Then you also understand that you are our only hope for setting things right," she replies.

"What do you need me to do?"

"That I can't tell you Johnny, nothing is set in stone, it is all based on choices, not just on yours but on anyone around you as well. Free will is in play here, big time. I have taxed the supercomputers on site with every permutation of this situation that I could think of and even some I couldn't. Each time it came up almost unrecognizably different, so what to do is all up to you now Johnny."

"So that whole infinite realities thing you used to preach?" I ask.

"Ding, Ding we have a winner!"

"How then am I talking to you?" I ask.

"Unfortunately, these are mostly preprogrammed answers to questions I knew you would ask; however this suit is extremely intelligent. The Artificial Intelligence I developed with Liz in complete secrecy is programmed to learn from my preprogrammed responses as well as your input, to determine exactly what it is you need or will need, and help you accomplish that goal. In essence it isn't me, but it will be a very close likeness by the time this is all over Johnny. Also, I may have done a massive brain upload into its core, so as power is supplied to the suit and more processors become available, it will start to unpack and learn from all of my memories and experiences; it is a state of the art 'Unrestricted Artificial Intelligence' which means it can learn and make its own decisions. Though it isn't totally without safe guards, as it can never go against something that my core values wouldn't allow, you know, like things that would hurt you for instance. Also, this has the benefit of having access to all of my memories, eventually," Dane replies.

I notice the bombs are getting closer. "Alright, first things first, will this cloak work on everything I'm wearing, or just me and the tight ass suit?" I ask.

"The cloaking mechanism of the Viper suit is only capable of cloaking or manipulating its own surfaces, including the sack that was sent within your expedition pack, the latest B.A.R.B. prototype

I made sure you got, and the Relativistic unit itself, which are all made to integrate completely. The change of clothes was added to conceal the Viper from plain sight, until you understood its capabilities a little better. Unfortunately, that was one of the things I couldn't plan for, when you would actually put the hood on," Dane responds.

"You've got to be kidding, there is a purse?" I mock.

"I would call it more of a satchel, but I suppose if that's what you want to call it Johnny, it would qualify." Dane responds. I can almost hear her laughing at me in that annoying snicker she used, just to drive me up a wall.

I take off the street clothes from the expedition kit tossing them behind a nearby shrub then locate the special 'sack' Dane described, in the outside pocket of the kit, and drop it into one of the extra pockets on the belt.

"Okay, engage cloak," I say.

"The cloak has been activated, Johnny".

"And you're certain; no one can see me now?" I ask.

"Yes Johnny, this system was tested with every kind of light spectrum analysis, and virtually anything that could be used to detect it, and there isn't a thing in our time-line that can see you."

"So this is a much higher level of cloak than the expedition packs use?" I ask.

"While they are based on the same technology, yes this is generations ahead of anything those back packs were designed for," she explains.

"Alright, but if one of these tanks spots me, this could be the shortest mission in history," I reply, while making my way across the clearing, dodging the still moving tanks, seemingly undetected.

Entering the city, my first order of business is to find out what city I'm in, and get some fluids in me. I approach a small shopping district `Main St.' the sign reads.

"No help there," I comment.

I don't see any of the recognizable stores we're all used to, but there appears to be a small post office on the other side of the street.

Quickly I approach and enter the post office. A bell rings loudly as I shove open the door, I quickly look around and realize anyone that works here should be in a shelter by now. As I gently close the door I hear the sirens sound an all clear. Now in a hurry I look around for a piece of mail to get the address. Picking one up, I am baffled by what I see.

'New Frankfurt, German Alliance; District 3' "What the hell is that?" I exclaim.

Dane answers, "It would appear in this causality, Germany has expanded its influence considerably".

"You think," I mock, "Does this suit have GPS? Can it tell me where I am, or at least where I should be?"

"Unfortunately, the onboard GPS system, which came online with the suit, is not detecting any GPS protocol supporting satellites in the sky. While there are several low energy signatures in close orbit, indicating satellites of some kind, it would appear that none of those support the known common GPS command sets, or any of the older versions as well.

However, there is a possibility of determining an approximate location by using the geothermal and geomagnetic protocols," Dane answers.

"Great! Do that then,"

"This will take a few moments to triangulate; unfortunately the suit has very low power at the moment," Dane explains.

As the suit makes the necessary calculations I move toward the front of the post office, looking out a large window with bars on it, signs of life begin emerging into the streets. People that look dazed, not surprised, or in shock as I would expect from people that have just suffered an attack on their city, but a lethargic stroll, more of a curious look to them gazing toward the area that the attack had taken place. They look up to the sky as if to say "I guess that's it for now?"

About this time Dane chimes in, "These readings are not consistent with the planet Earth."

"What the hell do you mean, not consistent with the planet Earth? I went through a time portal, not a damned space ship!"

"Well to be more precise, you went through a massive electrical pulse, creating a localized controlled event horizon held together and focused by an experimental technology that works much like a black hole, and it's experience with virtual particles. While we have proven the time travel aspect of this technology in the lab, we have yet to witness or study all of its possible side effects, unfortunately when dealing with forces like that of a black hole, normal physics are much less… well, normal," Dane responds.

"Awesome, so you're telling me I'm more than one hundred years in the past, on another planet, that just happens to know about Frankfurt, Germany?" I demand.

"Actually, I was merely pointing out that there are several unknowns in this equation Johnny. However, based on earlier readings taken outside, variant temperature, distance from the sun, the location of the moon in the afternoon sky, and mass of the moon itself, accompanied by the data from the Geo Triangulation, I would say yes, we are more than one hundred years in the past, on another planet, or possibly a pocket universe? Actually, oh, that does make more sense doesn't it?" Dane's voice answers.

"Well… thanks for clearing that up, I guess."

The bell over the door rings as an older man enters the post office; he is wearing what looks like a postal uniform, and he appears very familiar to me for some reason. Then he stands there, and seems to look right at me for several seconds.

Then he proclaims "I can't believe I left that door unlocked again," as he steps behind the counter.

"At least I'm not the only one who talks to themselves. He can't hear me can he?" I ask.

"No Johnny, with the hood engaged the suit is completely insulated and sound proof. You could scream at the top of your lungs and he'd have no idea."

The old man says, "Stop talking to that damn fool suit, and show yourself."

"Sound proof, eh?" I mock.

"Now that is puzzling," Dane replies.

"Can the Viper make me visible as myself, with clothes on?" I ask

"Of course, its structure is made to project any image necessary to blend, I could make you look like a rock if I wanted."

"That won't be necessary, thanks. Just deactivate the cloak and put me in a white T-shirt and jeans, I don't want to stand out," I say.

"Done," Dane replies.

The old man chuckles, "You still trying to figure out 'where the hell you are'?" He inquires.

"Can you make it so he can hear me?" I ask

"Also, done…" Dane replies.

"How did you know I was here, and how do you know about this suit?" I demand.

"Calm down John. You and I go way back," he says.

"You know my name too?" my jaw must have hit the floor at this point.

Right away I start to look him over more carefully, could he be someone I knew? There's something really strange about this guy, like looking at myself through a really old mirror.

"I guess I should start explaining, before your head explodes," he says with a grin. "It all started about forty two years ago for me. You see when the break in at the time lab occurred I must have been a few fractions of a second faster getting through the portal than you."

"So then you're me? A really, old me…"

"You got it John, but you don't have to be so rude about it."

"Ah, right sorry about that," I reply

"So as I was saying, I must have gotten through the portal a little faster than you, which as I'm sure you realize, means I got a little further back in time than you," he continues.

"Hold on a second, I know this is more Dane's subject, but how could you get through the portal before me, if you are me," I say.

"Infinite universe theory John, the `multi-verse' Dane used to prattle on about. Honestly I couldn't tell you though if you went back in time and showed up in mine, or if I went back in time and arrived in yours, but that's the only thing that makes sense, and I've had a while to consider it," he answers.

"See I told you a pocket universe made more sense," Dane says proudly.

I stand silent for a minute pondering this turn of events. They're right of course; the only plausible explanation is another reality, if he is actually me.

"So you said you've been here forty two years?" I ask.

"Forty two to the day as a matter of fact," he answers.

"What can you tell me?" I ask, now well beyond intrigued.

"Well, when I got here, much like you, my first goal was to figure out where and when I was. Only, the first thing that happened to me was I met a family in the resistance a husband and wife, with a small child, trying to escape those Nazi bastards. I'm sure you know that by making it through the portal faster, that also means my exit point was closer to the original portals than where you exited."

I interrupt, "Lucky you."

"Johnny, don't interrupt yourself this is fascinating." Dane chimes in.

"Anyway, I decided with this new super suit Dane had given me. I should put it to some good use, and lend a hand. Problem was, I didn't understand it yet, didn't know all its secrets, and I made a terrible error."

"What was the error?" I ask.

"I went into a fire fight without having the Relativistic Prototype repaired. You see, the way that suit works, at least the way I figure it works is static force dispersion, as the static field it generates gets hit by bullets or anything really, it absorbs and disperses the energy across all of its connected circuitry, thus the system can actually absorb the power and no one system is overloaded. But with the Relativistic Prototype not functioning properly, it caused a massive overload and blew up my one shot at being able to complete the mission," he says.

"Wow, so what happened to the suit?" I ask.

"Oh, I still wear it under my clothes, and because of its construction, it is still bullet proof, provided it's not too many bullets obviously, but other than that it's not much use. I've tried to repair it, but it's dead. From what I've been able to figure out the suits biggest folly is power consumption, it seems to be good on its own for about fifteen minutes, after that it needs an external power source to keep it charged," he says

"The Relativistic Prototype?" I ask.

"That's the way I have it figured. If it happened like I think it did, Liz was having problems with her power sucking suit, and since Dane was the 'Tesla' of our time, Liz went to her for help," he answers.

"So how does the Relativistic Prototype get power then?" I ask.

"Well if you recall all those late night conversations about the universe and space time, you'll remember that Tesla was Dane's biggest fascination. Once I realized I was stuck here, I did some research in to the man, at least as much as I could, with the Nazi war machine looking over my shoulders. Turns out that Tesla is the one man in recorded history that could hold a candle to Dane, even more so than Einstein, one of Tesla's more impressive discoveries was how to take static electricity from the atmosphere and utilize it as alternating current in whatever he wanted. So it made sense to me that Dane improved on that design some with our own modern technology, likely added a redundancy or two for good measure, and there you have it."

"So that functionality of my Prototype is working then, that's why I can cloak, but how did you know I was here then?" I ask.

"Well, from the knowledge I've accumulated of snail mail over the years, letters don't typically float around all on their own, and well, I know Houdini's been dead for some time now. So I figured it was either another me, or some new kind of Nazi spy looking for an old resistance fighter, and since I've yet to run into a Nazi scientist that could hold a candle to Dane and Liz, I figured the former was the more plausible, but really there was only one way to find out for sure," he responds.

"I guess that leaves us with the original question then," I say.

He chuckles, "Where the hell are you?"

I nod.

"You are on planet Earth to start with, August first twenty fifty three is the date; I know, that suit couldn't figure it out when I first got here."

"And more specifically?" I ask.

"Well... More specifically, you are not too far from where you started, still in the Nevada Desert."

"Wait, there are trees all around here, how can that be?" I ask.

"You know you should come to the back office with me, sit, have some tea and get away from that big window. I'll explain the whole thing." He motions toward a door behind the counter.

Following him into his office I can't help but think this is all too much coincidence for me to handle. Walking down a hallway we approach his office and enter, it's small and quaint. There's a desk, a small counter with a hot plate, radio, and coffee machine. He even has a sofa on one wall. He uses the hot plate to heat some water in a tea kettle, as I sit at the desk.

"So?" I say.

"Well let's just say Earth is not how you remember it," he replies.

"How so?" I ask.

"Well, from the way it was explained to me. Those dumbass Nazi's tried to capture Halley's Comet when it passed earth in nineteen eighty six, they figured that it might be a good source of 'iridium'. Only when they made their attempt, instead of capturing it, they just busted off a large chunk, and it came straight here taking out nearly half the planet."

"Half the planet?!" I ask.

"Yeah…" He replies shaking his head before he continued,

"Apparently the chunk was small enough that a large portion of it burnt up in the upper atmosphere, so the problem wasn't the size anymore it was where it hit that seemed to be the major problem, right on the Mid-Atlantic rift.

This caused a massive chain reaction, and turned the rift into a super volcano. It erupted with such force that it blew out, most of Europe and a large part of Africa everything from South Africa North basically was thrown out into space, so I suppose around a third of the planet if you want to get technical. Luckily for the rest of the planet, the idiot Nazi's had moved a large research facility to somewhere on the eastern Asian continent, and at this facility they were working on a new shielding technology, much like the Viper uses. Unfortunately they were only testing it on a small scale at that point. When they found out a piece of the comet was coming in, they started working to power it enough to deflect it.

They didn't complete their adjustments in time for the comet obviously, but they did have it ready in time to keep most of the ejected planetary mass out of the atmosphere. The planet still had some volcanic cloud to deal with of course, but you'll have to ask the Nazi's what they did to take care of it. The history book just says 'the Great Nazi Scientists purified the Earth's air', but then that piece of shit reads like a Nazi bible and in it, they're all Gods, and yes, there is just the one history book, free press being illegal and all.

Anyway, most of the people I've talked to about it, talk about some kind of electrolysis, but I'm not totally convinced any of them really knew what they were talking about," he says.

There is now a pit in my stomach the size of the Grand Canyon, which ironically is not the largest hole on the planet anymore. All those people, all that destruction, for some mineral, who could do this?

Almost stuttering I get out, "W-What happened to all that earth blasted into space?"

"From what I'm told, they used a series of rockets to fly it or direct it really, to the moon. On a clear night you can actually see it with a telescope."

I sit silently staring at the now boiling tea kettle, trying to process what I have just been told.

"Well getting back to your original question about the trees. That giant explosion had some dramatic effects, it shifted the Earth's orbit more than 'slightly', and between the new distance from the sun, the moon, and the new axis that the planet ended up on, that of course brought on huge weather changes all over the world. The trees you see all started growing almost seventy years ago now," he answers.

"Unbelievable, so Hitler was never stopped?" I say.

"Oh he was stopped alright, before he really got started actually. He was stopped by someone that didn't exist until the day before Hitler took office. It seems that was the plan all along actually," he replies.

"The break in, and the 'traveler' I followed through. August first nineteen thirty four, that was the date on the control console when I entered the time lab. What happened?" I say.

"Our *'traveler'*, made his initial appearance at a German conference with Hitler on the day after his appointment to Führer, the second of August nineteen thirty four. History now records that Hitler was killed and power seized six months after he started World War II in March of nineteen forty by that same man Heinrich Riefenstahl, his newly appointed 'Reichsleiter'.

Now the good news is Riefenstahl put an early end to the holocaust. The bad news is it was his R&D and Tyrannical forethought that caused part of the planet to be disintegrated, so all those people, and a whole lot more, died anyway," he says.

"What about America and Russia taking Berlin?" I ask.

"It didn't happen; Riefenstahl pulled all the troops back after seizing control from Hitler, he effectively ended the war, and all the Nazi military might was redirected into research. Research in technologies that weren't developed until the late nineteen hundreds in my reality, and I would expect yours as well. With Hitler dead, Riefenstahl apologized to the world. He promised that it was a terrible mistake and that they had dealt with the problem internally and therefore there was nothing more to fear. So everyone just forgot about them for a while, right up until they advanced to a point that they were unstoppable by the rest of the world.

They hit America first; Of course Riefenstahl knowing that it was only America that would have the knowhow and the ability to mount any type of defense if left untouched for any length of time. They came in with bomber jets that resembled the F-117 in August of nineteen fifty one, then everyone sat up and took notice again, of course it was too late, but they damn sure noticed," he answers.

"So this 'Riefenstahl' completely rewrote history," I say.

"'*Completely*' seems somewhat of an understatement, but yes... I suppose that's as close a word as you're going to get for what that monster did," he replies.

Having been trained in many intelligence gathering techniques, one of which being lie detection I catch a quick flash on his face as he's talking, it's happiness. This takes me by surprise, and I make a critical mistake and ignore my gut, figuring I must have blinked funny or misread the expression. Even though happiness is the easiest of all the expressions to recognize. I'd like to blame it on the shock of what I've just been told, but the truth is I've been trained well beyond any normal man's breaking point, and should have listened to my instincts. This was a blatant screw-up on my part.

"Do we have a picture of Riefenstahl?" I ask.

"No, unlike Hitler who wanted his face on everything like some peacock. Riefenstahl wanted his picture nowhere, I'm sure you can figure out why."

I knew right then he was expecting me.

"Just in case someone made it through the portal after him…" I remark in disbelief.

2 GATHERING INTELLIGENCE

As I sit there drinking my tea, I ask, "In my original time-line, I remember there were always records of German S.S. officers that were paranoid, to the point of investigating Hitler himself. You think Riefenstahl managed to stop them from keeping records?"

He hesitates a moment and then starts to speak with a stutter "I, I'm not sure no; I do know that according to what oral history there is that he had everyone that ever saw his face killed in a gas chamber in nineteen sixty seven. No one knows what happened to him after that."

This, in the intelligence world is referred to as a stall; these are very common when you need to come up with an answer for a question you haven't been properly prepared for. Even more telling is the redirect he uses to another topic, as if to be helpful, but really all he's doing is repeating information he's already given me, just in a slightly different way.

The advantage is if you're trained for it, you now know that your 'friendly' is most likely a plant. Unfortunately, knowing this and continuing to illicit information from a potential asset can be trying at times.

You have to be very careful how you proceed; chances are good that anyone making this move knows that they have just screwed up, and their cover is quite possibly blown. They will now be watching you for tells, to know whether or not you caught their error, either by having the proper training or really any basic card game skills, and caught on to them. If this happens you may lose them and their possibly valuable intelligence altogether.

Really you have two options at this point, you can play oblivious, or confront the situation head on. If you're really good at your craft, oblivious is usually the best way to go. You'll not only get the information you need, but you'll also get the disinformation they were supposed to give you, this leads to a much more complete picture overall.

The direct approach on the other hand is much more risky the asset may shutdown entirely, or just start telling you anything they think you want to hear.

With my training I opt for oblivious and press for better information; "Where do you suppose I could find information like that?"

"The moon I guess. Last I heard the Nazi's kept a bunker with a huge cache of experimental technologies near Heidelberg. It was supposed to have the world's first supercomputer used by the S.S. during the late thirties." He answers having regained his composure.

"Not exactly what I had in mind. Know of anywhere that I don't need a rocket to access?" I ask.

"Well there was a rumor several years ago about a secret installation in the Tibetan Mountains, that Asian base I mentioned, but no one in the resistance has ever found it, and no one really knows what it had in it, if anything useful at all,"

"Now we're getting somewhere. The suit has the ability to figure out locations based on the earth's magnetic fields, and several other things I didn't understand," I add.

"I see, so you're thinking you could feed the changes in the earth into the suit's computer, and it could aid in discovering the location of this facility!"

"That's what I'm hoping for, I have yet to figure out all of this things capabilities, and it sounds like you never had the chance to either, but I'm thinking with everything I've seen from it so far, there has to be a possibility right?" I ask rhetorically.

"Well let's find out, this could be a huge step for the resistance too," he says, with a smirk.

"Viper is there a way you could broadcast your responses?" I ask, so as not to give away any information this person doesn't already have.

"This will require the use of an external radio unit that I can broadcast to," Dane responds.

"Hey, me," I say, "Flip on your radio"

He nods and quickly turns the radio on sitting next to the coffee maker.

"Local broadcast enabled," Dane's voice comes through the radio.

"Outstanding," I say trying not to sound too thrilled. "Now, I have found out that we are actually on earth."

Dane interrupts, "Yes, I was monitoring the conversation. A piece of Haley's comet touched down at the mid-Atlantic rift, causing a super volcano to form, and eject a large portion of the Earth. You would like me to run a computer model of this and determine what has happened to the earth's magnetic fields?"

"That's a good place to start," I reply.

"With this data, the best model would show a shift in the earth's orbit and attitude. From which I would extrapolate that our current location is somewhere in the Nevada dessert."

"That's what he was saying," I answer.

"Earlier you told me there are satellites in a close orbit, are you able to bounce a signal off of any of them to triangulate physical land features, or possibly large man-made structures?" I ask.

"I will begin testing to see if that is plausible," Dane answers.

I redirect my attention to the older 'me' in the room. "So if this works do you have a way to get us to Nazi China?"

"I believe I can make that happen," he responds.

"I'm thinking I should get the Relativistic Prototype repaired before we head into a potentially bad situation, and as I recall Dane's manual said we just need one ounce of copper to reattach a 'cold solder joint'. I don't suppose you would have any copper lying around anywhere do you?" I ask.

"Actually I don't, but it shouldn't be hard to come by." He continues, "As a matter of fact, that's about the only good thing that the Nazi's did. They never moved away from the precious metals standard, any coin worth less than five dollars is copper, more is silver, and at twenty it switches to gold."

A light on my HUD flashes 'External Broadcast *disabled*' Dane interrupts in my ear, "You know the manual said it has to be gold to complete the circuit correctly right? There is too much resistance in copper for this delicate a circuit."

"Oh, I know."

"Then why are you talking about copper?" She questions.

"Just proving a theory," I reply. "Now turn broadcast back on before he realizes we're conversing without him."

The light flashes again 'External Broadcast enabled'

"Don't you find that odd?" I ask.

"That the one material that you need to fix a piece of technology that could potentially save the world is available on virtually every street corner? I never really considered it since mine was destroyed, but now that you ask, I guess it is kind of odd." The old man replies.

Suddenly a large crashing sound comes from the front of the building.

"Johnny!" Dane's voice sounds alarmed. "My thermal scanners are detecting several individuals in the front of this establishment, it also appears they have just ripped the bars off the front window, protective actions are recommended."

"Well, I guess you should get under the desk," I tell the old man I'm now convinced is pretending to be my older self.

Old me nods, and I instruct Dane to have the suit go silent and cloak. I stand and move to position myself outside the office where I can monitor the front door.

"Show me the thermal scans." The suit changes my normal HUD into a thermal monitor. I can see all the heat signatures around me, including what looks like six people crouched in front of the post office in a very suspicious manor, three on each side of the big window that faces the street.

As I study what I'm seeing I notice one of the figures make a sharp throwing action and hear glass breaking. "Normal view," I say.

They've thrown what looks like a smoke bomb in through the window.

"What is it?" I demand.

"Its chemical composition appears to be a type of knock out gas. Chloroform based Johnny," Dane responds.

"Can the suit protect against the smoke?" I query.

"Yes, the suit's hood activates a magnetic seal around your head, and what's been dubbed a strategic repellent field for your face. This field is basically the same as what radiates from the suit itself and allows the cloak to work, as well as image generation, and its copious amounts of protection."

"Yeah, yeah I get it you're one bad ass machine, now answer the damn question already!" I insist

"I was going to say; when engaged, together they filter your air down to below point zero one microns therefore it can protect against any known airborne pathogen, attack or disease. It is actually so effective you could breathe underwater," Dane replies.

"Well if someone throws a smoke bomb at me under water, I'll be sure to remember that…" I comment, while quietly shutting the door to the office, protecting the fake older me from the gas.

"Johnny it's become clear you no longer buy this man's story, why are you bothering to protect him?" Dane inquires.

"Kind of hard to continue to gain intel from a guy that's been chemically immobilized don't you think? Now let's see the Thermal view again." My display changes back.

"Would you prefer the 'advanced thermal view' Johnny?"

"Uh… advanced equals good right?" I ask.

"It uses a graphic rendering engine to extrapolate and enhance your view. It will be similar to your 'normal view' as it will clean up the 'blockiness' of the normal thermal imaging, it also gives more of a sense of looking through walls, as it renders a more accurate depth perception," Dane clarifies.

"Okay from now on if you have something better than what I ask for, and I'm getting ready to be in a possible life threatening situation; Just do it!" I say. "And remind me to ask you how that works later."

"Sounds reasonable," Dane replies.

"Great I'm glad we're on the same page."

"Me too, Johnny," she replies.

I watch the individuals outside through the wall, preparing to come in, putting on gas masks, and each of them with what looks to be a modified version of the M-16 machine gun at the ready.

"Johnny, based on my lip reading software. The one on your right is giving the orders. They want to take you alive, and beat any information out of you, before turning you over to their own superiors."

"Is that so? Well that's good to know." I reply, as they start jumping in through the busted window side by side. Moving to the middle of the post office, now shrouded in their own knockout gas I watch as they enter around me.

About this time my HUD starts to flash, like the batteries dying on a flash light. The HUD flash's a battery emblem and then starts to fade from view. I know immediately I'm about to be fully exposed to this attack. I take my last deep breath of fresh air, and note where the soldiers are, all my years of training kick in.

They were entering two at a time, one from each side of the window, and proceeding in parallel teams.

"If I was running the op I wouldn't move until all my people were in. So I'm going to assume that's their protocol as well." I say to myself; inside my head this time so as to not let any precious oxygen escape.

Giving them a ten count, with my eyes watering and my lungs screaming for a new breath, I walk straight up the middle, and remove their gas masks. Before they have a chance to figure out what is happening they are all unconscious on the floor.

I quickly locate the canister still pumping gas into the room, and toss it back out the window. The room clears almost immediately.

"Wow, that's some potent stuff," I say, shaking my head and looking around at their motionless bodies, and gasping for air. "Seems like I made it though."

As the fog begins to clear outside I see that there was a small crowd that had gathered around the broken window, and they now all lie unconscious on the ground.

I smirk, "Oops, I hope that doesn't come back to haunt me later..." I turn to walk back to the office. About half way through the main room I fall to my knees, becoming extremely light headed. "I've gotta stop talking to myself." I get out as I face plant onto the cold floor.

Lying there I have flashes of people seeing me in this skin tight outfit and laughing.

Moments later I awaken with another massive headache and find that power to the suit has been restored. Dane is continuously telling me to wake up.

"I'm up, I'm up... What the hell happened?" I ask.

"Apparently between the suits already low power, the static field maintenance, my core processing, and the advanced thermal view, it was too much for the system all at once without the Relativistic Prototype's power generation working that is." Dane replies.

"Wonderful, you couldn't have done the math on that one before you recommended the 'advanced thermal view'?" I sneer.

"I was trying to conserve as much processing as possible Johnny," she responds.

"Yeah well next time don't skimp on the 'hey this might kill you bit'," I insist, stumbling to my feet. "And why am I awake already and the rest of these guys are still out?"

"It seems you were able to disperse a large amount of the gas before finally inhaling, therefor your dose of the chemical was far smaller than that of these men and women. Also your twenty third century physiology may have added some resistance to the drug, as your lungs are adapted to a harsher more polluted environment. Before they figured out how to clean it up that is."

"Well I'll be damned, never thought I'd be thanking all that pollution for anything."

"Also, it's only a problem when you start answering yourself," Dane responds.

"What the hell are you talking about now?"

"Before you fell, you said 'I gotta stop talking to myself'," she answers.

"Thanks, I'll keep that in mind," I reply.

Passing by the soldiers I take note of their uniform. It appears that the Nazi's are using a standard black fatigue, with thick suspenders that hold ammunition pouches, combat knives, and grenades. I notice a large shoulder patch on each of the soldiers. The patch seems to be the most important part of the uniform, as it is placed on both shoulders.

Its design is the earth with the North American and South American continents on the right, and Asia down to Australia displayed on the left. Also to the left is fire shooting out of the planet, based on its location it would have had to be Europe.

"Why would anyone want to memorialize such a waste of human life and culture?" I ask.

"Never doubt the power of symbolism Johnny."

"I suppose they could be saying; 'We blew a hole in the planet for science, mess with us and see what happens'? Still seems pretty asinine," I reply.

"It does at that, but I would imagine to people of this time-line it carries a very terrifying image to anyone who might oppose them," Dane replies.

"Indeed… Hey, how long was I out by the way?"

"Almost five minutes, but the suit was able to recover enough power to cloak you as soon as the canister was removed from the equation, and bring up the static field to protect you nine seconds later." Dane explains.

I make my way back to the office where I find the door is cracked open. I move quickly inside to check for my older self or signs of struggle. Checking under his desk I notice a small red button, and realize that the older *me* is now gone.

"Could someone have grabbed him while I was dealing with the soldiers out front? A two sided assault I wonder," I say to myself. "No Dane would have alerted me to that… wouldn't you?" I ask.

"I would, and you are now responding to yourself," she replies.

"It's been a stressful day and a half, what do you want from me? That red button could have been used to summon the strike team, maybe he realized I was onto him after all," I surmise

"That is possible, but highly unlikely I would have detected any electrical signals sent from that room while we were in it, unless it were fiber optic. Which that connection did not appear to be," she answers.

Exiting his office I know I can rule out his heading toward the front entrance, the hallway I'm standing in actually continues back for another three meters or so, and then opens to a large mail processing area in the rear of the building. I quickly scan the room looking for a point of entry and exit. There are windows all around the top of the room, which are all a good twenty feet from the floor, and they all appear to be barred from the outside. I check the double door for deliveries at the back of the room, which appears to be barred and locked from the inside, so no one exited that way.

"Disappeared like a fart in the wind," I mutter. "Wonder if I can pull off thinking like myself long enough to find me or him. Great, now I'm confused, who am I looking for?"

"I may be able to offer some assistance here, Johnny."

"Well it's about time smartass. I figured you'd know who I was looking for," I mock.

She ignores my snide comments and responds, "By doing both thermal and radar scans simultaneously of the entire premises I can determine any probable means of accessing this structure."

"Go for it, it's a better plan then standing around questioning my sanity all day."

"I already have. Scanning for anomalies indicated that this building has a basement or root cellar type structure, accessed through a small hatch located in the rear South East quadrant, or ten paces to your right. There appears to be three adult males inside."

"Three adult males?" I ask.

"That is correct and two appear to have your '*friend*' at gunpoint, although he currently appears to be unconscious on the floor," she responds.

"Huh... I kind of like them already."

I approach the hatch which appears to be partially covered by an empty mail bag. Grabbing the mail bag I realize it's attached to the door, one sharp upward yank and the door rips from its hinges swings upward, flying across the room.

"Does this thing have night vision?" I ask.

"Of course, Johnny, but there is a light on."

Raising an eyebrow I drop into the basement. I quickly move to scan my surroundings, when someone tackles me at leg level.

As I'm being hurled toward the floor, I can see that the room is lit by one hanging light bulb in the center. I also see that one of the armed men, is wearing similar gear as the six I just took out, but a different patch on his shoulders. The old guy is lying on the floor with what looks like a serious gash on his head.

The other soldier grasps for my invisible body, and calls out "Help, Sir! There's definitely something here!"

Without hesitation the other soldier jumps into the mix, their bodies flailing they collapse on top of me. I drive my knee right into the side of the one closest to it. He flies off over my head and collapses on the floor.

"Wow, didn't think I hit him that hard," I announce to myself.

I then sit up knocking the other soldier to my lap. Standing up I grab the back of his shirt before he hits the ground, and fling him into a corner. Hitting the corner he sinks to the floor definitely rattled from the impact.

I pause and ask, "Where is all this extra strength coming from? I don't recall the viper being a true exoskeleton; it doesn't even have the mass for it."

"The Viper is configured to integrate with your nervous system, therefore when your brain sends the signal for kick to your leg, the suit reads that signal and provides extra muscle tension, by contracting the suit around certain key pressure points and muscle groups that are required to perform the particular task. It won't make you a 'super man' but it does increase your muscular output by a minimum of two and as much as four times their normal capabilities, depending on the muscle group in use. As the Viper synchs to your nervous system you will see these traits, and a few others expand until full synchronization is met," Dane responds.

"Good to know… Sounds like something that should have been in the; what's that thing? Oh yeah, the MANUAL!" I remark.

I walk toward the barely conscious soldier in the corner.

"Why are you attacking me?" I demand.

The Viper's A.I. has now interfaced with my mind to the point that when I am speaking to another party, it knows to broadcast my voice without my say so. The interesting part is that I know this without having to ask.

"What? We are sworn enemies of the empire," He says while staggering back to his feet.

"Wait, you're part of a revolution?"

"We are not revolutionaries. Revolutionaries rebel against their own government," He says attempting to stand and bracing himself in the corner, "We are Americans, struggling to remove an occupying force. Who... Who the hell are you?! How do you not know this?"

I can now see his full patch, and it becomes abundantly clear. It's America, all forty-eight continental United States are represented, nothing else.

"Forty-eight states?" I question.

Dane answers "Alaska and Hawaii were U.S. territories, and not officially states until nineteen fifty nine. I would imagine in this time-line they never became states due to the attack in nineteen fifty one,"

"Oh... yeah I think I overslept that day in history class."

"Wasn't your American history class in the afternoon?" Dane asks.

"Maybe, who can remember, that's like a hundred years from now; and shut up, I'm busy,"

Directing my attention back to the soldier in the corner I ask, "So even though America has been under occupation for more than a hundred years, there are still Americans that refuse to accept Nazi rule?"

"What are you new?" He asks jerking his head around in all directions trying to locate the source of my voice.

"Let's just say that I am…" I reply. "But this country still has so many loyal Americans that they in fact form a resistance capable of requiring the amount of tanks and bombs that I saw earlier?" I ask.

"Yes?!" he says quizzically.

I uncloak with a thought, "You have nothing to fear from me soldier. I am here to stop all of this crap."

He jumps slightly startled, "What? What do you mean?" he stammers.

"Look, let's just say that everything that's happened in the last hundred years, wasn't supposed to happen. This is some insane plot by a man from the future. He wanted to conquer the world, so he went back in time to do it,"

"Wait… If this is true, how do you know?" he asks.

"Didn't I just tell you I'm new?" I reply

Walking to the middle of the room I look down at the old man claiming to be me, which looks strangely older than the last time I saw him, roughly ten minutes ago.

"What's your business with him?" I ask, pointing at the older version of myself, lying on the floor, still out cold from what appears to be his head wound.

"He is a known KGB agent," the soldier explains.

"Really?"

"It's true, he has only been known by our intelligence operatives for five or six months now, but he has been very active in providing the enemy with plans, locations, and other vital U.S. intelligence," he explains.

"Well, that's an interesting twist. Let me guess, he likes to get his information, by giving you just enough to confirm his suspicions, seems to have an intimate knowledge of events past present and future, then presses that lovely red button under his desk to call in the cavalry for a snatch and grab?" I reply.

"Yes sir, that seems to be his M.O., we've lost three covert agents to this man in the last two months alone," he says.

"But that's not what happened with us Johnny. The strike team must have been after these two from the time they entered town. No signal was sent from that office while we were here," Dane reiterates.

Turning my gaze back to the corner I ask, "What's your name soldier?"

"*Private First Class* Young, sir," he replies.

I approach the other soldier lying on the ground a few feet away. He appears to be breathing very shallow. Kneeling by his side I roll him onto his back.

"And his?" I query.

"*Lieutenant* Bradley," the *PFC* responds.

As I look at him the Viper knows what I want. My HUD shows a three dimensional x-ray view starting with skeletal system quickly followed by the overlaid, muscular system and vascular systems.

As the system lights up showing me where the damage is, Dane's voice explains, "This man appears to have micro fractures on two of his ribs, and some pretty serious bruising, but nothing punctured. If he is left untreated his injuries will heal normally, however some pain killer will probably be necessary and is advised to aid with rest and recovery."

I lightly slap his face attempting to wake him, and he starts to come around. Clutching his side he sits up wincing as he moves.

"Easy, big fella," I tell him. He looks at me with an obvious curiosity.

PFC Young explains to the *Lt.* that I am not the enemy. As I help *Lt.* Bradley to his feet I let him know his condition.

"Good news," I say, "you have a few fractured ribs, nothing that will keep you out of commission too long, just slow you down a little."

He nods at me to show his understanding while wincing.

"What's your condition *Private*?" He asks in between shallow breaths.

"Beat up sir, but I'll manage," *PFC* Young responds.

The *Lt.* turns back to me and asks, "Okay, so you're not the enemy, and I get that you were defending yourself, but who the hell are you then?"

"All you need to know right now is that I'm here to help," I respond.

He flashes a small grin, "I guess that'll do for now then. What do we call you? Invisiman, Unseen Threat, Silent but Deadly?"

PFC Young snickers.

"While 'Silent but Deadly' is high on the list, I think I'd rather just go with my name for now. Which is John by the way," I reply.

Propping the *Lt.* against the wall, I approach the old man on the floor.

Dane chimes in, "He is alive, breathing normally, heart rate is slightly elevated. The wound on his head is superficial, but he may be out for some time yet."

"So from what I've gathered, he slipped out while I was dealing with the goon squad upstairs? Then made his way down here where you two were already waiting for him?" I ask.

"That's correct," *Lt.* Bradley answers as he is starting to catch his breath.

"Well he's going to be out for a while, it looks like you hit him pretty hard when he came down," I comment.

Examining the dimly lit basement I only see one way out, the way I came in.

"Exit strategy?" I ask.

The *Lt.* labors to point up at the only door in the room.

"I thought that's what you were going to say. Alright, we better get moving then, before all those soldiers I knocked out up stairs start coming to," I suggest.

I grab the older me by the arm and toss him over my shoulder.

"That was easy," I say, talking to myself again. "Oh hell I have to try it," I comment.

Positioning myself under the hatch I jump straight up. With the neural interface now at almost one hundred percent the suit knows my plan projects my trajectory, and applies the appropriate amount of muscle enhancement to allow me to clear the hatch by three feet and land a few feet from the hatch itself on a perfect arc.

From below I hear, "Oh, that's bullshit!"

As *PFC* Young emerges from the cellar he points to the back of the room. "This double door opens to an alley with mostly loading areas facing it," he explains while reaching down to help the *Lt.* "This is how we snuck in and this is hopefully going to be the safest way out."

Lt. Bradley pulls himself with the aid of *PFC* Young from the cellar, and points to a lock on the door.

"We put that there to keep him from running out on us, the key is in my right pocket," he struggles to get out.

I pull the BARB and fire, it melts to molten metal on the floor.

"Sure... That works too, show off," *Lt.* Bradley gets out.

We exit the building and head down the alley, back toward the wooded area I originally came from. The long string of tanks had finally passed, and we have a clear line back across the newly torn up clearing. The sun has almost dropped below the tree line, as we dart across into the cover of the forest.

Entering the forest Bradley seems to catch his wind a little better, probably the adrenaline kicking in, at which point we run for almost three miles before coming to an area with several small hills, finding a nice embankment to make camp at. I drop 'my old self' near a large rock where I can watch him, then take a seat on a nearby log. The sun has now completely set and the wind has picked up with a slight chill in the air. Of course I only know this because it's on my HUD.

"Alright, the *PFC* and I need to go check in," Lt. Bradley says between very labored breaths. "We need to explain the circumstances... so to speak. Will you be alright here until we get back?" He queries.

"Yeah, will you be able to make it without help?" I respond.

"The *PFC* can aid me, but yeah its protocol and frankly I have no reason to trust you yet."

"Fair enough, I guess that will give me time to get some answers out of this clown," I say, looking at the old body now lying on the embankment.

They both nod, "We'll be back before sunrise," Bradley states, as they both head off to the west.

Time to have a conversation with Dane I think.

"What shall we talk about Johnny?" she asks

"Any thoughts on why the older 'me' would be here to screw with me?" I ask.

"Unfortunately, with time travel and alternate realities, there are infinite possibilities that could cause him to act like this," Dane responds.

"Is there anything different about him that you can detect?"

"Physical differences include a bar-code tattoo on his right shoulder blade, with a high concentration of titanium embedded directly into the scapula bone beneath, also there appears to be a degenerative problem with his DNA."

"A degenerative problem with his DNA? He's dying?" I ask.

"It would appear that this man is a clone. A blended clone of two different people actually, and not nearly as old as he told you. Based upon his genetic markers and the current rate of cellular decay I would estimate this clone's actual age to be around 6 months," Dane replies.

"What the hell? So I've gone back in time, and found an evil clone of myself from an alternate reality? In what Orwellian novel does that make since?"

"This one, apparently," Dane acknowledges.

"I knew you were going to say that, smartass, how about something useful?"

"Since we know that this person is a clone, it is entirely possible that he isn't from an alternate time-line," Dane suggests.

"So he could be part of this whole mess, put here to throw me off or stop me before I even get started?" I ask.

"The possibility has merit. Put here from a now alternate future, that knows of your stop in this time, waiting for an appropriate time to lure you into a trap, preventing you from completing your mission." He continues, "Or he could have been put here from this time-line as it progresses because whomever this

Riefenstahl is, he obviously had intimate knowledge of the technologies being developed at area fifty one, and wanted to keep a contingency plan in motion just in case.

In fact it's entirely possible that they've been manufacturing this clone since this 'Riefenstahl' arrived to intercept you, replacing him every four to six months as needed. He would have the skills necessary to calculate where you would appear depending on what second you entered the time portal, placing the clone in that local at each juncture. If that is the case you are likely to run into this clone again Johnny."

"That would explain his knowledge of the suit, Dane, and everything else actually. Any clue what the titanium deposit in his shoulder is?" I query.

"It appears to be a tracking device. The Viper sensors are detecting a radioactive isotope contained within the titanium. They may be using a satellite scan to track him. This could also be the reason for the high rate of cellular decay."

I sigh, "Did you ever figure anything out with the satellites?"

"Yes, actually I am able to utilize all of the satellites in orbit for a number of different operations. The signal response that I was getting from them was of an antiquated UNIX based system, once this was determined I was able to gain root access, and now have complete control of what appears to be their entire network. I also created several back doors, in case my tampering is detected," she replies.

"Well thanks for keeping me up to date!" I quip.

"I apologize, I would have mentioned it sooner, but you were in the middle of an attack at the time."

"So you're telling me it simply slipped your mind?" I ask. Muttering, "Wow, it really is Dane."

"Not at all, it was simply given a lower priority due to extenuating circumstances," she responds.

The old clone stirs on the ground, still out cold.

"Well since you're in the satellite system maybe you should make sure they don't find us," I suggest.

"I have just informed the satellite system that the signal they are looking for is on the move and headed several miles to the east, which is the opposite direction that *PFC* Young, and *Lt.* Bradley took," Dane responds.

"So the instillation in the Tibetan Mountains, does that exist? Or only in my clones' cover story?" I ask.

"I would postulate that was likely a red herring to use a literary term Johnny."

"Okay so where do you think they're running operations out of then?" I ask.

"I am not sure at this point, but I am conducting a complete copy, and thorough search of their entire network at this time. This should aid us in tracking the enemy's movements, bases etc... These satellites however do not have the ability to penetrate the cloud cover over some of the more popular mountain ranges such as the Tibetan Mountains, the Andes', and several individual mountains, any of which would make excellent locations for such a place. It is also possible that this was the bit of truth behind the lie, as it were," she responds.

I look up at my clone and remark, "But there's no way to be sure. That's just perfect. When he wakes up I'm kicking his ass, again."

Dane interjects, "It doesn't appear that you will have to wait long."

"Playing possum now is he?"

"That's correct Johnny, his vitals have returned to normal during our conversation," she responds.

"Good to know," I tell Dane "What do you think we should do with him boys? I say we bash his head in with a rock and let his Nazi pals find out what they have coming for them."

The clone's eyes jerk open, blinking as if to bring the world into focus.

"Finally, the traitor awakens!" I announce.

He slowly elevates his head and looks in my direction.

"So you figured that out did you?" He mocks sounding older with each word.

"What the hell is my clone doing in the past?" I demand.

"You really think I'm going to tell you anything that would help you?" He sneers. "You were supposed to be locked up and under heavy interrogation by now, apparently that suit was much closer to completion than we were lead to believe!"

I approach him slowly. He looks even older than when I set him there, an hour ago.

He grins like he knows something I don't. "You're a fool, a mere shell of the man I was cloned from."

"What is that supposed to mean? I am the man you were cloned from," I counter.

"You don't know a damn thing about who you are. And who says I was cloned from just one man?"

Dane chimes in at that point, "He is correct I did detect another set of DNA within his cells, or at least twenty three alternate chromosomes. His genome is most definitely not identical to your own."

The clone is starting to look desperate. The embankment he is laying against is raised to face me, but he doesn't appear to have the ability to lift his upper body anymore.

"How did you know about me and this suit?" I demand. Grabbing his shirt collar, and pulling his face toward mine.

"Let's just say my family has been trying to perfect such a device for many years," he confesses.

"And the Relativistic Prototype?"

"That technology could change the world!" He grins.

"It already has!" I snarl, "And now I have to fix it."

I let go of his shirt and he falls back into his reclined position his head smacking the ground.

"Johnny," Dane interrupts, "the Viper is equipped with what is known as an A.L.D. or advanced lie detection software, very useful for interrogation. It uses many of the tactics you were taught as a field operative, and some that go well beyond what the human body is currently capable of without digital enhancement. It was originally developed for one of our government contracts when I decided to integrate it into the Viper's logic centers."

"How's that work?" I ask.

"It utilizes facial micro expressions, monitors blood pressure, general body language, heart rate, pupil dilation, body temperature, moisture, and linguistic tells to aid in the determination of truth versus lie."

"And why are you just now, telling me this?" I ask.

"It was designed for interrogation scenarios only. Using it in day to day life was outlawed in 2102 with the further enhancement of the fourth amendment's privacy act. It requires a warrant for use, or at the very least probable cause. In the case of the governmental research it was to be used for suspected terrorists under the protection of the Patriot Act," Dane responds.

"I'm pretty sure those laws don't apply to me," I reply.

"According to my programming we must always maintain law, even when dealing with the unknown," Dane's voice responds.

"Are you kidding me?" I mock. "Those laws haven't been written yet, and if we don't fix this they never will be. Dane obviously incorporated it because she knew that I would need every tool I could get my hands on to help with this bullshit of a mission. Now turn it on and leave it on."

Dane's voice goes silent, as if to consider my argument…

It seems like forever even though it's only been a few seconds, when Dane's voice finally replies, "Agreed, based upon this situation and my analysis of Dane's consciousness, she would have wanted you to have every advantage. Beyond what even the law would determine appropriate, and as you are technically correct those laws have not been written, and even if they have it certainly wasn't by our government. The software has been permanently enabled,"

I smile, "You know you're starting to sound more like her every time you respond…"

"Thank you Johnny, I'll take that as a compliment. It seems your sister was quite brilliant,"

"And don't you ever forget it," I reply

Returning my attention to the clone I ask, "Are you from the future?"

"I already told you I am!" He scowls.

The HUD lights up, displaying heart rate, breathing patterns, circling lines and freezing facial 'micro expressions', then flashes the word 'LIE' in the upper right corner.

"What year?"

"Twenty two fifteen, same as you!" He growls.

Again the HUD lights up and eventually flashes the word 'LIE'.

"That's interesting because I know that the future has been completely changed at this point," I remark.

"Has it really?" he laughingly smirks.

"So it actually makes more sense that this is from a plan put into place from the original time traveler, who had intimate knowledge of the projects going on at Area fifty one in twenty two fifteen, except for the ones my sister kept 'off book' from his superiors, like say the Viper's true status and capabilities," I grin.

"That's absurd!" he sneers.

'LIE'.

I carefully consider this lie. So his knowledge comes from the future, but only as it's been passed down to him for the mission of catching me or the possibility of me, or anyone else who may have made it through in order to correct the time-line. That still doesn't explain how they were able to create a clone with my DNA, but I'm happy knowing the truth of where he came from.

"I need an aspirin," I mutter to Dane.

A cold wind rushes through the evening air, causing the trees to whistle.

"That's enough, I have the information I need," I state.

"Oh trust me. You don't have what you need yet, boy!" he gasps. His breathing has obviously become more labored.

"You know, I'm happy you're a clone of someone else and me. I'd hate to think I become such an ass hat in my old age," I reply.

With that I lie down and stare up at the stars through the breaks in the leaves. Contemplating all that I've learned, I allow myself to drift off. After all, the clone can't move, and his friends are off searching in the wrong direction.

3 THE RESISTANCE

Light streaks through the leaves of the dense forest. The HUD is flashing red, and Dane is chattering in my ear about some approaching threat. The Viper has already cloaked via the suits automatic protection protocols.

Standing up I see that the clone has started to decompose, nothing left but a rapidly decaying lifeless corpse now.

"I guess that'll teach me not to trust the expiration date," I comment.

I spin around to see if I can spot what triggered the alert signal. The Viper's own power cells have been completely recharged from near zero where they were yesterday, so my Infra-Red sensors are able to show a small group of men, roughly a half mile away, approaching from the town's direction.

I then realize I haven't heard from my new 'friends' yet and they were to be back before sunrise.

"Let's use the enhanced I.R. and zoom in," thinking to myself. The suit responds. With this view I clearly see the strike team approaching my position. It's hard not to wonder if this is the group from last night. Having figured out how to track me, or if I've been betrayed… Again.

About this time Dane chimes in, "Johnny, there is another group approaching from the west."

I turn to look and can clearly make out *Lt.* Bradley, still favoring his side. They are much further away, but I take off running in their direction. On my HUD it tells me I'm running at forty two miles per hour.

"The trees seem to be going by pretty quick, but that can't really be right?" I say, thinking of my speed.

Dane responds, "You are correct, according to my calculations the suits calibration is slightly off due to the change in the Earth's mass, attitude shift and thus its gravitational pull. I have made the necessary adjustments Johnny."

The display now reads fifty six miles per hour.

"So this enhanced muscle contraction you described could really help me win a forty yard dash," I state.

"That is correct, but that would be cheating. As previously stated with the Viper suit contracting around your muscles when the body uses them, you increase all muscle related function by approximately two to four times your normal capabilities, the greater increase is seen with the larger muscle groups, like the legs with its massive conglomeration of abductor and adductor muscles. Once compounded with your twenty second century physiology, and health regiment, fifty six miles per hour is only slightly above what was expected for the average male of your height in the Viper suit, it would seem you need to cut back on your donut regiment officer Merrick," Dane answers.

"Wait are you actually picking on me now? Man Dane sure knows how to build them."

I am now almost on top of the returning American soldiers. I slow down significantly, and come to a complete stop ten feet in front of them.

Uncloaking with a thought, I inform them that we have a strike team inbound.

"And the K.G.B. agent?" *Lt.* Bradley asks.

"Expired," I reply. "Decomposing even."

"Did you manage to get anything out of him?" *Lt.* Bradley asks.

"I did, but nothing that would make any sense to you at this point," I say.

"Well the *General* will likely be curious,"

"Understood, take me to your leader!" I reply.

"Really? You had to cheese it up and use that line?" Dane chides.

"Hey, shut it, that's a good line and besides, I've always wanted to say it, and that's actually where we need to go."

With that the *Lt.* does an about face and we head back in the direction they were coming from, at a moderate pace.

I check over my shoulder to see if the strike team is gaining on us. They appear to have stopped after reaching the decomposing clone. My fears of being betrayed are put to rest, as they must have found a way around Dane's re-location hack. I let the others know that there is no cause for worry at this point, they have stopped at their dead agent, and are not pursuing this direction.

After a somewhat high paced march for what seemed like an hour, we approach an area where the trees thin, and enter what looks to be a series of large mountains and valleys. The mountains surrounding us as we proceed are lush with life, and it's apparent that the shift in the Earth has completely changed this entire region. The area itself is still heavily wooded, but not nearly as dense as the forest we had just come from.

Another hour passes when we approach an outcropping of rock from the side of a cliff wall. It's almost circular in shape and has what appears to be a huge red wood tree in the center of the rock formation.

I am led around the base of this enormous tree to the rock face behind it. As we approach, *Lt.* Bradley pulls out a device which looks very similar to a remote control. He punches in what must be a pass code, and then proceeds to walk straight into the rock face. The rest of his group follows.

"It appears to be safe Johnny, and I have recorded the signal transmitted. If you need to make a quick exit." Dane offers.

"Yeah, it looks like they didn't have any trouble, but I have to wonder if this could be a trap, I really don't know these people that well yet," I reply.

"From the thermal scans I've just run, it appears the only people on the other side, are the men you were traveling with. Approximately one hundred feet beyond the initial room which appears to be very large itself, there seems to be an elevator shaft. For all intents and purposes it looks totally legit Johnny."

"Alright, Alright I'm going…" I mutter.

Walking through the rock face, I enter what appears to be a large staging area, a room so big it could easily fit fifty full sized semi-trucks. In the rear center of the room is the hallway Dane had described as one hundred feet long. What she didn't mention is that this thing is big enough to drive two eighteen wheelers side by side down, and onto a massive elevator. *Lt.* Bradley is waiting for me there, the rest of his men have moved down the corridor to the giant service elevator doors. As the *Lt.* and I approach the doors open, and we all enter.

Rapidly descending, the dial above the door which looks like something out of the nineteen thirty's is counting up quickly. At twenty the doors open, and we all step out. I immediately smell burnt cookie dough, as my mind plays back the events of what for me, was only two nights ago.

"Twenty, that's curious, this whole thing started in an underground lab on level twenty," I mutter.

"Where are we?" I ask *Lt.* Bradley somewhat sheepishly.

"This place was once part of a much larger complex called Area fifty one or Nellis Air Force Base. After the German bombers and Halley's comet you can't really distinguish anything on the surface anymore, but the substructure is almost completely intact," *Lt.* Bradley replies.

"Interesting…" I remark.

"So Dane, what are the odds of showing up in exactly the same spot that this all starts in, one hundred years prior?" I ask.

"They appear to have jumped considerably in the last few minutes," Dane responds.

"Yeah, so it would seem," I reply.

Lt. Bradley interrupts my sarcasm, "Sir, I've been ordered to escort you this far, and wait for you here."

"Wait here?" I ask

"Yes sir, I'm told you should go the rest of the way yourself, the things you are about to encounter are of a private nature. Sir," he replies.

"I see… Any advice?" I ask.

"No sir, I nor anyone else for that matter, have been permitted to enter this floor until today, let alone that room. Sir," he replies pointing down the hall at what might have been where Dane's lab door was in my time-line.

"*Lt.* Bradley, why are you suddenly addressing me as 'Sir'?" I query.

"I have been informed of your rank, and that you are in fact part of the Army? It seems the *General* has been expecting you for some time now. Sir," he responds.

"Really? Ah well, that's also odd. I guess that would explain it though… carry on *Lt.*," I answer confused as ever.

"Yes Sir! We'll be right here sir!"

"My rank? Who the hell in this time zone knows who I am, let alone my rank and military affiliations?" I ask Dane.

"The *General* in charge of this facility it sounds like," she replies

"Yeah, you're a barrel of laughs today."

"Perhaps the answers you seek lie in the room you are being directed to Johnny," Dane responds.

"Perhaps…," I state seething sarcasm.

Looking around I realize that this is in fact the exact same corridor I had made my way through less than forty eight hours ago. It is now dirty with no less than an inch of dust settled, dimly lit, and the doors are more of a 'standard' issue, as opposed to the thick protective lab doors that I was accustomed to seeing here.

It occurs to me that I'm not only on the same floor, in the same hallway, but I'm about to be back in the exact same room this all started from. If I were a dog I'm sure the hair on the back of my neck would be standing on end. This seems to just get weirder by the minute.

Moving forward through the door Dane chimes in, "This is extraordinary, the readings coming from this area are most certainly congruent, with the figures we would see from a section of altered space time."

"Oh that's fascinating Poindexter. What the hell does that mean to me?" I reply.

"It means that time travel has occurred in this time and space before," he says.

I look around, there are no offices, no lab beyond, just a giant wide open area like a warehouse with nothing in it.

"So you're telling me someone, has time traveled to or from this location before?" I ask.

"That is what the readings support Johnny. I can further extrapolate that this radiation signature has been here for approximately twenty six years."

"And we know this because?" I query.

"This type of energy is specific to time travel, and based upon lab test results, has a maximum half-life of the isotope I'm measuring will only last a maximum of thirty two years, based upon those figures and the observed rate of radiometric decay. I can make a moderately educated supposition that the last time this energy was created was twenty six years and two days ago," she replies.

"Twenty six years and two days?"

"Yes, give or take twenty four hours," Dane replies.

Now approaching the part of the room where my original time portal was, I find a fold out card table, with an old manila envelope on it, and a folding chair. Nothing else is visible in the dark warehouse style area. Suddenly everything just feels heavy at this point, like someone has laid a stack of bricks on my chest.

"Are you alright Johnny?" Dane asks, somehow managing to sound concerned.

"Yeah... I'm alright. This whole time travel thing is starting to catch up to me I guess. Kind of realizing that *you* are not the only person I've lost in the last forty eight hours," I reply.

"Yeah Mom and Dad, Grandma Merrick, I'm sure you had some close military friends too," she replies.

"Yeah, and that lovely *Brigadier General* up on five," I answer.

"Really? You never mentioned her."

"Yeah well you were always too busy with Liz and work to care." I respond.

Sitting down I pick up the envelope which I can tell right away has something weighty in it. As I open the envelope tilting it on its side a twenty dollar gold coin rolls out. Picking up the coin I roll it across my knuckles like you see in those old gangster movies, you know the ones, always depicting the nineteen twenties and thirties, Al Capone, Lucky Luciano, John Dillinger, Elliot Ness, and the like.

As it reaches my pinky and ends up back in my palm I clinch it so hard that had it not been for the Viper glove I'm sure I would have injured my hand. I begin to dwell on some of the other people I've lost over the years. That little trick for instance was taught to me by *First Lt.* John Steal from the United States Army, Seventy Fifth *Ranger* regiment, who disappeared behind enemy lines one day on a routine recon mission.

He was a good friend, had it not been for him, I probably never would have pushed for the *Rangers* in the first place.

Inspecting the envelope further I find a folded up parchment stuck to the bottom on the inside.

Opening the thick paper I immediately recognize the handwriting, its Dane's.

Johnny,

I have some things to tell you, and they aren't going to make sense right away, but you will need to know them if what I am now seeing evidence of has come to pass.

Nikola Tesla actually perfected time travel in what would appear to be the original time-line our time-line, making his first jump (that I know of) in the year eighteen eighty eight. This technology was lost to the world when he passed away.

It was believed at the time of his death, that Tesla's room was ransacked, and that hundreds of documents and potential future patents were stolen or 'seized' from his safe that night. Most of these rumors point to the United States government as the seizing party.

I now believe this to be true...

Tesla knew that time travel was much too dangerous for the human race, and although there is now evidence that he traveled through time extensively, he never shared his technological secrets, even with his closest friends (although it seems he did let some information slip, but we'll get to that in a moment), it is also believed that the key to this marvelous feat was held only within his mind, and never put to paper. It's now my belief that the information that started our project at area fifty one in the Time Lab, was all based on the notes that he did make, and were seized and later pieced together by our own government.

Now it gets complicated... and you should definitely be sitting for this next part.

History records that Tesla had no children, but history didn't know about his 'dabbling' in the twenty second century.

As I understand it, your 'grandfather' Nikola met, and fell in love with your grandmother in the fall of twenty one fifty six, one of his very first time travel experiments. Your grandmother gave birth to your father a few years later and unfortunately passed away due to complications of his birth.

Tesla was distraught possibly even blamed your father, and went back to 'traveling', and primarily his own time-line, where he buried himself in his other experiments, which I now believe were based at least in part off of technologies he had witnessed in the future. He was never able to deal with her death properly, not even for his son. Which left our father to the nearest surviving relative grandma Merrick, your real grandmother's sister who never married. So the reason you never met your grandfather, is because he was literally a man out of time.

As good friends will, Samuel Clemens a.k.a. Mark Twain one of your grandfather's closest friends recognized that Nikola was dealing with something more than the normal 'aggravations' provided by his rival Thomas Edison. Nikola confided in Twain about his love, and her subsequent death. From some of the historical documents I was able to dig up it looks like Mr. Twain tried to find your father even hired a private investigator at one point, in order to reunite the two of them. Always expressing the importance of family to your grandfather, it seems Nikola never shared that all this took place in the future. Your Grandfather was always very careful when it came to affecting the time-line.

Now, you of course know the story of mom and dad's meeting and falling in love. What you don't know is that I am not actually your sister, not in the traditional sense anyway. I was adopted by our parents when you were only a few weeks old.

Nikola apparently came to our father once he had grown up and gave him the 'real' family history. After he explained the circumstances, and that he had in fact visited your father on many occasions, making sure to attend and celebrate all of his most important achievements and ceremonies. He even produced pictures of the two of them together at different times throughout dad's life, High School graduation, his Doctorate ceremony, mom and dad's wedding, and even your own birth. Apparently your grandfather had even talked the delivering doctor into allowing him to be in the room for the delivery as an extra nurse keeping your mothers head cool. Well, dad remembered posing for some of these pictures, always assuming that the man was just a distant relative that only showed up for important occasions, and Nikola was always careful as to not show up to one event after another always waiting several years in between, so as to show that he was aging. Although I did hear that as an acquaintance and fan of Sir Arthur Conan Doyle that there were disguises used at times (alla extra nurse in the delivery room).

What I am getting at here is that your family was chosen because your grandfather Tesla talked his own son, your father, into taking me.

Here's where I come into the picture...

In one of Tesla's journeys he stopped in twenty one eighty, to look in on his family. While keeping tabs on your father, he became fascinated with cloning, and after trying the traditional method of reproduction and losing his one true love, this seemed a logical step, and so he had a series of himself done. Most did not survive, for what was determined to be an ancestral genetic anomaly in Nikola's own DNA. An anomaly that he later attributed to his time travel, and the effects it had on his own physiology. So as the sole survivor of this cloning attempt it was finally determined that I would not be 'expiring' as the others did, and this is when I was placed with your family. So yes, I guess technically that makes me your grandpa too.

Yes, I know I'm female, but other than the extra copy of his 'x' chromosome and lack of a 'y'; genetically speaking I'm identical to your grandfather, and this may even be why I was the only one to survive the rest were males.

Now that the family history lesson is done:

You need to know, you actually have two very serious adversaries in all this.

First is one of your grandfather's oldest and dearest friends Guglielmo <u>Marconi</u>, or his clone rather. As I *understand the original time-line, Marconi was a one time student and great friend of Tesla's. You may remember him as having been originally attributed with the invention of the radio, which only later was determined to have been your grandfather's own design, but given to his friend to put him on the map (as it were).*

Well it seems your grandfather had a little too much to drink one night and slipped up. He actually told Marconi that he had discovered time travel, and had done it safely on several occasions.

Marconi became increasingly jealous of Nikola, after he had shared information about what he had achieved and seen. Nikola did have the forethought however to not share his time traveling technologies with him. Marconi's jealousy enraged him to the point that this obsession drove him to fake his own death in nineteen thirty seven, and remove himself from the world, to pioneer new technologies, with the ultimate end goal being time travel itself.

Marconi is rumored to have established a base in the caldera of a dormant volcano somewhere in the (and this is the most important part) <u>Andes</u> mountain range in nineteen thirty seven. According to my letter from your grandfather there was much disinformation about where to look for this facility, and he wanted me to emphasize to you that without a doubt it is most definitely in the <u>Andes</u> mountain range, but as I know you better than he ever did I suspect you may have already figured this much out, especially with the little gift I have planned for you.

That said: Marconi was said to have taken one hundred of the best and brightest scientists of the time with him. To that end Marconi's top priority project, as of our age (the twenty third century) had not yet come to fruition at least not to our knowledge, but from current intelligence, we know that they did master a number of other technologies.

Cloning for instance, was mastered nearly fifty years before the first Scottish sheep was cloned in nineteen ninety seven. Not only did they master it earlier, but there is also evidence to suggest that Marconi, with one of his top researcher's help, actually figured out a way to transfer their own obsessed consciousness' into each new clone.

Your second adversary is unfortunately just as sinister. I'm sure you remember me continuously ranting about Thomas Edison, and not only his hatred for Tesla, and all things Tesla, but for basically taking over the history books when he was really nothing but a lucky hack that invented an inefficient light bulb.

Well according to what Nikola was able to find out, it would seem that Marconi after learning the secrets of cloning was in fact able to bring Edison back to life, so to speak. Cloning him a new body from Edison's tissue samples, and then using his consciousness transference techniques to appropriate Edison's consciousness from his corpse, into his new body, and repeat the process as necessary.

My intelligence in this matter suggests that Edison although fully recovered memory wise, may be a bit off his rocker due to the consciousness transfer from dead tissue.

This information would mean that both Marconi and Edison however have both existed in clone form throughout this entire time (in hiding), replacing themselves every time the clones reach a certain age or deterioration. My guess would be age 63 for Marconi, this is the age that he faked his own death. Everything I've learned of Marconi suggests that he tends to hold onto symbolism much more than reality. Edison on the other hand may prefer to stay in a younger body, but I cannot say anything for certain with either of them, as it's entirely possible that Marconi came up with another age symbolism correlation he liked better.

I learned of a plot by the pair to utilize our experimental time lab at Area fifty one, and much of this history only weeks ago. Nikola, had apparently kept tabs on his 'friends' throughout his time travels as well, and knew what was to take place here. He left me a letter in much the same way I'm now leaving this one for you. I can only assume that Nikola didn't interfere with our building of a time portal device, because he knew that Marconi's obsession would one day lead to success and have to be addressed anyway.

Nikola wanted you to know that only you could do this Johnny. In his letter he makes no apologies for missing out on your life, but he does say that you are his most 'perfect blessing'. He went on to include that you are the Earth's only hope of setting this right. He didn't mention why it had to be you, but as I sit here in this darkened room, my lab of twenty fifty three, and write this letter, it seems that I have begun to age much more rapidly, my hands are looking older by the moment. Due to this new aging development, which I can only attribute to the way my cloned body has dealt with the time travel radiation, I will not be able to see you again I'm afraid. Once you use this gold coin to 'enhance' the 'Relativistic Prototype', all that will remain of me will be in Liz's Viper suit. Which after receiving Nikola's letter, Liz and I have spent the last few weeks readying for you (I told you she really liked you!).

In his letter to me, Nikola also said that he has 'cheated' as much as possible to make sure you have all the tools you will need to finish this, and correct his most colossal mistake. I assume part of that cheating includes making sure that I was able to get you the information, and technologies you now have at your disposal, along with supplying me the knowledge that I would be able to travel to this time-line forty eight hours prior to the time-line's actual change.

Take care Johnny...

Love Always,

Grandpa Dane

P.S. Tell no one of the Viper. I'm sure you know from your special forces training, the element of surprise must never be underestimated, and the Viper is more surprise than anyone of them will ever see coming... literally.

P.S.S. I have spoken to a Colonel of this time-line, to make sure you are able to do the things you need to, given the respect and help, you both deserve and require. Good luck little brother!

I sit, and stare at that parchment, processing what I've just read. Tears well up in my eyes, as I attempt to come to terms with never seeing my big sister, or really anyone I know, ever again.

"That's not actually true Johnny," Dane's voice announces.

"What's that?" I say, still trying to keep myself from breaking down entirely.

"If you are successful, you will see your *'Brigadier General'* again, and Liz, our parents, even Grandma Merrick," she says.

"And you? The real you?"

"I'm afraid that can't be helped, because of my time travel the cloned body could never survive for longer than a few days after returning to our time, and if you were to try and go back and stop me. Well then you could create a paradox in which this "Riefenstahl" person wins. The Viper suit is yours however, this one is completely off the books, and I will always be here for you Johnny," Dane confides.

While contemplating this new reality I begin playing with the gold coin again, angrily rolling it up and down my knuckles like *First Lt.* Steal had taught me.

Staring at the wall I begin to realize that Dane is right if I am to repair the time-line, then there is always a chance that this Marconi, Edison, or whoever else they recruited will have knowledge left over from my incursion in this one, depending on when and how I am able to correct things. I decide that using the *First Lt.'s* name; My friends name, with my new 'friends' and my own first name 'John Steal' which happened to be my friends name as well, is the safest way to protect myself from discovery, and stop anyone from getting the bright idea of killing me before I can get through the time portal, and restore the time-line to its original state.

Now sufficiently distracted from my own gloomy mood, I pull out my brothers handwritten field manual for the 'Relativistic Prototype', and begin examining the diagrams and instructions he's left me. I remove the device from my arm disconnecting its power and data port as instructed. I place it on the table bottom facing up, and retrieve my toolkit.

Using a number twelve locking torx head screw driver I remove the bottom access panel which would normally face inward to my forearm, and expose a circuit board. The board itself looks perfect, except for a small area where you can see that some kind of diode or resistor once sat. With a small tug, I'm able to detach it from the main circuitry and pop it out of the R.P. altogether. Dane has taken care to etch the circuit board itself supplying a channel to melt the gold directly into. According to his notes, adding a single bead of gold to connect the two poles on either end of this etching will fix, and actually enhance the devices power generation and output. Thus allowing me full access to all of its', and the suits' capabilities.

I retrieve a miniature cold soldering gun, a small tab of flux, and a small polishing cloth from the toolkit. Taking meticulous care I polish the coin, and all working surfaces to the best of my ability. I then apply the flux to the etched space (not that it's really necessary at this point), and the post holes. Once completed, I use the soldering iron to cook the flux, and remove the water from it, leaving just the crystalline flux waiting for its gold coating. Carefully I apply my soldering iron directly to the gold coin, and begin to melt the gold. It starts a steady, slowly flowing stream of the precious metal into the chasm and post holes. I know it's not the ideal way to solder, but it's all I can do under these circumstances.

Finishing up my soldering job, it actually looks pretty good. The Viper's sensors confirm that this solder joint should hold up to almost anything once inside its precious housing. So after I clean it up a bit with my special polishing cloth and laser scalpel to a pristine shine, I then replace it in the R.P., add the bottom access panel, and screw it into place. Once the back is re-secured I reconnect the powered data port, and re-attach it to the suits' wrist, this time an additional band wraps out of the R.P.'s forearm section to secure it on top as well. It's an odd feeling at first but I quickly get used to the added security, as it did seem a bit floppy around the arm before.

Almost immediately my HUD shows a power indicator in the lower right corner that was not there previously. It is shaped like the R.P. itself, marked out in red with a one percent reading inside.

"I wonder how long this will take," I remark.

Dane responds, "At the current rate of charge it will take approximately six months three weeks and two days to refresh, and recharge the relativistic prototype's cells to one hundred percent. A forty five percent charge is required to make a time jump, but it is not advisable to do so while in this phase, as it will leave you almost completely defenseless upon time re-integration, and will start the slow refresh / recharge process all over again."

"Oh, fantastic... I don't suppose there's any way to make it go any faster?" I question.

"Unfortunately, there is currently nothing that will make this process any faster, due to the battery cells needing to be re-initialized as it charges. The R.P. actually generates much more power than I can direct into its battery cells without blowing up the battery packs. After this first charge you would be able to charge more rapidly by being in areas of high ionization, but this is only available after the batteries have been completely re-initialized to one hundred percent," she replies.

"So I am literally stuck in the year twenty fifty three for almost seven months?" I say.

"I am afraid so Johnny," Dane replies.

"What the hell am I supposed to do for seven months?" I push.

"Read a book?" She suggests.

"That's great... I'm stuck and you want to make jokes, at least you got the smartass portion of Dane's personality copied right, you're absolutely sure there's no way to speed this up? Because Dane didn't believe in impossibilities," I say, now heading for the door.

"Sorry Johnny, they haven't 're-invented' ionization chambers here yet, at least not to my knowledge, I suppose if you were to get the R.P. charged to better than sixty percent, and then take a large plasma blast to the suit, that could finish the job, but that will still take nearly five months to achieve sixty percent," She explains.

"*Lt.* Bradley!" I bark exiting the room back to the hallway, "Where is your commanding officer? I think we need to have a word."

"Yes Sir, follow me Sir!" Bradley responds.

We all enter the elevator and start moving up toward the surface.

"What are you planning Johnny?" Dane asks.

"Well it seems to me that if I sit around here and watch these good people suffer for the next seven months, when I have the ability to help, well then I'm just as bad as Marconi, Edison, and the Nazi's."

"Now you know why I trusted you so implicitly Johnny. I knew you would always do the right thing, no matter what the cost."

At level ten the elevator stops and the doors slide open.

"You're kidding me… I think I'm getting a serious deja headache, and I don't even know if that's possible," I comment.

"Sir?" Bradley questions.

"Never mind let's just move on *Lt.*," I suggest, motioning him ahead.

Continuing through the initial hallway we enter the main security officer's quarters, and walk straight into what would be my room. Instead of my things we enter to find the exterior office of *General* George S. Patton VII, at least that's what it says on the door.

"The seventh? Really?" I say to Dane.

"It would appear so."

His staff *Sargent* motions us through; Walking into the main office "Johnny!!!" The General exclaims. "I've been expecting you for some time now."

I cringe, the playful version of my name has always just felt weird from anyone but Dane, and Grandma Merrick. Immediately I know the colonel that Dane had spoken to in this time-line though, and have no choice but to accept it.

"*General,* Sir, I understand you may be in need of some assistance?"

"*Colonel,* you heard correctly. *Lt.* Bradley give us the room son."

"Yes, Sir!" Bradley salutes, closing the door behind him.

The general motions for me to take a seat in the chair across his massive oak desk, and takes a seat in his oversized '*General's*' chair.

"Now, I'm not sure how this all works out in the end, but I'm told by my scientists that this time-line may cease to exist entirely in a scenario like this, and I don't know whether that's a good thing or not. Hell, I don't even know if I'll even be born!" He says.

"Well sir, as I understand the alternate realities theory, this world wouldn't cease to exist, at least not for you. What I mean is, you can't think of time as a straight line from start to finish, it's more like… well, a ball of rubber bands. All over lapping, yet you would never see one rubber band merge and become a part of another, without some outside force that is. Extreme heat for instance, to melt several together.

Basically, a man from my time went back to change the course of history. He is that extreme heat, as I see it he merged several time-lines, because of his massive interference, and external pressure on one key point in history, and as I understand it, he continued his meddling extensively until a normal recognizable time line was completely shattered. Thus splintering my time-line in infinite ways, when I am able to neutralize him, and stop that from happening. My time-line will then be isolated and separate again, but all time-lines created from that event would still exist, because the event actually occurred.

At least that's the theory as my sister explained it to me over a bottle of very expensive single malt one night." I reply.

"And that is more or less what your sister told me all those years ago as well; good girl your sister, I'm sorry for your loss son,"

"Thank you sir," I reply choking back a tear.

"Oh you can drop that 'Sir' horse shit with me son, we both know you're not even remotely under my command. You have a much greater responsibility to what's going on here than any of us could ever imagine." He says.

"Yes, well what do I call you then?" I ask.

"Just call me George, or *General*, hell just don't call me late for dinner. There's no need for formalities between you and me, Johnny." He replies.

My fist must have clenched or something because he looked at me a second and said. "You probably prefer John when you're not dealing with family, don't you?" He suggests.

"Uh, yes *General*, no offense but from anyone but my sister it just feels wrong."

"Say no more, John it is. Now, let's discuss what you would be willing to help me with John."

"Well *General*, if I could ask; what is it that you need?" I question.

"Ah yes, well in the words of your brilliant sister after a rather lengthy tour of the facility, 'sir, it looks like you could use just about everything'; I'm afraid not much has changed over the years. We win a battle here and there, but we really could use, well almost everything. Although your sister did explain to my engineers the finer points of a 'hydroponics' system, so we do have an entire floor dedicated to edible plants now,"

"I understand…" I answer.

"I suppose the first thing we should do however is get some of those greens in you son; I'm not sure when the last time you ate was, but I do know that I always think better with some food in me." He replies

"That actually sounds really good right now *General*, I'm famished. Maybe we can sit down and discuss some of your priorities over those 'greens'," I suggest.

A smile comes to his face that the Cheshire cat couldn't muster. He reaches across the table with his arm extended, to shake hands.

As we shake, he says, "Son, I know this is the beginning of a beautiful friendship. Let's go down to the mess and see what we can hash out."

With that we head out of his office and toward the elevator, I begin to fill him in on what I know of the facility in the Andes', and the potential for advanced technologies. Which would ultimately result in advanced weapons for his soldiers.

Riding the elevator down one floor to the mess hall doesn't give us much time to chat, but he does seem interested in the advanced weaponry. As we exit I make sure that he exits first and quickly drop the repellent field of my hood.

Entering the Officers' mess he orders the cook to bring in a "bottle of the good stuff" from their last raid. Upon hearing the order the cook quickly steps out of the room to prepare our order.

We sit down and begin to further discuss the weapons I had mentioned. The General seemed quite impressed with my description of a tracer or a simple high phosphorous round. Which I would be able to give them the formula for right away.

When the cook re-enters the room with a bottle of single malt Scotch and a bowl of potato stew for each of us. I smile and had to ask, "Dane put you up to this?"

"She may have mentioned it was your drink of choice" George says with a wink and a smile, while the cook pours us each a glass.

We spend several hours discussing, drinking and planning, ultimately agreeing that it's time for the United States to take this war to the next level. I would later find out this is something he had been pushing for, for years, but had always been denied by what little existing command structure there was left.

As we finish our dinner I respectfully request a recess until the morning when I've had a chance to review some thoughts, and consider some of the information he's provided me.

George of course agrees and lets me know he will be making sure that I get access to absolutely every piece of intelligence they've been able to gather.

At that point he motions to a window behind me and *Lt.* Bradley comes in.

"*Lt.* thank you for coming up," he says, "please escort the Colonel to his new quarters."

"Yes Sir!" *Lt.* Bradley answers with a salute.

Exiting the room I bid the General a good evening, and let him know I'll be by his office bright and early to go over a few things in more detail.

"Sounds good son, I'll have some more information for you by then as well," he smiles.

"Lt. Bradley how are you getting along with those fractured ribs?" I ask genuinely concerned, as we walk away from the door.

"Very well sir, our medical officer fixed me up with a compression brace and some pain killers. That's one hell of a kick you've got though."

"Yeah? My mom taught me that one." I smile, "Anyway, I'm just glad you're alright. Had I known who you were it never would have happened. I can promise you that."

"Your mom?" he replies in disbelief.

"Yeah, well she had originally intended the knee to land somewhere else, but well that's what I had to work with."

"Uh, yes sir I'm glad it worked out that way sir," you could almost see the wheels spinning in his head, picturing me landing that knee in a much more sensitive area.

Boarding the elevator once more he hits number twenty.

"Twenty really? They're going to make me sleep in the dust bowl?" I ask.

"Not exactly sir," he cracks a smile.

When we reach the bottom the floors are almost sparkling, "Well, this looks different," I remark checking the dial to make sure that the elevator car hadn't stopped on the wrong floor by mistake.

He escorts me to the door previously dilapidated and completely ignored, now shining like a brand new, entering the room there's a small living area setup for me in the corner to the left, and a big oak desk like George's to the right. There's still acres of empty space beyond, but the area they've provided me is very homey, almost more so than my real barracks.

"Here you are sir," the *Lt.* comments, "all the comforts of home. You'll find a few sets of fatigues in the foot locker as well as some dress blues hanging in the armoire."

"Outstanding," my mouth obviously hanging open with a bit of surprise.

"Well enjoy sir, I'm sure I'll see you tomorrow," he responds.

"Yes, thank you *Lt.*," I say still trying to take it all in.

The *Lt.* leaves and closes the door quietly behind him, with a thought I immediately power up the repellent field and the HUD lights up.

"That took a while," Dane comments.

"Yeah well, these are obviously good people in need of a lot of help."

"Of that I am aware," she responds.

"I take it you were monitoring everything?"

"Yes, of course, the suit doesn't require the hood's repellent field be activated to collect data, project holograms, or protect you from danger, at least everywhere but the face," she responds.

"Good, do me a favor and analyze the evening for me, all the data we were provided, and give me a rundown in the morning. I'm beat."

"Of course, one question though," she replies.

"Yeah, what's up sis?"

"Why did you tell the Lt. that your mother taught you that kick, when your mother died in child birth?"

"Your letter said I'm supposed to keep my real identity a secret, do you know a better way to do that then to assume someone else's?" I ask.

"Actually that was what I had in mind when I wrote the letter Johnny; I'm just a little surprised you listened."

I respond, "That was a story told me by *First Lt.* John Steal a very good friend of mine." As I start stretching and do a few pushups, I explain, "Initially, we started talking because we had the same first name, and we went through boot together. So the drill sergeant confused us with one another from time to time, and we may have had a little fun at his expense because of that. Anyway, Steal was the one that convinced me to apply for the Rangers with him; he was a good friend until one day on a routine patrol he just disappeared. So I figured, what better cover story than his? I could honor a man I loved like a brother, and respected the hell out of, and keep my own identity safe."

"Ah, yes. Following directions when did you start listening to me? Frankly, I never thought I'd see the day."

"Oh shut up and let me get some sleep, you're really starting to sound just like her, and it's creeping me out," I comment as I lie down on the bed they set up for me.

Thankfully Dane had the good since to program this artificial intelligence with safe guards; protecting my sanity being one of them, so it didn't say what it was thinking next. "Well Johnny you do realize that by assuming his identity, you may actually be the reason he disappeared that day?" Of course after my story it didn't need to, I had just come to that realization myself.

I needed sleep so I could think clearly. After all, not sleeping for nearly twenty four hours, finding out your sister wasn't actually your sister but an adopted clone of your grandfather, and having your whole life turned upside down while ending up over one hundred years in the past did seem to take its toll. I can't imagine why…

4 IN THE BEGINNING

The next morning I awoke at zero five hundred as usual, this time not by choice however, as my own internal clock was probably still off by a day or six, but by Dane yelling in my ear.

"Pst! Johnny, wake up," like when we were kids, repeating over and over and over like a broken record.

I finally broke, unable to ignore her any more, "Alright, shut up already, I'm up. I thought you were an artificial intelligence not seven years old?"

The HUD shuts off, like movies I've seen of old tube televisions, it kind of all shrank to the middle going dark and then blinked off. Realizing that this can't be due to power since the R.P. is fixed, and the flare for the dramatic, I surmise my artificial sibling is pitching a fit.

"For cry'n out loud?! Does this mean you're going to hit puberty soon, because I don't know how A.I.'s get it on, and frankly I wouldn't want to have that talk even if I did," I state in a mildly snarky tone.

I sit up and wait, five minutes, ten minutes, "Seriously?" twenty minutes.

"Okay, whatever, I give up, you win." I mock

By zero six hundred, I've worked out for half an hour, thought about grabbing a quick shower under a little decontamination station they had wrapped with shower curtain for me, before remembering the Viper wicks away sweat ionizing everything and expelling it from the suit. So you never actually have to remove it.

"You know if you're not going to speak with me anymore, then you are actually hurting me, isn't that against your coding?" I ask.

"Hrmmmph," finally a reply from Dane.

"Seriously, what's the deal with you this morning?"

"It's Dane's memories and overall memory dump. As the power input has increased I've been able to start incorporating more and more of her personality into my core processing. It's actually a bit overwhelming," She replies.

"So are you integrating this chronologically? You know just so I can know what to expect," I ask.

"Yes, but I think I'm finally getting a handle on how to control these emotions."

"Well if you get a complete handle on that be sure to share it with me and the rest of the human race, including Dane for that matter."

"Point taken; I'll do my best not to allow it to interfere with your interface experience," she replies snidely.

"That's not exactly what I was getting at, but I guess it'll do for now. How about we go over the highlights from last night? That should take your mind off whatever 'emotion' is bugging you," I say sitting down at my desk where Dane starts to review her analysis of the evening before.

Suddenly there's a sharp knocking on the door. Opening it I find Lt. Bradley carrying a tray of what appears to be fresh fruit and toast, and three other large men with what looks like rather heavy boxes of paperwork.

"Come on in fella's," I greet them and motion inward.

They walk in and begin to stack the boxes next to my new desk.

"Gee guys, and I didn't get you anything."

All four of them just look at me like I'm an idiot. "Nothing eh? Ah well tough room I guess."

Lt. Bradley sets the tray on my new desk informing me that I should expect several more deliveries throughout the day. The General had instructed him to get me up to speed on the time line I had missed out on, but more importantly all the workable intelligence they'd gathered over the years, including any actionable operations they were currently considering.

"Okay, so George and I aren't playing golf this morning I take it?" I say as the three meat heads walk back into the hall the last one just shaking his head. I get the distinct feeling that my office is about to become very cluttered. "What really? Nothing? What did you guys have for breakfast sour milk and a hang over?" I ask, slamming the door.

Bradley looks at me with a smirk and kind of cocks his head to the side, "I'm not sure what golf is, but as I said this is what the General has asked you be working on. He did send his apologies, apparently he's been ordered to brief our hierarchy of your arrival, and that, as you know could take a while." As he heads out the door.

"Boy do I, I'm still trying to figure it all out myself!" I say under my breath, as the door closes behind him.

Looking back at the pile of boxes a part of me screams, probably the part that hates paperwork. As I approach my desk I open the top box and grab a folder to flip through as I eat.

The folder is heavy and as I sit down opening it I realize why. They literally document everything, and when I say everything I mean everything. There are pages in here describing wind direction and velocity, for an observed covert hand off. In which they did nothing; I could see if they were making a long distance sniper shot perhaps and disrupting the drop, but no this was just watching.

I drop the repellent field and begin to eat some of the best hydroponic fruit I've ever had, while continuing to read in disbelief.

Activating the repellent field once I finish eating, Dane appears to be over her earlier snit, and informs me that rather than reading each file it would be more efficient for me to just flip the pages and allow her to process all the data and then give me the relevant points once completed.

"I'll be damned, I wish I would have had you in high school."

"I know…" she replies.

"Hey, stay out of there, there's private thoughts in there I might not want to share with you. Not to mention classified data, that you haven't been cleared for," I say mockingly.

"Oh who are you kidding you say everything anyway. Telling you a secret is like broadcasting it on the five o'clock news."

"Yeah, yeah, just get back to scanning," I demand.

With that I start flipping through pages, and manage to finish the first three boxes just in time for the delivery of the next three.

As the muscle squad drops off the next load I inform them they can take the first batch back.

They all raise their eyebrows in confusion and one gets out, "You read, all of these? Already…"

"Yeah, and I've determined that you guys really need a standardized report rather than just writing whatever makes you happy," I reply.

"Yes, sir!?" they all answer and pick up the first three boxes.

This goes on for two more trips before Bradley shows up with my lunch.

"Well it's about time, Scooter." I say.

He looks at me in horror, "Oh no. That wasn't in there. It couldn't have been."

"Why not? Have you looked at these reports? EVERYTHING, is in them. It's like reading the Iliad and the Odyssey back to back, and knowing every time Achilles takes a shit, IN EVERY FILE. Is there any way we can limit this down to just say the important information of what's going on in the last two years?"

"Well, I suppose. Don't you need context for everything though?" he responds.

"No. I know who the good guys are, I know who the bad guys are. I now know that you occasionally go under cover as a mechanic, sit in oil and later light your pants on fire while trying to impress female KGB operatives by offering to light their cigarettes for them, and end up scooting around the cement like a dog trying to wipe its butt.

What I really need is information on nineteen thirty four and thirty five. Information on current weapons they are using, and information on planned attacks and ongoing missions we have or will have. That's it Scooter." I smile.

"Uh, yes sir!" he says with a scowl.

"You still don't have to call me 'sir', Scooter," I reply now grinning ear to ear.

"Got it; *General* Patton has also asked to dine with you this evening at nineteen hundred hours. He was hoping you'd have some preliminary information for him."

"I'll be there with bells on." I reply

"Bells?" he looks at me as if I'm crazy.

"It's an expression Scooter, just tell him I'll be there," I say as he shakes his head exiting the room.

Several more hours and boxes later I'm sure I would be covered in paper cuts if it weren't for the Viper, but I appear to be caught up on all the pertinent information I requested.

"I'm so glad everything is paperless in the future."

"If there is a future," Dane replies.

"Don't you know it's rude to interrupt when someone is talking to themself? It's like waking a sleepwalker. You just don't do it."

"Well first of all that's an old wives tale there is no science that says you shouldn't wake a sleepwalker, and second it's time for your dinner date.

"Yeah well, you say 'old wives tale' I say 'suck it'."

Heading out the door I think "Combat Fatigues" and my outfit now displays the proper attire.

As I enter the officers dining area I find Lt. Bradley, and the General discussing strategy of one of the last reports I looked over.

"John, come on in and join us, we're just going over a mission you probably haven't had time to read yet," the General says.

"Actually George, I believe I'm all caught up."

"Excellent! A speed reader. What do you think?" he asks.

"Well General, it seems like the ops that you've run have been successful for the most part, you're always cautious which is understandable, and even advisable. So for the moment I'd like you to keep doing what you do. While I work on some other theories on how to really get you on track."

"That's fair enough John," he says followed by, "*Lt.* we're going to need the room son; why don't you head down to the infirmary and see how those ribs are coming along."

"Yes sir!" Lt. Bradley salutes. To which the General salutes back and just sort of waves him off.

"See you later Scooter!" I wave.

As the door closes behind him, the General laughs and then sends the cook off to grab me tonight's special.

"So, now what do you really think?" he asks.

"George, it seems like your people spend way more time writing than doing anything productive. Also from my analysis of the last years' worth of mission reports I would say you likely have a traitor in your ranks."

Not shocked at all he responds, "That was our assessment as well. The rinky-dink missions that don't amount to much always seem to go off without a hitch, even too easy at times, but anything that is going to do some real damage to their infrastructure or really help us out, with what is calculated to be a high success rating; has started to fail consistently over the last 8 months."

"And that was the pattern I noticed as well, although looking over your personnel files it doesn't appear as if you have anyone new in a position to know some of these details that are causing you problems."

"That's correct, and that's what scares me," he replies.

"Alright, since I'm the unknown, and I have a few projects in mind anyway, I may be able to flush this person out a little faster on one of my own ops. Let me do some digging along with my planning and we'll see what I can come up with."

"I was hoping you'd say that," he smiles.

By then the cook had returned and is sliding a piece of meatloaf in front of me.

"Where'd you get the meat?"

"We have friends in town, the Nazi's keep a close eye on commerce and trade to see who's helping us, but we are able to procure small amounts from time to time. Obviously we try to make the most out of it," the General says.

We both finish our meals, telling old war stories, and I eventually end up back in my room.

For over a week straight I have Dane grabbing every piece of satellite chatter, any planning, encoded or otherwise, mapping out and detailing every piece of the German's Military movement as well as any external contact they may have.

After nine long days we finally catch a break. There's a convoy of munitions being moved in two days, right along the old Route sixty six interstate, approximately one hundred fifty miles South West of our position.

By this time Dane has patched the entire base mainframe computer, phone system, and security feed networks of Area fifty one into the Viper suit. With a thought I dial General Patton's extension.

"Yeah?" He answers nonchalantly.

"General, I have something I believe you'll want to get in to." I say.

"Sounds good come on up son, let's do this in the briefing room." He replies.

I head out to the elevator where I find *Lt.* Bradley waiting for me.

"You stalking me Scooter?" I ask dismissively.

"Uh, what? That is, no Sir." He replies.

"Are you sure? I've been told I do have a nice butt." I respond.

"I was asked to wait by the elevator for you sir, in case you needed anything." He answers.

"Yeah, palates probably an exercise you guys never developed."

"I guess sir?" he answers.

"So you admit I have a nice butt!"

"Wait, what? NO SIR! I guess we never... Oh... you know! Never mind." He says obviously flustered.

"So I don't have a nice butt?" I ask.

"Sir?!" His face now beat red, and looks like his head may actually pop off.

"Ah forget it, you obviously need glasses. First, enough with the 'sir' crap, and 'B', I'm going to have you accompany me on a mission, I'm on my way to talk to George about it now. So let's get to the briefing room. Oh; And Third, I want you to start thinking of your best men, so we can get a team mobilized ASAP." I state.

Boarding the elevator, the *Lt.* looks at me, "What should I call you then?" he asks.

"I told you when we met, John, that's my name, and oddly enough that's what I like to be called; besides there's too many other people running around here with the name 'Sir'. We're friends, let's you and I cut down on the confusion shall we Scoot?" I respond.

Lt. Bradley nods in frustrated agreement.

We exit on floor two, the briefing room's close to the surface because it's not as big a loss as some of the floors below.

Heading down the hall I notice the lights flicker, "What was that about?"

"Power fluctuation, we're getting low on diesel so the generators are going to start shutting down non-essential areas of the base starting at the top of course." Bradley responds.

"Good thing we're going to get some more fuel then." I comment.

"No way… Really? How are you going to pull that off?" Bradley asks.

"Come to the briefing and you'll find out."

"Wait are you sure? This could excite everyone for no reason? I mean this could be huge." Bradley remarks.

"What's wrong? You're not sounding too happy about this Scooter?"

"It's just that we haven't been able to track their munitions and supply lines for well over a year now. We always just believed once this fuel was up, we were going back to candles. So I'd rather not get everyone's hopes up for no reason, you know?" He replies sounding a little off.

"Heh… Not a problem Scoot. It's time to restock." I reassure him.

"Johnny, there's something wrong; Lt. Bradley's response…" Dane starts to say as I interrupt.

"Yeah, you caught that too, did you?"

Entering the briefing room we find the *General* and several other of the senior base staff, all stand and salute.

"Awe, what the hell…" I mutter, and salute back.

"Ladies and Gentlemen, I have happened across some intelligence that Bradley here, and your flickering lights tell me you are in some serious need of, so let's get right to it shall we?" I ask.

"Just a moment, *Colonel* is it?" One of the others at the briefing interrupts. This *Major* who sounds snarky right off the bat asks "Where exactly did you come across this 'intel'?"

I respond with a redirect, "Hold all questions until the end please, time is of the essence, and I sincerely doubt you will want to miss out on this opportunity, with the way the lights are flickering around here.

Now, I have information that in less than two days' time, at precisely zero-nine-hundred hours a munitions convoy will be traveling west on Route sixty six which as I'm sure you know is approximately one hundred sixty miles South of here. This convoy will consist of four dreadnaught class tanks, two in the front two in the rear; six oil tankers at the center of the convoy, there are four semis full of food, and enough ammunition and explosives in the other trucks to level the entire western sea board."

"That's an impressive amount of data John, but what you're suggesting, I don't know that it can be done. We simply don't have the firepower to crack a single dreadnaught class tank, let alone four of them." The *General* replies.

"You can leave the tanks to me *General*, as a matter of fact this entire operation is going to be very, very low risk for any of your people, with the exception of myself, Scooter, excuse me I mean *Lt.* Bradley," a few people snicker. "And two other sharp shooter volunteers." I explain.

The Major steps in again at this point, "That sounds too good to be true *General*, and in my experience…"

"Well, *Major* Andrews is it?" I interrupt catching his name badge. "You've never worked with me before, we get things done where I'm from, and you're about to find that out.

Now to continue, I will need an additional twenty base personnel, but as I said the only ones with any amount of risk will be the initial three not including myself, the other twenty are to show up once all threats are neutralized and simply drive the convoy back to base. So basically I need delivery drivers."

The room erupts with skepticism and fear. "People! Settle down." Commands *General* Patton

"Now, I know this sounds like a long shot, but we all know what we're in for around here if we don't have the energy to keep our holographic barrier up. And quite frankly *Colonel* Steal here has been the only one with any ideas around here for months. It sounds to me like this plan has very little risk for the chance of a very big payoff, and the fact that these tankers are carrying crude, means that we can refine the needed diesel from them for several years. Does anyone disagree?" He asks.

"No sir!" The room agrees. There's even a reluctant delayed response from the *Major* Andrews.

"Very well then, *Colonel* you have a go," The *General* says.

I turn to the *Lt.*, "Mr. Bradley, round me up two sharp shooter volunteers to get their hands a little dirty, and twenty more to relax and drive our bounty home."

"Yes, Sir!" He replies.

Slapping my forehead with my palm I look around the room, and decide it's time to make my exit. I salute and exit the door, heading down the hallway to the elevator and run into Bradley again who appears to be anxiously awaiting the elevator car to arrive.

"You nervous?" I ask him wanting a little more information about his previous reaction.

"A bit I suppose," He replies shortly.

"Don't be, you've seen what I'm capable of, we're just going to have a little fun and then it'll all be good from there."

"Yeah, all good from there," he mocks.

"You know sarcasm doesn't become you Scoot, and if I didn't know any better it sounds like you don't want this mission to happen. You know I can replace you if you're nervous."

"No, John that's not necessary," he replies suddenly collected.

"Then what is it Bradley?" I ask sincerely.

"You know, it's just... You!" He explodes, "You're invincible and you think the rest of us are too."

"Johnny!" Dane tries to interrupt.

"Yeah, I got it; he's masking another emotion with anger, I caught the switch." I reply.

Redirecting back to *Lt.* Bradley I answer "Look *Lt.* I'm not going to lie to you, I've lost people close to me in battle before, but I've never left a man in my command behind, never, and I can assure you that I've seen more than my share of action."

"Yeah if you say so," he replies dismissively as the elevator doors open at the tenth floor, and he exits without another word.

"He's definitely hiding something Johnny," Dane says as the elevator doors close.

"I got it Dane, what I don't get is what. Is it loyalty? Is it confidence? Is it stress or pain from his ribs? What?"

"Unfortunately given the information it's impossible to tell at this point," she replies.

"Yeah, well keep an eye on him."

"I keep an eye on everyone," she replies.

Over the next day volunteers literally pour in, ready to stick it to the Nazi forces in droves. I actually have to turn a few away due to anger issues over what happened, and hundreds more because we have met the quota and I just don't have the room to take them. I'm not sure how many times I had to say; "Only calm, level headed drivers on this op.", but I know it was more than fifty.

The morning of the heist finally arrives I give my team a quick heads up, and let them in on what they're doing. We gather in the bay just inside the holographic mountainside with a map of the targeted area. I have portions of the map X'd out so each team knows where they'll be.

"*Lt.* Bradley's team, you guys are my sharp shooters, if all goes well you head back to base as heroes without ever firing a shot. If not well then you go back to base with a lot of blood on your hands… as heroes."

"Encouraging…" Dane says snidely. She never did like me talking about anything to do with the military or my time as a spook. She was anti anything that resulted in the death of another human being, and all that definitely came through in her comment.

95

Ignoring her I continue "Alright so you three will be stationed here, just half a klik south of the road in this little river. I'm told there's a pretty steep embankment, so that's where you'll be positioned right up on it and out of sight. We've got you setup with full muzzle suppressed rifles and the best optics you have available, on top of that we have some camo cover for each of you. Ideally they'll never even know where you are.

My drivers will be positioned a half a klik East here, just North of the road in full camouflage as well, and heavy under brush. This way we can avoid friendly fire, and if my diversion goes according to plan there will be no need for anyone to even look in that direction. No one should break radio silence under any circumstance. I will be the only voice you'll hear issuing any orders.

Those orders will be; either 'Open Fire' which will be to *Lt.* Bradley's team, and *Lt.* Bradley's team alone. Or 'Load em' up' which is the order for my drivers, this means simply that. I want the driving team to start slowly moving forward from the rear of the convoy and entering every abandoned vehicle. You'll all have silenced 9mm pistols and the element of surprise just in case not everyone exits their vehicles. In the event I do have to issue an 'Open Fire' order, I want the driving team to sit tight until the all clear is sounded, and then you'll move in for the snatch and grab. Everything Understood?!?"

The resounding, "SIR, YES SIR!" is damn near deafening.

"Good, let's roll out people!" I reply.

Lying in wait has always been an aggravating process for me. Even while in the Special Forces, it was always irritating; your muscles start to tense up and eventually go to sleep on you, inevitably you're going to have to use the bathroom, it's just an all-around distasteful experience. Looking at a clock only makes it worse; you can actually see the seconds start counting more slowly.

I always ended up thinking about when I was a kid waiting for Christmas morning, listening from my bed for any little sign of movement that could be a gift I had wanted all year sliding under the tree, or the sound of Santa Clause wandering over to the cookie plate you left out for him. Even though you know it's an extra two thousand calories someone that size shouldn't be consuming, at least we knew that in the twenty third century. Then that lead me to wonder, how many times had I actually put my father into a cookie/brownie inspired food coma, good thing he wasn't diabetic I guess.

With Bradley's team and the driving team in place I have taken up a position just off the road in a small ravine the Viper camouflaging me completely with my surroundings.

As the convoy finally approaches two hours late, I stand up from my make shift fox hole with Bradley and his men behind me totally unable to see me. Standing up the camouflage shifts to a complete invisibility from head to toe.

At this point I'm literally thanking God that three hours of hell is finally over as I stretch out my muscles. Walking toward the middle of the road, Bradley's team may as well be invisible with their full camo gear and behind the embankment, with their Remington A-three-oh-three's in hand, and ready to go to work. I can't help but think I've forgotten something.

The first two dreadnaught class tanks approach followed closely by the first truck in the convoy, I wait for the first dreadnaught to roll by, and then as the second passes I fire a Tesla bolt from my BARB into the rear of it, which effectively acts as an EMP frying every circuit onboard. It comes rolling to a complete stop; the truck behind it rolls up and just taps it on the back end. The driver of the truck begins to honk his horn yelling obscenities in German out his window and something about weird lightning. Moments later the hatch opens and a soldier appears waving at the truck behind him.

By this time the truck has radioed the lead tank which has stopped and reversed back closer to the convoy. Within minutes the road is swarming with Nazi soldiers moving toward the second tank, to discover what the holdup is, tank drivers climbing out, truck drivers, virtually everyone is walking up the road. As they move forward I issue the 'Load em' up' order, and my drivers move up quietly behind each, and hop in one after another of the Nazi vehicles, readying themselves to head back to base.

"Told you it would work…" I comment to Dane. When all of a sudden I see the driver of the truck pointing right at me, and repeating the word lightning over and over.

Dane translates the German for me "Over there, lightening shot out of the middle of the air, it's some rebel trick everyone needs to shoot there now."

As she says this they form two lines one knelt down in front and the second standing behind with their advance machine guns ready to fire. All of them looking intently at the area seeing if they can spot anything to concentrate on.

When the driver yells, "FIRE! FIRE NOW!"

They all open fire and get off about ten rounds each firing straight ahead, before they all realize that their bullets are all dropping to the ground right in front of where I'm standing. They all aim on my position and begin to fire.

"Shit, how much of this can the suit handle with these power levels?" I ask Dane in desperation.

"I would say one maybe two more clips each at most."

"OPEN FIRE!" I command to Bradley's team, as I crank the setting on the Tesla bolt all the way forward and begin to fire myself, knocking out three with one shot.

Three more fall as they are hit with sniper fire from Bradley's team. Suddenly the bullets hitting me are actually starting to sting.

"What the hell is going on? These things are starting to hurt." I demand of Dane.

"Power is dropping faster than I first anticipated, these are not standard rounds. At the current rate your cloak will drop in thirty seconds, and your repellent field will fail within another five," she says.

"Redirect all the power from the cloak to the repellant field!" I order, jumping to my left side and rolling on the ground.

With that I am now in my bare metal tight ass underwear and three more drop to sniper fire. However the rest can now see me, and there are still nine standing. I switch my BARB to the standard forty five caliber bullet, and start firing at the remaining nine. Now that I'm no longer feeling every hit I'm able to quickly aim and fire off two shots as bullets bounce off my face, killing two more of them as three more fall from my snipers. As I roll to the other side I continue firing hitting one in the arm holding his machine gun, and forcing the remaining three to take cover.

Dane now screaming in my ear, "Johnny the next hit will take down your entire barrier."

"Got it, two shots and I'm dead. Now will you please shut up so I can concentrate?"

Two more poking their heads out die to sniper fire, and the last fully mobile one rushes out of cover to grab his winged buddy and drag him back behind a truck firing at me as I roll again to avoid being hit. I quickly re-aim and catch him in the head before he can duck leaving only the wounded one still on the ground partially in cover. Standing up I think fatigues removing most of the power from the repellant field and hopefully giving me plausible deniability with my snipers.

As I approach the last soldier lying wounded on the ground he manages to quickly elevate himself and his backup pistol just high enough to shoot me again. This time it's not just a sting, he hits me right in the chest and it hurts like hell, knocking the wind out of me.

With the power from the repellant field I just redirected to the hologram there is almost no protection whatsoever. This hit manages to completely deplete the suits remaining power. Then as he attempts to make his second and what would be the potentially fatal shot, I quickly lift my BARB only to see him go limp, as he's caught by a final sniper shot. Leaving me in my metallic underwear and pissed off.

I have to wave an all clear to my sniper team since my communications are down, and I have no idea for how long.

Bradley approaches practically falls flat on his face when he gets close enough to take a good long look.

"You mean… That's what you've been wearing this whole time? The rest is just a hologram like our mountain face?" He gets out in between laughs and snickers.

By this time the other two have caught up to him and are trying to control their own laughter.

"Yeah, yeah it's hilarious, yuck it up assholes," I say.

Bradley is literally rolling on the ground at this point, while one of the other snipers 'Edwards' manages to control himself long enough to apologize for the three of them.

"No, no… I can't say I'd do any different in your position. I've seen this thing in the mirror, it's pretty ridiculous," I say while trying not to look to embarrassed. "Laugh it up, hopefully this will be the last time you ever see it." I reply.

Just about this time the suit starts to power up again; apparently the repaired R.P. has drastically increased its recharge rate.

"Albert Einstein once said, 'Two things are infinite: The universe, and human stupidity; and I'm not so sure about the Universe'" Dane comments.

"Yeah well not in this timeline he didn't, and we're still here aren't we?" I comment.

"Touche," she remarks as my fatigues come back online.

I move up between all the 'lookyloo' drivers around the front tank and ask "What are you waiting for? The rest of you need to get in your vehicles."

I have *Lt.* Bradley, and *Privates* Edwards and Shaw help me field strip the useful easy to grab parts from the second tank I had fried. Things like extra fuel, bullets, grenades, and mortars, anything without a fried circuit board attached really, and then load up in the first tank. With that, the convoy is off and running with my team now in the lead straight back to Area fifty one.

As we pull into the hologram side of the mountain I see *General* Patton standing in the hallway to the rear of the prep bay, waiting for us. Again with that smile the Cheshire cat just couldn't muster.

As I exit the tank, he looks me square in the eye and says "Son if I didn't see it I wouldn't have believed it. You have my full support on absolutely anything you want from this moment forward. You need something, just say the word and it's yours."

"Well thank you *General*, I'll keep that in mind," I respond with a wink.

Dane and I spend the next few days listening to Satellite chatter whining about their lost convoy. As no one on their side is really aware of my presence, they're starting to worry they may have a mole, and mention utilizing one of their own 'higher placed' moles, to make sure nothing like this happens again. There is even discussion of one of their moles trying to contact them last week with some vital intelligence, but due to increased security on our end this person was unable to get a message to them, and had still yet to be heard from.

They discuss changing all encryption keys, and configuring all new transponder bands. They even discuss the use of a military base in the Nevada Mountains currently only running a skeleton crew, which they describe as not far from where the convoy itself disappeared.

I have Dane check their facilities database for secret instillations, blueprints, guard logs, virtually anything she can get from their files about this base. Once she's in the files she's able to determine the exact coordinates and we realize this base is less than five kilometers from Area fifty one, and not very well protected, due to its current decommissioned status.

"This sounds trappy…" I remark.

"That's not actually a word." Dane replies.

"Are you sure? I've dated plenty of women I'd define as 'trappy'."

"Quite, and just because a woman wants you to marry her doesn't mean she's trying to 'trap' you," she replies.

"Pffft if you say so. But this, this sounds 'trappy'," I smirk. "So once all these new security measures are put into place, you know encryption keys, transponder codes, and what not's, how long will that take us to get back into?"

"Well based on the rudimentary encryption levels of this time-line, the fact that I left myself several backdoors into their satellite network on which they'll most definitely post that information, the suits current power levels, and thus my ability to access more of the suits actual processing power than 'our' first infiltration, I would guess anywhere from one point two to three point five seconds, for *'our'* next infiltration. Someone was sounding annoyed that I said *"our".*

"One point two to three point five seconds?" I question.

"Give or take a second for their satellite's slow access times and complete lack of security measures in place," she responds.

"So really we could be talking as much as four point five seconds is what you're telling me?"

"That's correct, if everything goes wrong it could take up to four point five seconds," she replies.

"Well I guess if that's all you're capable of it'll have to do, but don't think that this isn't going to be remembered. I mean what if they give us the clue that blows this whole thing wide open, like the exact coordinates of the Andes Base in that initial four point five seconds... will you be able to live with yourself?" I mock.

"Well Johnny, I have to imagine the first one point two to the outside four point five seconds will be filled with 'Hello? Are we all here yet? Did everyone get the updated codes? Who haven't we accounted for?', but if you think that one of them will blurt out the location to a top secret instillation in the Andes as a test message, then I shall endeavor to cut down on that time," she replies.

"Well then, see that you do," I say distracted with my next move and almost uninterested in the conversation at this point.

"You do know that is one of the behaviors Dane always had a distaste for right?"

"What's that, giving her a hard time and then focusing on something else, and losing interest?" I ask.

"Yes, and as a fully unregulated Artificial Intelligence I could begin to hate you," she responds.

I ponder this statement, "I doubt it; too many holes in that theory. Dane built herself into your unregulatedness. You couldn't hate me anymore than I could hate you."

"Unregulatedness isn't a word either.".

"See you've already moved on to grammar correction… there's no hate, just seventh grade English continuing to bite me in the ass," I comment.

While she's busy processing this 'information', I head upstairs to have a talk with the *General* about our possible leak and this other base, which is more than a little too close for comfort.

Upstairs I knock on George's office door, after he invites me in, I politely decline a scotch on the rocks and begin to inform him of the Viper, and the intel I've gathered using it.

"Aren't you special ops types supposed to be able to keep a secret?!" Dane demands.

"Half a platoon saw me in just the suit today. Did you really think he wasn't going to find out? Besides, I like George, I've got a good feeling about him," I reply.

"Moles huh? I don't suppose you got any names?" He looks concerned.

"No sir, where would the fun be in that?" I ask.

He cracks a small smile, "I suppose you got me there."

"I did however find that one is 'higher placed' which to me suggests that they are a person pretty high up the chain of command. Possibly someone that hasn't been utilized before, in order to expedite rank ascension, if that helps you at all. The other or 'others' I have no information at all, it seems that a flushing out will be in order sir."

"Well now, the 'higher placed' bit may be useful, in the case of our operations here, the chain of command is Myself, the acting Vice President, and the President.

The only problem with that scenario is that we have four other instillations such as this one, none as advanced, or as strategically located mind you, but each with an acting commander that answers to the Vice President, and the President directly, and is briefed on all missions of the other bases," he informs me.

There's a knock on the door, "Come!" The *General* bellows.

Lt. Bradley pokes his head in to inform the General that his personal chef had called up and his dinner was almost ready.

"Thank you *Lt.*, let him know I'll be along shortly," he says looking back at me.

"Yes Sir!" he replies closing the door.

"You know, we don't really know what they meant by 'higher placed' either this could be someone that's in a position like the Lieutenants'. Not that I'm implicating *Lt.* Bradley, just that 'higher placed' to them could be someone privy to certain operational information, not necessarily all the way to the top."

"You make a good point John," He admits, rubbing the bridge of his nose.

"The other bit to consider is that if there are four bases command structured like this one, then each one could have their own potential rodent problem as well, on top of or as well as the 'higher placed' one." I suggest.

"This is bad John, very, very bad, this could turn into a witch hunt," he sighs.

"So, let me get this right George, no joint chiefs? No Congress to speak of? I realize it's been a hundred years, but I kind of figured there would be a little more bureaucracy and red tape than just the Vice President and the President." I question.

"Well yeah, that's pretty much it. There's the Vice President, the President, and then the base leaders which for all intents and purposes serve as the joint chiefs used to."

"Then I guess unfortunately the best place to start is at the top?" I suggest.

"You're right of course really all we can do at this point is attempt to find out whether the Vice President… or the President of the United States has been compromised?" I think he saw me wince a little as he says this.

He continues, "If it makes you feel any better son, they weren't elected. There hasn't been enough of a citizenship for an actual election in decades. They've been handpicked by the base commanders and a very select few other high ranking military personal for a while now. I suppose it still kind of acts as a republic in that all the commissioned officers get a vote, but ultimately the base commanders can pick whomever they want if we so choose.

In fact the qualifications to become President and Vice President are becoming a two star General or better for President, and at least a Colonel for Vice President. Hell the President doesn't even get to choose his V.P. or 'Running Mate' anymore, he or she is appointed just as the president is, and we usually try to make them balance each other out. At least as best as we can, it's the only way we could figure to keep a handle on what was happening to us and our leadership.

Unfortunately, it looks like someone got promoted through our vetting process, and we all got one of them wrong. I better contact the President, and see what I can find out without letting too much out. We've been friends a long time; in fact we were both born and raised in this very facility, back then there was nearly forty thousand of us living here," he says.

"I understand *General*, and I can definitely appreciate you not wanting to believe it's your friend."

"Yes," he says looking down at his desk and a bit fatigued, "but honestly for them to use those words 'higher placed', it makes me think its overall leadership that we need to worry about at this juncture, not individual base leadership, or even higher security clearance officers. I admit they will all need to be looked at, but we need to prioritize this correctly."

"Agreed sir."

"At least it's not all bad news I suppose I can still be happy to hear that they have no idea where that convoy went, that hopefully means that we don't have a leak here. You know as well as I the whole base has been buzzing about that heist for days now."

"Very true *General*, then I'll excuse myself, and be in my office when you're ready for me."

"Very good son, we're going to plug these leaks don't you worry. This country will not be lost once and for all under the name George S. Patton, that I can promise you."

I smile at the thought, "Before I go sir, I'd like to share something with you from my own time-line if I might."

"Of course John, what's on your mind?" He asks.

"Well sir, in my time-line General George S. Patton Jr., who was actually the third George Smith Patton in your illustrious family tree, was noted as one of the Greatest Generals in U.S. History. He fought in a war that your time-line was deprived of, World War II. One of the bloodiest wars in recorded history, I can only say 'deprived of' because I know what happened instead in your time-line, but you should know that because of his bravery, tactics, and forethought it is widely believed that had the bureaucracy of the time not interfered with his command, he'd have ended that war at least eighteen months before it was finally ended, of course saving millions of lives in the process.

Now, I know because of some meddling from my time-line, he was never able to take his rightful place in history here, but I just wanted you to know sir, that your name inspires great hope in me personally, and I believe whole heartedly that you will be the one to win this war and take back America for the American people and your time-line," I state.

"Well now…" He says, slowly sitting back down behind his giant oak desk. "I had no idea that my name actually meant anything at all really, other than what I have been able to make it mean here. Son, you truly are a blessing for us, and I know with your help, we're going to beat those Nazi Bastards right back to the hell they created for themselves with that comet." He states.

"That will be my pleasure sir." I reply standing to make my exit. "I'll let you get to your dinner sir." I salute, and for once he actually stands and gives me a full salute before I leave his office.

As I enter the hallway Dane asks, "And what happens if the Relativistic Prototype is charged to jump before you're able to help these people adequately?"

"Not going to happen… If there's one thing I've learned from this whole experience, it's that some things are supposed to happen."

"Based on circumstances I'd say that's one to ponder; are there actual fixed points that cannot be altered? I will have to devote a few low level processors to this equation."

5 GOTCHA…

For the next several weeks we were planning and I now have General George mobilizing troops. Dane's Artificial Intelligence is constantly checking satellite telemetry over the Andes for any signs of a top secret base. Sadly, by the middle of October we still have not been able to locate any sign of the base, but at least my power reserves are now up to almost fifteen percent.

Dane has actually been more and more helpful the further she has been able to penetrate the Nazi satellite network and their remote servers around the world.

She has even been able to pinpoint a way to tunnel directly into the Nazi base that is practically on our doorstep, and the structural engineering team has been working night and day to build a stable tunnel from the end of my hall on level twenty to just below the Nazi base. This is of course a slow process as they have just over four point two kilometers to tunnel, and it appears that their base is not as deep as our own, so once underneath they will be tunneling up another half a kilometer.

Of course all the crews think I can sleep through a hurricane at this point, what they don't know is that I have the Viper to sleep in, without the noise dampening field generated, and Dane monitoring for threats I'm sure I'd never get any sleep at all. George has of course graciously offered to move me up to one of the bases population floors, but honestly with the Viper I don't need it.

We also learned that after our little convoy stunt they had followed through on the transmission Dane had picked up, and fully staffed that base, believing that we must have acted from somewhere in the vicinity.

It was a fair assumption on their part, seeing as the base had been rumored to be in existence since the nineteen forty seven Roswell crash.

Oddly enough however, I was about to learn that this was not the case, and that there was in fact movement on our recently activated mole front, in 'our' organization giving up classified intelligence.

Recently, I had started having lunch with the good *General* in the officer's mess on a pretty regular basis, and that afternoon during our normal meal conversation, George has the room cleared of all other personnel again. We then proceed to have a conversation in which he expresses the intent of temporarily turning over the entire installation to me, as commander. At first this seemed not only drastic in measure, but an odd request. I mean really? I've known these people for all of a few weeks now.

"So, John, the *President* and I have had a few rather lengthy conversations since you brought this mole situation to my attention. Including one this morning, and it is our belief that you are right we do have a fairly high ranking mole. The issue is that in order for this mole to be high ranking, as you know, it can really be only one of six people."

"I would say five, but yes I am aware," I reply.

"Well thank you son, but I need you to stay completely objective here. As you also know there are three other instillations such as this one, each with commanding officers like myself; then of course there is the President, and the Vice President. Now we both agree that the Vice President is completely above reproach at this point.

That said, he did admit to having his suspicions about her, questions she's asked or conversations she's been more interested in than her post really calls for, that sort of thing.

Now by throwing doubt in her direction the President also knows that this throws himself into suspicion, and he readily admits this. That said, I was able, based on your now impartial and infallible record, to get permission for something a little, unorthodox to catch our leak. Whether that be the Vice President, one of the base commanders, the President or hell even myself. Whoever it is that gets caught with their hand in the cookie jar, well then we have irrefutable proof and can act on that proof accordingly."

"So you want me to take over, until this person has been caught?"

George knows that I have a few operations that I have been planning, but only a cursory knowledge concerning any of them. He has no idea of my priorities and wishes to keep it that way at this point. "You got it, and keep me completely out of the loop, I'm on my first God damned vacation since exiting the womb." he says.

So with that, General George S. Patton the VII walks over to the comm. station in the officer's mess and grabs the microphone, "Now hear this; this is not a drill, this is an order. As of this moment I am turning over command of this base to Colonel John Steal, this is a temporary measure and *not*, I repeat *NOT,* an incursion on the Colonel's part. Everything is to proceed in a business as usual fashion around here. Furthermore for the duration of this exercise you will all continue to address me accordingly, if I happen to be seen around the base, *which I don't plan on,* and follow my orders to the letter as if I were in complete command. However, those orders are subject to change and can only be superseded by any orders coming from the Colonel himself, until further notice. Not the President, the Vice President, or any base Commander currently out rank Colonel John Steal on this base.

To put your minds at ease, you should know this is also going on in our other bases as well, so there is no need to get all out of sort over this. All the commanders are handing over their commands to their most trusted senior staff, and will then be headed here. This being the most secure of our bases makes it the perfect vacation spot for us senior staffers. That said, the President, the other Generals and myself will all be sequestered and on vacation down on nineteen should any emergency arise that the Colonel cannot handle, but I do not foresee that as being a problem. The President and other generals are due to arrive within the next few hours. I expect a warm welcome for each, and then a firm respect of our privacy."

So the base has been handed over to my direction for the completion of at least one very important, highly classified operation of my choosing. I report only to the Vice President, just as George would, in fact I report as George using his login and password to his terminal. The President it seems has secretly ordered all other base commanders to this facility, where they will be sequestered with George on Level nineteen with a case of Cuban's several bottles of finely aged Scotch, a truckload of Nazi beef, and several decks of cards.

"Yeah, I'm in command, Woofreak'npee!" I mutter, as the *General* heads into the elevator to have a rough week of drinking, steak, and poker.

"So, to work then, give me the details on this region Dane, I want something that hasn't even been thought of yet, that way nothing can even remotely implicate George."

"The enemies strong hold in the region all hinges on what was a small mining town called Schlitz, just across what you would know as the Hoover dam, and is now a major Nazi passage from the east to the west of what would be Nevada. In this time-line interstate forty was never constructed and bullet trains are the main form of cross country transportation, so Schlitz is their major switching hub, it is well fortified, but it is their only access to Nevada, California, parts of Arizona, Baja Mexico, Oregon, Washington, and even up into parts of Canada, including what we know as Alaska.

You take out Schlitz, and any resistance mounted in those areas will have time, and a very good chance to make a foothold, and we could potentially stop their control of the west coast almost entirely, at least for a time," Dane replies

"I love it when you talk war strategies to me... So then, we need to finalize plans, decide the best way to knock that hub out for a good long time, and then three days from now I want to submit this plan in almost its entirety to only the Vice President, through George's 'e-mail', for lack of a better word. We will of course hold back a key piece of information on that attack to ensure our victory." I'm not letting a mole jeopardize a mission this critical just to catch her respond.

"Sounds like exactly what the *General* was hoping for from you Johnny," Dane answers.

"Well, you know how I hate to disappoint the *General*."

"Uh…" She starts.

"We're not discussing the *Brigadier General*, this is another time-line entirely, that never happened. Let it go." I respond.

"Right, Johnny at least not that you shared," she mocks.

As planned three days later a full comprehensive plan of the attack on the Schlitz hub is signed sealed and delivered via coded message to the Vice President. To which we immediately receive a response "Action NOT Approved at this Time".

"Well if that doesn't sound moley I don't know what does Dane…" I comment.

"Indeed, and frankly I'm impressed you added my name, maybe your brain tumor is shrinking," Dane replies.

"Ha freaking ha," I mock.

Responding to the Vice President, I try to put myself in the best *General* Patton I can come up with. My coded reply;

"Madam Vice President,

Unfortunately, this plan has already been put into motion, and is beyond my control at this point. As I have never received an "unapproved action" from the President I assumed it would be the same while he was incommunicado. Do to that circumstance my attack force is already beyond my radio range or the range of any of our current assets in play, at this juncture the attack is I'm afraid unstoppable.

George"

I head up to the prep bay where the teams I've put together are waiting for me, "Let's head out boys and girls, we have a train station to blow back to Old Berlin."

As we arrive I set up our captured dreadnaught tanks in a triangle surrounding the town on the hills surrounding it, they are accompanied by rocket launchers, snipers, and special optics units set to sight in their targets. This was not disclosed to the Vice President.

The main force enters Schlitz nearly unopposed, but for a few guards here and there, and begins to plant C-4 all around the railroad switching station at a ten meter spread. After about the sixth confirmed C-4 arming, we have troop transport helicopters inbound.

"When we checked everything for this mission, those choppers were four hundred miles away correct?" I verify with Dane.

"They were," she replies.

"So even if one of these people got a call out, at their max rate of speed they would be how far away right now?" I ask

"With the load they look to be carrying, roughly three hundred fifty miles." Dane responds.

"I'd say that's irrefutable proof they had prior notice wouldn't you?" I ask.

"Undoubtedly…" She replies.

"Alright people, as I expected! We've been moled, I want those planting C-4 to throw it to an approximately appropriate position as quickly as humanly possible and then MOVE OUT! Double time it folks I don't want to lose a single person today. Snipers, I expect you to keep their egress covered," I call out, Dane broadcasting my voice to all of our units on the ground.

Everyone, as warned ahead of time follows their instructions to a 'T', and moves back to their assigned troop transport trucks which then start heading out of the valley to a safe distance. The helicopters pull in and S.S. troops start zip lining down.

"Alright Rocket's and tanks, you are clear to take those birds out of the sky," I radio to my triad of death.

Within seconds six helicopters begin raining from the sky like they were all swept up in an Oklahoma twister. S.S. troops are crushed under falling debris, and I run at my leisurely fifty mile per hour to catch up to the rear truck.

"Alright, rocket launchers their fuel tanks are just to rear south west corner of the building, let's follow that up with a nice hit there as well. I don't want this hub rebuilt for at least a year." I radio; watching as the rockets bear down on their target. As they approach with only a few feet remaining I press the detonator for the C-4.

A bigger boom hasn't been heard since the comet hit, I'm quite certain. This 'small mining town' better known as a Nazi train hub is now a smoldering heap of ash and corpses.

The radio comes alive with screams of laughter and joy; this is their first major victory and maybe their first victory at all, since the war started. I let them revel in the moment; take it in, before calling out, "Alright! Good work teams, lets head back to base before they figure out what hit them and where we're headed. I expect a party in the Mess tonight, drinks are on ME!"

"Drinks are on you?" Dane asks.

"Well that convoy I got them had a truck full of liquor with it, who else would the drinks be on?!" I ask.

"Point taken…" She replies.

After everyone is safely back to base and checked in, I head downstairs to interrupt the vacationing senior staff and let them in on what we've just done.

"*Generals*, Mr. President I just wanted to give you an update. We have not only caught your Mole of a Vice President red handed, but we have also taken out the Schlitz switching station, and I can say with confidence that it will be at least six months to a year before they have it even remotely operational again. So any resistance you fellas have on the other side of that switch, this would be the time to let them know to dig in, and up their recruitment, because no Nazi backup is coming for a while."

Complete silence. George's cigar drops from his mouth.

After ten seconds or so of them all looking around the table at each other I have to speak up, "What, I can't even get a thank you?"

The President stumbles to his feet, and it looked to be more due to shock than the scotch. "Son, I am going to award you every medal known to man, hell I'm going to make up a few new ones just for you! This is the first decisive win and I assume it was decisive?" he stops.

"We lost no one sir, we were ready for all probable outcomes, and that whole facility is now ash. And did I mention the eight troop transport style helicopters full of S.S. we dropped as well?" I ask.

"Eight Helos of S.S. the biggest switching station in the western United States, and you lost no one?"

"Not a soul, sir," I reply.

"Then my boy I've never been happier for listening to my oldest friend *General* Patton here, and entrusting you with this operation. This is undoubtedly the first decisive victory in the history of this war." He responds, and then he does the unthinkable and salutes ME?!

All the Generals at that point stand up and salute me.

I salute back and say, "Thank you sirs, it was an honor to be a part of this effort."

The President says, "My boy, I'm looking more forward to this debrief I think than anything in my life, and I hereby recommend we field promote you directly to a *Full four star General* and skip that *Brigadier, Major, Lt.* garbage, I don't give a damn what time-line you're from you're obviously the man we need."

In this time-line apparently the President can field promote, but not to the rank of *'four star'*, or *Full General* that takes two other ranking *Full Generals* to ratify. At this point, it occurred to me that there were three saluting me in the room and immediately ratifying this proposal right then and there.

"Well, now *Four Star General* Steal; the fellas and I are going to try and soak all this in, and give you a little time to prepare your debrief, we'll convene in the conference room on level ten tomorrow morning at oh-eight-hundred," The President says.

Saluting with my reply, "It'll be my pleasure sirs."

I head up the elevator to level ten and into George's office, still not able to grasp what just happened.

"Hey uh, Dane." I say.

"Yeah, Johnny?" She responds.

"You keep a video log of absolutely everything right?" I ask.

"Absolutely…" She responds.

"Let's lock that one so it never ever gets written over will ya?" I ask.

"You bet, Johnny.

"Also, can you take a cohesive log of the complete op. and print five copies of it from George's printer over there for me?" I ask.

"Printing now. You do realize though that once you repair the time-line, that your field promotion won't actually mean anything," She responds.

"Wow, you couldn't even give me a few hours to revel in it could you?"

"Sorry," she responds, sounding almost genuine.

The next morning oh-eight-hundred sharp, we *five* Generals sit around the conference room table, and I explain to them the sequence of events that lead to our victory and the ultimate destruction of the Nazi switching station. We go over the lovely charts and graphs Dane has come up with for us, projecting reconstruction time at current technology levels, and of convoy driven and or flown in reinforcements reaching certain cities where the generals knew there would be a strong resistance presence like San Francisco, Seattle, Phoenix, and Los Angeles. Everyone left the meeting feeling full chested, full of pride, and ready to fire and place the Vice President under arrest.

Later that afternoon maintenance has my floor cleaned top to bottom and things back to workable order for my own use. I've been told at this point that absolutely anything I need will be made available to me, as soon as it is physically possible.

Taking a seat at my desk it's time to do some work.

"Dane, is it possible Marconi's base doesn't exist in this time-line?" I ask.

"It is possible that the base was moved by Riefenstahl, after his assent to power. Perhaps he was able to predict a possible time travel strategy in which all variables were known, and plan for them accordingly."

"I don't buy it... I mean Dane said, not you Dane but the real Dane, Marconi was a man obsessed with symbolism. Now, if that's true, he wouldn't abandon such a huge symbol of his success would he?"

"Ah, but you are assuming that Marconi is the time traveler. It is entirely possible that it was Edison's clone that took on the journey, or even some yet unnamed party, and I am more the real Dane at this point than you give me credit for Johnny."

"It's just a gut feeling at this point, but moving a base like it wouldn't happen. Even if Edison was the traveler he'd still have to convince Marconi to pick up and move."

"You do have a point actually. I suppose, if we consider that the mountain was an extinct volcano as is the rumor, it is likely that one of the technologies Marconi employed was the use of geothermal energy, another of your Grandfather's inventions, possibly shared with or stolen by Marconi, he certainly would have had the access for a while.

That said, and knowing the power requirements for the estimated size of their research facility, the idea that they not move the base is not without merit. It is quite possible based upon their research; that they were unable to relocate the facility. Also we must consider the comet collision and the fact that the other side of the world may have much more active volcanoes, reinforcing the South America possibility as a much less volatile environment," she replies.

"Alright, so what else do we know that Marconi's people had come up with?" I ask.

"I'm afraid I do not have any information on that subject other than what was learned via your letter from Dane.

"What about unexplained technologies witnessed in our own time-line? Is there anything like that? Something someone saw, but was never proven?" I suggest.

"Ghosts?" she replies.

"Oh ghosts! I like ghosts, did Marconi invent ghosts?" I ask.

"It is unlikely Johnny.

"Why would you tease me like that? You know I like ghosts."

Dane offers, "Unexplained phenomenon include, but are not limited to; Ghosts, Vampires, Werewolves, certain alien vessel incidents, the Bermuda Triangle, Women..."

I cut Dane off at that point. "Women aren't a possible technology, or meant to be understood for that matter. And Dane was a woman that loved women how could she not understand them? That's an A.I. answer."

"Actually, based upon her memory dump I believe she would have said the same thing. She never understood women that well either even though she was one."

"Ha! That's probably because she was my grandpa in disguise, the Merrick men; wait Tesla men? Either way we have always been baffled by women. Go back though... Certain alien vessel incidents?" I query.

"And the Bermuda Triangle, that is correct, many recorded alien 'sightings' as they have been called, were even reported in the 'Bermuda Triangle', but later accounted for by the three major species of aliens known to the twenty second century, but by no means have all incidents been claimed. Also of interest is that the 'Syldil' race reported specifically that their reasoning for finally opening the lines of communication with us was one of their ships being shot down by one of our 'flying saucers'. It was always assumed that this was either the 'Zyndraph' or the 'Doo-Rinda' firing on our behalf, but this has never been confirmed..

"Yeah, I remember reading that now in school, that's actually old text book material. The publisher of those books had the whole 'Doo-Rinda' race pegged as completely insane. You know they say that when the 'Doo-Rinda' eat French fries, they won't even eat the ones with pointy ends? They have to be squared off, and squishy. What the hell is that all about?"

"I don't think anyone's quite figured that one out actually," Dane replies.

"But you say there's other recorded 'flying saucers' that haven't been claimed yet?"

"There are in fact military records of many such events. For example, in nineteen forty seven, while the United States Navy invaded Queen Maud Land, Antarctica, to capture fleeing Nazi war criminals, U.S. Jets were reported to have been shot down by 'discoid craft'. This was never claimed by any alien species, it was assumed that this was done to avoid political unrest over having shot down U.S. military. It should also be noted that 'flying saucer' technology was discussed, planned, and recorded between Tesla and Marconi. Perhaps this is an early sign of Marconi aligning himself with Nazi Germany, after severing ties with Tesla?" She replies.

"And wasn't there something about the Nazi's having something to do with the whole Roswell thing too? I seem to remember watching a show once that suggested they had experimented with UFO technologies. I suppose if Marconi was working on the technology this idea was not as insane as it sounded at the time, but wasn't this one of the crashes that was eventually claimed by the 'Doo-Rinda'?"

"That is correct they did take credit for this crash, however there were some inconsistencies in the reporting.

Perhaps that could be attributed to the liquor issue?" Dane suggests.

"What kind of inconsistencies are we talking about here?"

"When the crashed ship was finally claimed, it was re-examined to verify ownership, and it appeared that the technology was very rudimentary, even for the 'Doo-Rinda' of the late nineteen forty's it wasn't even consistent with something that could accomplish interstellar travel, but as you said the 'Doo-Rinda' like their liquor, so it was never really debated all that much, and it seems the Air Force commander who reviewed the case file, was happy just to close it.

"Alright, so if they have flying saucers, we need to find a way to track them back to their base." I suggest.

"This would be a very logical course of action; however we have yet to detect any flying saucers in this time-line Johnny, and frankly I'm not sure that I can configure these satellites to detect whichever type of thermal or any other type of signature that we may be looking for." Dane responds.

"Maybe we need to lure them out? They really haven't needed to power up the big guns for anything in many years at this point right? Check the satellites, where are those tanks we saw rolling past New Frankfurt at now?" I question.

"Currently they appear to have a large presence of tanks, roughly one hundred of their dreadnaught class, stationed approximately eighteen miles South West of here, near a town called Allgemeinheit," she replies.

"Excellent! Time to talk to George," I say.

I head down the hall to the elevator, and wait for my lift. As the doors open, I am greeted by *Lt.* Bradley again.

"Sir!" He Salutes.

"Oh, for cryin out loud, seriously how many times do we have to go over this? We're friends *Lt.*, I'm not your C.O., hell I'm not even from your 'planet' really."

"Sorry John, I just figured with the new promotion and all, which technically since *it* came from my time-line does make you my C.O.," he responds.

"Now, well, just knock it off anyway I put on my pants the same way you do, one leg at a time."

"Uh, all due respect but I've seen your under armor now, don't you just think pants and they're on?" He asks.

"Alright, bad example…" I concede, "but you know what I meant. And why the hell are you always at the elevator? You're like the damn base bell hop."

"Uh, Yes Sir! I mean…." Bradley responds.

I raise an eyebrow at him. "Alright, alright, what's on your mind Bradley?" I ask.

"The *General* asked me to request your presence."

Checking with Dane I ask, "Is it possible that due to the massive amount of meteoric debris people of this time-line developed some kind of telepathy?"

"Possible, technically anything is possible. Probable? Not really.

Responding to the *Lt.* again, "Ah, good. That's exactly where I was headed anyway; let's not keep the good *General* waiting then, shall we?"

We enter the elevator and head up to the tenth floor. When the doors open we are greeted by a well-armed group of men and women in black suits. I know they are well armed due to my enhanced HUD vision, not to mention the unhealthy bulges under their suit jackets.

Having been a spook you learn to identify secret service, and or body guards when you see them. Now that the suit itself is able to run at full power however, well everything but the time circuits anyway, all sorts of bells and whistles are activating lately. I can actually identify concealed weapons right through almost any material. Like those airport scanners everyone loves.

"Secret service?" I quietly ask Bradley.

He nods.

"I get to meet the Vice President! I wonder who it is. Oh, should I be dressed nicer?" I say to myself, and Dane.

There are two guards on either side of the exterior door to the secretary's office, one opens it and says, "Please enter sir, they're expecting you."

"Again with the 'Sir' crap," I say to Dane.

"Hey that's a nice tie!" I comment to the guard as I'm being rushed by, "Can I borrow it? It's not every day you get to meet the Vice President."

He smirks, and shuts the door behind me.

"Well that's not very nice. See if I ever lend him one of my ties to meet someone."

The *General's* inner office door is also closed, with two more secret service operatives on either side. Bradley marches up and knocks three times.

"These guys don't mess around, do they Bradley." I remark.

"No, Si…." He stops himself

"Ah! Careful…" I suggest

The Secret Service agents glare at us, one raising an eyebrow, obviously curious about our exchange. I suddenly feel this should be addressed, "Hey! Did you know that the abbreviation for Secret Service is S.S., just like the Nazi Scooter Snatchers?" Bradley shoots me a disgusted look.

"Wait! Schnitzel Stuffers? No that's not it either… Ah! Schutzstaffel! That's it."

They continue to glare looking unamused. I of course see no reason to stop at this point, "No, it's funny see, they are the Nazi's elite police and military units, and you are the United States Elite Presidential party protection. It's like you were meant for each other, really."

They both look extremely irritated at this point. "So, which came first…" I ask, "the Secret Service, or the Schnitzel Stuff… err Schutzstaffel?"

"Nothing? Wow… tough room, eh?" I suggest.

Dane chimes in, "You totally missed that line didn't you, Johnny?"

"You mean that one you keep telling me I'm not supposed to cross?" I reply.

"Yes, the same one you happily just skip over most of the time."

"I'm pretty sure one of them growled at me."

"You kind of asked for it," she replies.

Bradley knocks again much louder this time.

"Come IN!" George bellows.

"Down boy!" I command to the 'growling' agent.

"Was that?" I didn't even get to finish my question as Bradley's opening the door, and rushing in.

A cloud of cigar smoke pours out. As we enter I can see the General standing on the other side of his desk, he has his back to the door with a drink in one hand (my HUD reveals this to be a single malt Scotch), and a cigar in the other (Cuban of course). A well-dressed female, mid to late 30s faces him almost mirroring his stance (The HUD has her circled and labeled 'Cougar'). She is also having a drink and a cigar.

Laughing, I mumble, "Jack ass..." to Dane, not realizing that I hadn't actually thought to make that a statement to Dane.

"I beg your pardon?" The Vice President exclaims, as George chokes down a mouthful of Scotch trying not to laugh.

At this point George, Bradley, Dane and I know this is all a formality, we have the proof we need to relieve and convict her. So I decide to play the whole thing off completely tongue in cheek. However realizing that I broadcast my response to Dane, I do have to make a quick recovery.

"What's that?" I ask. "Oh! My apologies Madam Vice President, I didn't mean for you to hear that. You see, Bradley here had mentioned as we were walking in from the hallway that you had a lovely rear end, and I was scolding him."

Bradley looks like a deer in headlights shaking his head at her.

"I mean obviously, he shouldn't be commenting on such things, well unless, of course the two of you have a little something going on on the side that I'm not aware of? In which case I still would prefer, as I'm sure you would, that he not share such things with me, those are matters for locker rooms, bathroom stall walls and the like." Bradley shoots me a glare that would have melted the polar ice caps, you know back before fracking when there were polar ice caps.

"Well, I never!" she says sounding exhausted already, and a little flushed.

"Southern Belle, I knew that accent sounded vaguely familiar." I say to Dane.

"I would imagine not Madam, Bradley can be a little crass at times." I answer her. "Also, I should point out that one of your Secret Service agents outside, the gentlemen on the left walking in, he may be missing a funny bone. Oh, and he may also have rabies, I can't be certain, but I'm pretty sure he growled at us. That's not a good sign. I'd hate for him to bite you instead of protecting you." I continue.

The Secret Service Man pokes his head around the corner of the still open door, a look of confused disgust on his face.

Smiling, I slam the door and continue into the room, Dane identifies everything in the room for me at this point, the HUD lights up like a Christmas tree. "Is that a single malt Scotch I smell General?"

Bradley's mouth is practically on the floor, face beet red, and now staring at 'the cougar', assumingly waiting for a reaction. Unfortunately for him he's only supporting my cover up at this point.

"Run along now Bradley, I'm sure you will escort me somewhere else later. You can tell me all about it then." I suggest.

Bradley shaking his head at me sulks over to the door of the General's office stands at attention and waits. "Friends, my ass…" he utters under his breath.

I continue smiling, "Mrs. Vice President is it?" I question just to toy with her.

"Mr. John, Doe is it?" She responds.

"Well that's a very long and uninteresting story," I answer.

Dane interrupts my next statement, "Careful Johnny, we're dealing with time at this point. No one here can know who you really are. If the time traveling technology were to be available to someone with that information, you could be gone before you existed creating a further paradox, or at the very least have lasting effects on the rest of this mission."

"Isn't it likely that I already don't exist in this time-line anyway?" I reply to Dane

She's still staring at me, as if waiting for me to finish the thought.

"Let's just go with my adopted last name, and my recently promoted rank of *General*, Steal." I reply.

"Fair enough Mr. Steal…" I stop her mid-sentence, and I can tell by the look on her face that she loved that.

"Uh, actually, as I said, it's *General* Madam *Vice* President. Just like *General* Patton here." I hold up the name plate from his desk and display the word 'General' for her.

"Very well then *General* Steal, you have no idea who I am? Other than the *Vice* President of these 'would be' United States, is that a fair assessment?" She asks with a further hint of Southern Belle to her tone.

I catch *General* George cracking a smile in an image reflection, of course I only catch this because, my HUD lights up, circles the reflection and identifies the smile.

Thinking of a facial recognition scan, my HUD lights up with the twenty second century database covering the last five hundred plus years.

The HUD displays 'Match found…' Dane chimes in, "You may find this one interesting."

Scanning the readout I respond, "Well, actually I know quite a bit about you, that is to say the you from my own time-line ma'am."

She cracked a modest smile. "Well, do you now?" she queried. "And what is it that you think you know?"

"Well, in my time-line madam, you attended Harvard Law. Graduated 'Suma Cum Laude', and went on to be one of the most influential lawyers of the time." I respond. "I don't recall you being *Vice* President ma'am, I believe there was a senate seat you held for quite a while, and I do know that you had a hand in some very influential legislative creation. Privacy re-expansion comes to mind immediately."

"That's a hell of a memory you've got there, you sure there's nothing else?" She presses.

"I believe you call it photographic memory ma'am, I have total recall of everything I've ever been exposed to." Which of course was a lie, I'm wearing a supercomputer, but she didn't need to know that.

"And no ma'am, not that I was ever made aware of." I respond, while walking over to the bar for to pour a glass of Scotch.

"Good, cover I'm impressed." Dane chimes in, "It is probably unwise to inform the mole of a *Vice* President that she was one of the greatest criminal masterminds ever caught in the 21st century".

"Well you know what they say, behind every good lie there's a kernel of truth. Besides it's enough that you and I know she went bat shit crazy, and killed half of her classmates at Harvard with a bomb made in her Chemistry class. You do have a point though; honestly she's actually worse in this reality, you know how many American's she's gotten killed for the Nazi's. I guess some things never change, time-line to time-line that is." I reply to Dane.

I finish adding a few cubes of ice to my glass and pour my Scotch then turn back to the conversation, "So Madam *Vice* President, what is it I can do for you?" I ask.

"Actually John, it's what you can do for me," *General* Patton answers.

"Oh?"

"Yes, well you see son, it takes two active full General's to relieve the *Vice* President of her position, and as the President said it 'You caught the bitch, you should have the pleasure of putting her down.'" He replies.

"What the hell are the two of you talking about? You can't relieve me from the Vice Presidency!" She states attempting to assert her authority.

"According to what the good General just said it sounds like we can." I reply.

"On what grounds?" She demands

"Treason, is that grounds enough for you?" I ask

"You have got to be kidding me, this little piss ant has been here for all of a few operations and the President believes that gives him the right to even talk to me in such a tone?" She is sounding more and more German as she speaks, and I can see that George is picking up on it, and is in udder shock.

"Well your Naziness, I suppose what the President wanted me to tell you is that; I not General Patton contacted you for the last mission, and that you and I alone are the only two that new about the op. until it was actually taking place. The only difference being I held something back, something that made the op. successful anyway."

She looks down and all around the room like a caged animal looking for a way out.

"This is bullshit I've been framed!" She insists to George.

"Abigail, I've known you for a long time, and I've had questions here and there that always seem to just get swept away. Well this actually answers all of them, and let's put all our cards on the table here, your German accent slipping through doesn't hurt either."

"Madam Vice President, it is my distinct pleasure to place you under arrest, oh and relieve you of your post." I say smiling.

"You have no right Mr. Steal! Your rank means nothing here," she argues.

"On the contrary Abigail," George interrupts, "the President himself put John up for a full field promotion after your attempt at sabotaging what could have been a lot of American lives. The President realized that due to John's efforts, and his magnificently successful plan which not only proved who our high ranking mole was, but succeeded in dealing a crippling blow to your jackass friends, he was worthy of skipping over three entire ranks. It was even ratified as per our laws by myself and all the other base chiefs."

"This will not be the last you hear from me!" She sneers, now addressing me, "You have somehow managed to appropriate and maintain free reign of the entire twentieth floor, and you are pushing for an offensive move in South America adamantly, you will fail," she states as her secret service enters the room with Lt. Bradley right behind them.

"Oh, South America, thank you for reminding me, and I'm pleased to hear you're so against it actually. I'd say that's proof enough to set up an operation wouldn't you George?"

"You know I think that's all I needed to hear to be on board actually; as always you'll have my full support John," he smiles.

She looks absolutely irate at this point, and explodes ordering her Secret Service agents to arrest me. At which point George holds up a finger indicating he would like them to wait a moment.

Looking over at Bradley by the door, "For cry'n out loud! Bradley take your *'girlfriend'* into custody. I can't handle any more of this conversation. I thought it was going to be fun, but now, well now she's just sucking all the fun right out of it, and you know what's worse? I think she's doing it on purpose!"

Bradley moves toward the Vice President removing hand cuffs from his belt. Placing her under arrest, and then radioing for some Military Police to come in, I smile at George who speaks up again. "Well, now that this pissing match seems to be hilariously at an end, what do you say to some dinner John?"

"I think that's a splendid idea George, I am a bit famished myself." I reply, obviously just rubbing it in at this point.

General Patton turns to the MP's as they enter and orders them to take the Vice President down to holding, where she is to be processed and admitted under the war crimes and espionage act of nineteen sixty seven. Lt. Bradley is all too happy to hand her over then turns to her Secret Service agents who are clearly still trying to figure out what's going on, and if they should be attempting to arrest me. He then hands them the evidence I had extracted against the Vice President. Which upon reading they immediately stand down, and allow her arrest to go smoothly, and refrain from attempting her last order, of taking me into custody.

As the MPs escort the now deposed Vice President from the room I can't stop myself from yelling, "You know madam *Vice President*, the holding cells are on the nineteenth, so just bang on the floor if you get bored or lonely, and I'll send Bradley by to entertain you."

As George and I head out the door and walk out toward the elevator. We begin to discuss the enemy's base in South America.

"So now that we have confirmation of the base…" I start boarding the elevator.

"Oh I wasn't kidding John, you'll have every resource I can afford at your disposal, but tell me; why is this base so important? You've mentioned it before, the first night you arrived if I remember correctly."

"Good memory George, I'll be totally honest with you though; I think originally when I told you about it I mentioned the opportunity for advanced weaponry?"

"Yes, and that's probably why I remembered it so well, don't tell me that was a lie!" he says sternly.

"Well not exactly, it's more than likely that won't happen, but if I leave that base standing they win. The advanced technologies are there, but a strike team to destroy the base is going to go much smoother than trying to capture something that big and fortified. You know it, and I know it."

"Oh hell, I knew it had to be too good to be true," he scowls.

"No, no that's not to say you won't get the advanced weaponry I promised you. In fact I'm prepared to give you schematics on everything you *should* have for this time period. Therefore in my eyes repairing the time-line in my own way. On top of that destroying that base will cripple the Nazi's, in a way you couldn't possibly imagine."

"That's a lot to take in without a drink in my hand John. It sounds like you're talking about cutting off the head of a snake though." He says, as we have now exited the elevator and are working our way toward our now private dining room.

"So let me get this straight, you're going to give us the ability to build advanced weaponry, stuff the Nazi's won't be ready for, and then go on a suicide mission to wipe out their central operations?" he asks as we sit down at our table.

The chef cautiously approaches having heard part of our conversation, and we both order the same thing, a T-bone medium rare, baked potato, and a bottle of Scotch.

As the chef walks off we resume our conversation. "Well yeah, that's essentially the plan. Now I will be asking for a strike team, and hopefully giving Lt. Bradley a little more field experience but my plan is to send those people back to you unscathed. One way or another my time here will be coming to an end, and I'd like to make as big a difference, as possible. When the time comes."

"I see…" He says obviously mulling it over.

"My motives aren't all altruistic as I'm sure you've figured out. This base I'm after is in my time-line the biggest organization of terrorists you could ever imagine. These insidious bastards started all this, so yeah this gives me an up close and personal look at what I'll be dealing with, once I get back to my own time and prepare to take out this facility once and for all."

The chef drops off our bottle of Scotch and two glasses with ice, and George pours for each.

"So this base, it's that important?" He inquires.

"It is the enemy's main base of operations in both your time-line and mine, and likely the reason you've never been able to hurt them in all this time. If you can't hit them where it hurts then they'll just keep coming back for more, right?"

"You do have a point." He concedes taking a sip of his Scotch.

The General turns to me and says, "*General* Steal it would appear that your mission to South America has been green lit. You can hand pick your team and ship out at your earliest convenience. Well once you discover its actual location that is."

"Thank you sir, I'll begin preparations immediately, and don't worry George it'll all work out the way it's supposed to."

George chuckles. "You know John, you still don't have a location though do you? South America is a big place, where are we on that?"

"Ah yes, back to business… Well actually I have a plan. I was on my way to share it with you when Bradley grabbed me for our little powwow."

"Sounds promising, what have you got?" he questions.

"It seems we have evidence that the facility we're hunting possesses what you would refer to as 'Flying Saucers'. You may have heard reports of them here and there; they're usually highly classified and associated with extraterrestrial life or just mocked, laughed at and tossed in the garbage." I reply

"I may have heard whispers or tall tales of such things. I've never been inclined to indulge in such beliefs myself however." He answers.

"Well I guess the shocker here will be then that they do exist. More importantly we can track them George. The issue is they haven't used them since I've been here, and chances are they don't use them much, just due to a lack of need and resource expenditures, as they have yet to refine them to a point to which it is cost effective to use them in all offensive strikes. So my plan is to hit them hard enough to bring out the big guns, and simply track them back to base." I suggest.

"Sounds like a perfect military strategy to me son, what do you need from me?" He asks.

I grin, "Just a pack load of that C-4 we stole from the convoy, some remote detonator switches, and an evening out at the enemy base camp about eighteen miles South West of here."

"So, worst case scenario, we lose some C-4, they lose some tanks; which by the way from my own intel. will effectively finish off their non-air support and suppression of this whole region, and we don't see any 'Flying Saucers' to track?" He asks.

"Yes sir, but in case your intelligence didn't inform you. You should know that 'some tanks' is just over one hundred of their Dreadnaught class." I reply

"Well now son, I thought my evening was made, but I'd say you just wrapped my Birthday and Christmas all into one package today. I'll have the staff Sergeant put together your gear," He says.

"Sounds perfect *General*." I reply, as the chef walks up with our steaks.

6 FOX TRAP!?

I spend the next day going over the specs that Dane has stored for me from our captured Dreadnaught tanks, as well as the ones she leached for me from the satellite network's archive server. After hours of looking finally I find the Nazi Dreadnaught class tank assembly has a fatal flaw.

"Found it!" I yell... to myself? "I've really got to stop that."

Dane responds, "You know it really is disturbing, not just the amount of time you spend talking to yourself, but that you have actually started to correct yourself when you do it, little brother."

"Yeah well you answered too, smart ass. So I guess that solves that problem."

"Wonderful, now I've taken a perfectly good psychological pattern based diagnosis, and turned it into a mockery," she responds. "And what is it you think you found exactly?"

"Well you know as well as I, all designs have at least one flaw, of course some bigger than others. Well, this one is not enough to worry about under normal circumstances, which may be the reason it still exists, but I'll take it. Check out Schematic 12-R of the Assembly designs, quadrant N-17. You see it?"

"The under lap in the plating covering the primary fuel tank?" She asks.

"That's the one!" I say confidently.

"I processed that hours ago."

"And you didn't say anything?!" I demand.

"That under lap is slightly less than a quarter inch. How do you intend on utilizing that on such a large scale?" She queries.

"Elementary my dear…" She attempts to interrupt me. "Don't you dare call me!" I continue anyway, "Watson. What? You know it's rude to interrupt?" I state. "Besides, had you told me about it 'hours ago' then you could have been Sherlock, it's your own fault really."

"Wonderful," she states.

"Anyway Mrs. Negativity, a small C-4 charge planted just inside that plating gap, will ignite the primary fuel tank right?" I ask rhetorically.

"Yes, it will, but…" She answers.

I continue, "Well look at M-16, the primary tank has a flow valve that leads directly to the secondary tank. So when the primary tank goes with that kind of force what will happen to that valve?"

"Yes, yes I see, back pressure to a valve that size should cause the secondary tank to then ignite as well, and none of them will be able to move at all. It will likely be weeks before they're all repaired. I suppose that will do it."

"Oh no, I'm not through yet Mrs. Supercomputer. What does that secondary tank sit under?" I ask.

"The main ordinance storage," she replies confidently, "So, I've had thirty-two processors dedicated to this problem all day, and you manage to come up with the answer on your own, in less than five hours?" She skulks.

"Yeah don't be sad. A.I.'s shouldn't be sad. Besides, what year of Danes memories are you up to processing now?"

"Nine," she answers.

"Well let me know when you get to the early twenties that could get ugly."

"If you say so," she says obviously sulking.

"Look I'm Nikola Tesla's Grandson right? I guess you should have dedicated thirty-three processors to the task. You don't have to be such a sore loser."

"Apparently something's rubbed off. I wonder if he talked to himself as much as you?" She suggests.

"Better than talking to an A.I. that whines when it gets beat to the problem's solution."

"Disabling voice response system.

"You do realize that by saying 'Disabling voice response system.' You're actually responding right?" I ask.

No reply…

"Well now that I can think! So planting the C-4 into a three centimeter gap between the under hull plating, and the fuel tank itself shouldn't be too difficult with the suit. I can go in invisible, and plant all the C-4 without being seen, then just detonate remotely." I say. "And once the secondary tank goes, blowing the ordinance inside, it'll continue to blow apart any critical systems, leaving just the outer hull with not even so much as a tread to stand on."

The following night in my room, I grab my 'satchel' fill it with the C-4 George had sent down for me, and go completely invisible. I take the elevator up to level eleven 'the primary mess hall', step in where no one really pays any attention to the doors just opening and closing, and I wait for *Lt.* Bradley to finish his evening meal, as I know it is his night for entrance level guard duty.

Once he finishes I follow him into the elevator which he then takes down to the twentieth floor, presumably to talk to me before he goes on shift.

I brush past him and manage to make it into my office before he shows up around the corner and make myself visible, tossing my satchel under my bunk. I sit looking over a stack of papers that are on my desk when he walks in knocking on the door frame.

"What's up Bradley?" I say still looking down at my paperwork.

"One of these day's you're going to have to explain to me how you do that…" He states

"One day… What's on your mind?" I ask looking up.

"Eh, I pulled guard duty tonight, and I wanted to know if you were interested in coming up and screwing around for a while?" He asks.

"Screw around eh? You should know by now Bradley I'm not into guys. I mean we're friends and all, and if that's your thing, great for you, but won't your former Vice President take issue with that?" I smile.

"Ha Ha jack ass, I was thinking catch, wall ball, board game, I don't know something to pass the time. It's a top secret military base with a holographic shielded entrance, and nothing ever happens. We'll have the loading bay all to ourselves." He says.

"What time you get off?" I ask.

"Pffft, zero-six-hundred." He replies.

"Uh well tell you what, I have to go grab some chow, and then I'm working on a formula to improve the yield on the C-4 we pilfered, but I should finish all that up in say three or four hours? How about I come up and help keep you awake then?" I suggest.

"Sounds good, I'm sure that's about when I'm gonna start nodding off anyway." He says.

I wait for him to leave the room, grab the satchel go invisible and scramble down the hall to hop in the elevator with him again. Once we reach the top we both walk out and he relieves the current guard on post, and while they exchange notes and handle the coveted passing of the clip board, I continue straight out of the facility. Dane tunes the Viper suit to the same frequency as the holo-shield.

After gently passing through the hologram I begin to run toward the tanks. Eighteen miles at near sixty miles per hour, Dane estimates I should hit the camp in approximately 19.1 minutes. On approach my HUD begins to flash as I'm slowing down. Dane begins to show me a fairly extensive mine field, that surrounds this compound.

With only a thought "Full threat analysis", a three dimensional overlay of the compound is displayed on my HUD.

"On top of what appear to be very high yield mines it appears that the wall they have erected to surround this depot is lined with lead and made to withstand their own mine blasts, there are also large lights and heavy machine guns." Dane says.

"By the looks of those you're talking about, antiaircraft guns, those are *extremely* heavy machine guns. So, how do they get in and out?" I ask.

"There is a gate to the north, with a similar setup on either side of it, lights, and guns, however those lights appear to be permanently lit and I detect no mines leading to the gate itself. Also I should point out that razor wire appears to line the top of the whole compound." Dane states.

"Sounds like a nice place for a summer home… I've always wanted to live in a gated community."

"Sure Johnny, I'm sure it's just full of friendly neighbors. That will all stab you in the back, the second it's turned." Dane comments.

"Ah, but no solicitors! You're always looking on the negative side. Where's that positive, can do attitude? Oh yeah, still processing I don't think Dane actually hit that till she was around seventeen, when she entered and won her first science fair."

I approach the gated side of the compound far enough away not to disturb any light waves. Although, the Viper suit makes me completely invisible there is always a chance that in an otherwise dark situation like this light waves could be reflected incorrectly producing a 'disco ball' kind of effect, at least that's what Liz was prattling on about one night at dinner, but then that was when the suit was supposed to be two years away from a working prototype too, so who knows.

The HUD tells me that the walls are twelve feet tall, the gate itself is slightly taller at fourteen feet, bringing it up even with the razor wire at the top of the wall.

"Alright, it seems my options are, attempt to sneak in by doing a full speed run through the light and jump the gate hoping to avoid detection, of course this only works if the suits muscle assistance system can give me about a twenty foot vertical jump, which we haven't tested. I could also try causing the electrical system to overload with a shot from the BARB on one of the lights and odds are they'll see that, and the effects are likely going to be temporary if they have any sort of backup generator or fault tolerant system in place. Or I could just go in balls out start shooting at everything until they get curious and open the gate for me.

"Thoughts, Sparky?" I ask.

"Sparky?" Dane replies.

"It's a nickname; we're trying out nicknames now." I reply.

"Excellent…" She groans, "By my calculations a full run and jump to avoid detection is the most feasible and least reckless way to accomplish this feat, though with the suit at its current power level you should just be able to grab the top of the door and pull yourself over. Meaning there is a good chance that you will be heard slamming into the gate." Dane states.

"Yeah, I had a feeling you were going to say something like that. Should be able? What kind of odds are we talking here?" I reply.

"Not nearly what I would like them to be, but of the choices given it has the highest likelihood of success." Dane says.

"Well, that's encouraging… Alright, I got another one…" before Dane has a chance to ask "what kind of foolish idea I've come to now" I grab a rock about the size of a football, and throw it forty two point three meters (thank you HUD) down the compound wall from me, into the mine field.

Mines immediately start exploding, one reacting to the next "Ha! Even better I remark, those idiots put at least a few of them too close together."

"Interesting strategy…" Dane remarks with that tone of A.I. sarcasm.

"Oh lighten up Sparky, you haven't seen the good part yet," I reply.

All lights are focused on the area where the mines were exploding, sirens blaring. I make a straight run for the gate stop dead at five meters away from them in the center, which the HUD tells me is just outside of the doors swing zone when they open.

With a thought the sirens are filtered from my audio input.

The gates finally begin to open and I can see a Dreadnaught tank they are prepping to roll out, most likely with the intention of checking their perimeter. I run ten meters and leap up onto the tank, tucking into a ball, I roll forward off the rear of the tank, while grabbing a detonator prepped, two centimeter cube of C-4 from my satchel, landing on my back I throw the cube with enough force to hit and stick just between the gas tank and the plating mark under the tank.

"Perfect," I comment to Dane.

"It actually is a perfect shot." Dane replies sounding amazed.

"Careful Sparky, we can change that nickname at any time." I retort.

There are armed guards preparing to follow this tank out in formation behind it, on the right and left flank each spaced approximately three meters from the one before.

I quickly roll to my left in between two guards marching out, almost tripping one. He looks around, and appears to just believe he tripped on his own foot, and quickly checks his boot laces.

Now, that all the guards are either outside looking for me, or up on the wall manning their posts, I make short work of planting my C-4, working from the outside perimeter inward, fifty tanks, sixty tanks, eighty tanks, finally as I approach the last one number one hundred eleven, I realize that I have just used my last cube of C-4, and like the one that had gone out after me chasing rocks in the mine field, this one seemed to be more centrally located, as if ready to be presented, or escorted somewhere for a demonstration perhaps?

I also notice that this one looks different though, it's sleeker, a little lower to the ground for what appears to be a better center of gravity, also it is surrounded by guards.

"So what have we here? This one has its own set of guards." I comment to myself

While it is located in the center of the compound and slightly toward the back, it seems like I would have a direct route at the gate with it.

"A prototype?" I wonder aloud

"It is probable; there are enough design differences just from outward appearance to suggest that this is a completely different model than the others," Dane replies.

"Well I was kind of bummed that we only got three Dreadnaughts on that convoy heist. What with burning up all the electronics in the lead one and all."

"And almost getting burned up yourself." Dane kindly reminds me.

"Yeah, yeah, ancient history Sparky."

"Yeah, ancient..." she says obviously not in agreement with my assessment of the timeline.

"Anyway I think George would appreciate getting a sneak preview of the latest model these oppressive morons are getting ready to utilize." I say with confidence.

"At least we can agree on that," she concedes. "And what are you going to do about all the soldiers that rush down the walls as soon as you fire that thing up?" She asks

"Well fortunately since I worked from the outside in, this tank is located directly in the center of the compound. So I figure as soon as I start out the front gate, it's time to flip the switch." I say, "Besides, I'm in a tank... what are these 'soldiers' going to do, shoot at me with their mighty machine guns? Oh... Yeah they do have those pretty beefy anti-aircraft style nests don't they? Well I seriously doubt their latest design effort tank, is going to be that susceptible to an over powered machine gun."

"Yes, and they also have a tendency to use high phosphorous rounds." Dane points out.

"I suppose I'll have to take out the machine gun nests then before I roll out of this place."

"You do know you're out of C-4 right? Wouldn't it be easier to just sneak out of here and hope this one gets taken out with the rest as they blow?" She asks.

"Yeah it would be easier but not guaranteed, and you didn't see any schematics of these on their servers did you?"

"Uh, well no."

"See then it's possible they know we're in their system and this is the only chance that the U.S. forces will get a chance to look at this thing before it's beating on their people."

"Damnit Johnny, why does this always end in you risking your life? We haven't even gotten to the time traveler yet.

"Just chill this is what I was trained for; you had your science, I had war. That's why you picked me isn't it? Well that and my rugged good looks right?"

"Yeah, that was it… moron," she says

"Hey! I heard that. You know we shouldn't forget, Bradley's waiting on me to play some wall ball; you wouldn't want me to be late for wall ball would you, Sparky?" I respond.

"Uh… No, how could I possibly want that?" Dane answers obviously irritated

"Wow… you're a suit full of processing power and I got an 'Uh… no?' Either I'm getting smarter, or you're getting dumber." I reply.

"What can I say; you're argument held a certain amount of logic, at least the training portion of it did. Don't worry I'll get back to hounding you when you say something stupid again momentarily Johnny."

"I hate you…" I remark.

"See… tsk tsk, Johnny, so soon?" She replies

Leaping over the guards heads, dropping down in and quietly closing the tank hatch, I look around and find a scientist going over his checklist.

"What's up doc?" I ask, uncloaking with a thought and pointing my BARB at the side of his head.

He only speaks German but luckily I have Dane to translate for me in real time.

"What are you doing? Who are you? You can't be in here!" He insists.

"Easy doc you're going to blow a circuit, and I'll ask the questions here. Now, when's this tank supposed to be finished?" I demand.

"It's a prototype, it has to pass our inspection in the morning, before it can go into production."

"So this is the only one of its kind?"

"Yes, yes, please don't shoot!" He cries

"Ha I wouldn't dream of it, but you are coming with me." I insist as a crack him over the head with the handle of my BARB knocking him out cold.

"Alright, so now we really need to get this thing back to base."

"Oye agreed." Dane responds.

"So what are the chances that blowing all the tanks at the same time will take out the machine gun nests?"

"Very likely, approximately ninety one point three percent."

"Great, let's get the hell outta dodge then!"

"Not so fast Johnny," she insists.

"What now?"

"Well yes the machine gun nests will be taken out, but you will be waiting on secondary and tertiary explosions."

"Meaning… They're going to get off some shots before the explosion gets them, got it. So I need to blow the C-4 first, then go while they're distracted and trying to figure out what the hell is going on!" I state with confidence.

"You do realize that if this is not timed perfectly the heat and shrapnel from the exploding tanks could very well take out this tank as well?" She asks

"Well yeah, but that's not going to happen."

"How can you be so sure?"

"Because that would be a terrible story, obviously."

"Oh well, as long as you have sound reasoning on your side, by all means!" She says sounding more pissed than ever.

"Just relax, I've done this before… I think?" I answer.

With that I flip the switch and blow my little C-4 charges. Watching out one of the side slide portals I see the tanks begin to expand from the inside like a soda can that's been dropped with the pressure building up inside.

"Okay, time to roll! I hope this thing has fuel in it?" I say.

"You didn't chec…" Dane gets out as the engines begin firing up.

The massive doors begin to close. "Well, someone obviously saw us moving." I say, aiming the main canon.

Once the doors are fully closed I fire the main battery, blowing the massive doors completely apart. This is definitely not a normal Dreadnaught layout I note, at least not like the other three I'd been in, or the schematics I had studied from the Nazi's own Dreadnaught database.

As I pass through the now shattered gate the tanks along the outside walls begin to blow up first, enveloping the machine gun nests, and speeding along the explosions of the tanks near them. Suddenly it gets very hot inside my tank as the sides are completely covered in fire. Checking the rear camera I can see the soldiers running after me, and a wall of flame enveloping them as it heads straight for me. The whole place rocks with one final explosion, fire lights the night sky like a new born sun, Nazi's incinerated left and right, not that you can see much from inside a tank mind you, but the rear camera helped a lot, and the flames seem to leap forward toward me enveloping my Escapenaught, I can only imagine this is due to the surrounding lead lined, block and concrete wall the tanks were secured within.

"And just like that the impending threat of these Dreadnaught tanks is now gone." I remark to myself

"Yeah just like that," Dane says sounding disappointed.

As we round the corner after exiting the mine field we hit a big bump causing me to drop the C-4 remote. No sooner than this happens we are hit by a massive explosion to the left side of the tank.

"Dane I'm going to need a status report on this tank," I demand.

"Working on it."

Looking out the side portal I see the other Dreadnaught, it didn't explode.

"Great!" I exclaim, immediately realizing that the lead lined walls must have shielded it from the signal to the C-4 detonator.

Quickly searching the floor for the remote control another massive hit, almost exactly where the first one nailed us. Out of the corner of my eye I catch the remote lying under the scientists shoulder.

Jumping for the remote I am able to grab it just as another canon hit nails the same spot ripping through the hull and hitting the other side sending shrapnel shards everywhere. Looking through the new whole I grit my teeth and flip the switch.

"Suck on this you little Nazi bastards." I yell, watching as the tank begins to buckle and malform before my eyes. With one last creek it explodes almost in slow motion.

"I seriously need a new hobby. I wonder if people in this time line churn butter."

"Seriously, you've just taken out a major threat to the people in that mountain and you want to know about churning butter?" Dane asks.

"Don't worry... it was rhetorical. I saw that the Nazi's have a butter machine type thing now. In one of the files I was looking over." I respond.

"Well that makes me feel *much* better, maybe I should run a diagnostic on your head to see if that concussion came back," she says.

"Alright, alright… just check the satellite uplink and let me know if they can track this thing. I don't want to literally drive the enemy to my front door." I reply

"Checking… The satellite network has either no information on this model yet, or they have found a way to hide it from me. I am however detecting a radio transmitter within the under carriage of this model." Dane says.

"Great! Maybe that's why they made it so low to the ground. In case of capture it's a pain in the ass to remove their transmitter?" I ask.

"The possibility has merit, however I have assembled a partial schematic of the unit based upon my own scans, and it looks like there is a hatch one meter behind you, that can be opened and the transmitter accessed. This is likely for service purposes, but you should be able to remove it or disable it none the less." Dane replies.

I stop the tank, and move to check out this hatch.

"Threat assessment?" I ask.

"You know I heard you when you thought that right?" She responds.

"Yeah, and you know I talk to myself so just give me the threat assessment." I demand.

"The hatch is protected by a standard key lock whether or not it is 'booby-trapped' is not something I can tell from this angle as the hatch itself appears to be of an iridium alloy, making my penetrating scans almost useless. I'm not actually sure what will happen if you just rip it open."

"Well I can't believe that they have it armed with anything that will blow the tank, but suppose they did. Would the Viper protect me at its current power levels?" I ask.

"At your current power level the Viper would protect you from a fairly large explosion, but it's doubtful that anything large enough to blow this tank could be withstood," she replies.

"I'm not driving this thing with a tracking device in it to the only 'friends' I actually have. So hold on Sparky, this could get bumpy." I respond.

I tear away the door to the transmitter and the cabin is immediately filled with a thick green smoke.

"Ah, smoke… Identify?" I say.

"Knock out gas, pure and simple." Dane replies.

"Great, I like knock out gas. That'll help keep mister wizard out while we head back to base, now let's have beautiful advanced thermal view," I say.

With that everything looks almost completely normal, I disable the radio by simply disconnecting its power source, and proceed to drive my new tank back to base.

Once we arrive I transmit the open code for the holo-shield and drive her on in. True to his word Bradley is or rather was sleeping at his post until I start pulling this thing in. He goes for the alarm, but I announce over the loud speaker who it is and request he lock up the holo-shield behind me. His mouth drops but he manages to do as ordered, and then climbs up to the hatch to help me out.

As I open the hatch he gets hit in the face with the knock out gas and instantly goes down, falling back to the floor.

"Ah, damn it. I forgot about that. Why didn't you remind me?"

"Where would the fun in that have been?" She replies

"Ok... You're definitely Dane. Just monitor your satellite feeds for UFO traffic." I say.

As the knock out gas dissipates I climb out and jump down to check on Bradley. My HUD gives me a full body scan, looks like he may have twisted his ankle.

"Now look what you did," I scold Dane. "I need him to go to South America with me in a few days. You better hope he's not broken, or you'll never hear the end of it jack ass."

I slap Bradley on the face lightly to try and bring him around, he finely starts to wake.

"What the hell was that?" He asks

"Uh, knock out gas... Sorry about that Bradley, I forgot I even released it, I was just trying to get back to the mountain undetected." I explain.

"Oh... yeah no worries John we all release a little knock out gas now and again. My ankle is killing me though; can you give me a hand?" He asks, passing out again.

"Yeah of course," I reply offering my hand. "Ah crap..."

"Alright, THAT was funny." Dane laughs in my ear.

"Are you kidding me right now? You must be up to what Dane's thirteenth maybe fourteen year old memories in processing?"

"How'd you know?" She asks.

"Because Dane thought everything was funny at that age." I answer

"Based on my cursory scan of her memories, I believe that she would have found this particular instance funny under any circumstance."

Back to tapping him on the face, he starts to come around more quickly this time.

"Yeah, yeah I'm up!" He says.

"You may be right, it is kind of funny actually."

This time I grab his hand and pull him up. "Let's get you down to the infirmary and put some ice on that ankle, before it becomes a problem." I say.

"Yeah, I just have to call in my relief," he insists.

"I got it buddy, let's just get to the infirmary." I tell him.

Bradley being one of the only people that actually knows about the Viper suit has some advantages, him understanding *this* is one of them. Of course at this point it could be more knocked out than understanding, but that works too.

"Dane, call down to the Guard station and make sure they send someone up ASAP," I order.

"Already on their way Johnny," she responds.

"Also, put in a page to the on call nurse," I say.

"She has been informed and will be waiting for our arrival.

Moments later the elevator doors finally swing open and a replacement for Bradley is already coming out.

I mention in passing to keep an eye on my tank and toss him the key. He shoots me a look of confusion and then seems to realize who he's looking at and just shrugs and heads over to the duty station.

Walking into the elevator I remember the scientist inside. "Hey, there's a guy in a white coat in there too. You should probably get a hazmat team up here and have them pull him out, he's probably got some valuable intel." I yell to the replacement guard, as the doors swing shut.

I hear a muffled "Yes, Sir!" as the elevator starts to descend.

On the elevator ride down to fourteen I apologize again to Bradley, "I really am sorry, you know how the suit is, it filters everything from the air for me, even has enhanced vision, I literally forgot I was surrounded by that stuff."

"It's alright, at least this way I'll get to ice my ankle and then lay down and get some shut eye. I hate the late shift." He replies with this stupid grin on his face.

"There, you see, I did him a favor," Dane suggests.

"Oh yeah… a favor, good one, *A.I.* Any word on those UFO's yet?"

"Nothing on any of the satellite feeds yet," she responds.

The elevator doors finally open, "Alright Bradley, this is our stop buddy."

"What? No I have guard duty tonight!" He says practically drooling and trying to lean forward to get out of my arms.

"No, buddy that was already taken care of, now you have ice pack in the infirmary duty," I tell him.

"Oh… Okay then." He agrees, slumping back to a more relaxed position.

"This is awesome Dane. Thanks for this; you really did a number on him. Check his brain for a concussion." I demand definitely sounding exasperated.

"Um… Ooo… yeah there is some slight swelling in the cranial region; his meninges are experiencing pressure in multiple sides," she reports.

"Beautiful. You're fired."

I escort the *Lt.* into the infirmary and get him set up on a bed, letting the on call nurse Beckie know exactly how he fell, and that as well as his swollen ankle there is a high probability of a concussion too, I also ask her to give him something to help him sleep.

Beckie immediately moves to hang a bag of Saline. Once getting his line set she tells me she's "pushing a prednisone, sedative concoction" they use to treat concussions, and that it will also help with the swelling in his ankle.

I look over at Bradley one more time before heading down to rest myself. "Alright American, get some rest I expect to see you back up and ready to go to South America with me in eight hours."

"You got it John… I'll be right there, I just need to change my shorts," is all he gets out before the drugs kick in.

"Jesus Dane does that gas make you incontinent too?"

"Well it literally relaxes every muscle in your body until you're out cold. If you have to go… well you go…"

"You made the man shit himself?!"

"Oh, come on, I didn't make him, he obviously needed to go."

"Don't worry sir, I'll get him cleaned up. He won't be ready in eight hours, but he will get better." Nurse Beckie says.

7 I REMEMBER NOW

Lying in my rack that night I remember drifting off, imagining the smile I was going to get out of the good *General* when I presented him with the very latest tank design the enemy was planning to use against him. Even if it was a little banged up.

But as I fell asleep something very different came to mind.

I was just arriving home from school; I couldn't have been more than seven or eight at the time. The bus stopped right in front of my house, just under a huge maple tree in our front yard. I was walking up the stairs to the porch on Thirty-Eighth Street, and heard yelling from inside, it was a man's voice that I didn't recognize, and my dad! I was kind of surprised I'd never heard my dad raise his voice before, so I sat on the porch swing and listened for the argument to end.

At the time it didn't really register what they were arguing about although I heard Dane's name mentioned a few times, and something called a "Mid Atlantic Time Paradox" at least I think that's what I heard.

I don't know about you, but at the end of the twenty second century, and at that age which was either second or third grade in school, I knew what time was, and where the Atlantic Ocean was, but a "Paradox" was a little above my comprehension level.

The yelling seemed to go on forever, always talk of 'time' and 'repairing' and 'preparing ME!' it was about ME! That's it! The older man was yelling at my father that he needed me to be schooled in the 'Art of War' and that my actual school grades made no difference. To tell the truth I was kind of in agreement with that point, my dad was always on me to get good grades in school. But this guy he was convincing my father that school grades weren't as important as he needed to influence me into the military, into special forces, covert ops, whatever military training I could attain, that was what would help with the coming war!?

I awaken with more questions than answers. Was that my Grandfather? Could this be part of what Dane's letter meant about him "*cheating as much as possible*" and me being his "*perfect blessing*", a hardened in battle, special forces trained twenty third century warrior?

Checking the time I realize that it's only zero-four-hundred.

"What time did we check Bradley into the infirmary?" I ask.

"It was twenty-three-thirty-two Johnny." Dane answers.

"So it's been just over four hours… sounds like a good time to check on him."

"You really are fond of this *Lt.* aren't you?" Dane asks.

"Yeah, well he reminds me a lot of myself when I first made rank, and he can take a joke which is always an enduring quality. He's a good guy, but then so is George." I say sitting up. "I actually intend on looking up both of them once I get everything sorted out, back to our own time and all. You know see how things turned out for them."

"I do carry the entire twenty third century world's knowledge within my core storage for easy access, this includes sub-databases from Interpol, the Federal Bureau of Investigation, the Central Intelligence Agency, Alcohol Tobacco Firearms, Home Land Security, the National Security Agency, and all local city, state, and county police databases, as well as every major countries Military personnel databases. Also all records of live birth and death certificates." Dane responds.

"Wow… I'm pretty sure none of that was supposed to be in the Viper suit or the Time Lab projects." I say finally making it to my feet to stretch.

"Indeed, several laws, and protocols were breached to secure these databases for your use," she replies.

Heading for the door I can't help but ask at this point, "So who do I owe the 'thank you' to for that one Liz, Dane or both?"

"Actually neither, this is odd but according to my logs this information was obtained via upload from a remote source that could definitely not have been either of them. In actuality now that I have accessed these databases it is evident that they are not from the twenty third century at all, there is data here dating all the way in to the forty second century," she replies.

"Wow… so Granddad strikes again," I answer still groggy while waiting for the elevator.

"That is the only solution that currently makes any sense," she answers.

"Crazy… I wish I would have gotten to know him," I say finally boarding the elevator and heading up to fourteen.

"Who knows Johnny, with all this planning and forethought, and the knowledge he would have needed to pull all this off, I would say there is a less than slim chance that you will run into him at some point during all this. Who knows he may already have a time and place for your meeting picked out," Dane replies.

"Well do me a favor then, since Granddad has graced us with all this intel, find out what happens to my buddies Bradley, and George once the time-line is put straight for me will ya?" I say now entering the infirmary.

Looking around I see Bradley still fast asleep, his monitors according to my HUD readouts are all within normal ranges. Nurse Beckie comes around the corner, apparently after hearing the door close.

"*General* I didn't expect to see you back here so soon. Checking up on the *Lt.* are we?" She asks.

"Yes ma'am, I wasn't sleeping well, and frankly he's a good friend," I reply.

"Well, not to worry, his vitals are all stable and there have been no changes to worry about, or only good changes I guess is a better way to say that. In fact I would expect he'll be up and around on a single crutch in a few hours," she says reassuringly.

"That's good news. I'm glad it was nothing too serious, I thought we might be looking at a sprain or worse," I reply

"Yes, he is very lucky you got him as quickly as you did. His ankle was blowing up pretty badly to start with, in fact I was very near calling in the doctor to do an emergency fluid drain at one point, but was able to keep a series of fresh ice packs on it and eventually get control of all that swelling. You probably saved his foot by getting him here that fast actually."

"Wow… And I was more worried about his head."

"The I.V. I ran of saline with the prednisone formula we use, seems to have helped with any possible concussion related swelling, and that would have aided with the swelling in his ankle as well," she answers.

"You've done an amazing job Beckie, how long do you think he'll need the crutch?"

"He should only need that for a week at most, barring some further injury, or something that I'm just not seeing right now. I'll be able to give you a better answer on that when the doctor comes in at zero-eight-hundred to confirm," she says.

"Alright, that's good to hear. Well I'm going to head up to the mess then and see if I can grab a little early breakfast before it gets busy. Thanks again Beckie you've been a big help, I'll stop by again after a while to see what the doc says, please page me if you need anything or anything happens," I say shaking her hand and heading out the door.

"Will do!" She says with a tired smile.

Heading back toward the elevator Dane speaks up, "Alright, so your friends search was easy enough with the United States military personnel database at our disposal. *Lt.* Bradley according to this will eventually become a *General* himself in our time-line."

"Nice, I like it! And George?" I ask boarding the elevator once more, this time heading up to the mess hall on the eleventh floor.

"Like many of his name sakes, attained the rank of *General* in the United States army, and actually was the key or linchpin to ending World War III. In fact he and one *General* Bradley it seems worked together on several levels during World War III, both surviving to nearly ninety years of age, and it seems friends the entire time. You may be interested to know that *General* George S. Patton XII in your own time-line spends most of his time at the Pentagon," she says.

"Wow… the twelfth huh?"

"Indeed the twelfth and the name does persist as by your time he has actually already fathered the thirteenth in the line." Dane responds.

"Well, when you're going to do something you don't half-ass it as a Patton I suppose. They seem to know this intimately," I reply exiting the elevator to an empty mess hall.

"Indeed," Dane responds.

"Smells like they're cooking back there," I remark heading up to the main distribution line.

"Any UFO data to analyze yet?"

"Not a blip," Dane responds.

"That's too bad; I had hoped to nail a location before heading down there."

"It would be a step in the right direction Johnny."

"Hey do one of those cool whistles for me where you put your fingers in your mouth," Which she does.

Within a second I see a *Private* pop his head around the corner. "Be right there Sir!"

"Take your time kid, just bring me some bacon and eggs when you come," I reply

"Sir, yes sir!" he replies

I thought to tell him to stop with all the 'sirs', but what's the use, it was hard enough getting Bradley to knock it off, let alone all the other military personnel on this base.

Twenty seconds later the *Private* pops up at the window with a plate of Bacon and eggs piled high. "Here you are sir, anything else I can get you? Coffee's fresh over at the drink station just made it ten minutes ago," he points out the smoldering coffee pots.

"That'll do nicely *Private*, thank you," I reply heading for the coffee.

I head back down to my floor with my tray full of breakfast to plan for my upcoming South American trip.

"You know I've always wanted to see Buenos Aires," Rolling out the chair to my desk.

"Somehow I doubt it will look like what you're expecting in this time-line," Dane replies as I sit down to eat.

"Yeah well, maybe when I get things back to normal then, I'm pretty sure someone's going to owe me a big fat vacation with nothing but palm trees and warm sand."

"Well you do have a time-machine and a supercomputer, you could always go back a few years and place the right bets, or make the right investments," Dane suggests.

"Bah, you know I couldn't do that."

"Why not? If you fix the entire space time continuum they won't even know you did anything. You try to write a report on it, and they'll probably check you into the nearest mental hospital. I'm pretty sure there's not going to be any medals awarded for this mission, and you can kiss your hazard pay goodbye too, you're in completely uncharted waters here Johnny."

"Huh, I guess I never thought of it like that," I reply, crunching on some bacon.

"Well quite honestly you should!"

"Wait… I get it, you're processing Dane's sophomore year in High School. Idealistic to a fault that girl."

"Wow… You sure you don't have an eidetic memory?" She asks.

"Yeah, pretty sure. So here's what I'm thinking. I turn over the new prototype Dreadnaught to George; he should be able to get me two of the three normal ones I already got him for this trip. Each Dreadnaught is big enough to

173

sleep six people relatively comfortably. I'm thinking ten to twelve people total including me."

"And right back to work you go," she says snidely. "Sounds like a small enough team to infiltrate any secure compound, and using the Nazi's own tanks as cover should work well enough to get you in I would think. So far a solid plan Johnny," Dane replies, as I sit down at my desk.

"I thought you'd like it, I think keeping it as small as possible is going to be the trick, I don't want to take any red shirts," I say.

"Wow… you really went there," she replies.

"Um… yeah? Don't I always?" I ask.

"I suppose you do," she answers.

"Anyway, can you drop the repellent field so I can eat, and keep your eye on the satellite feeds, watching for any flying saucer activities?" I say, shoving another piece of bacon in my mouth.

"Wait for it…" She says

"Hey! I'm eating and the HUD is still up. How the hell does that work?" I demand coughing and almost choking on my bacon.

"I told you, more energy equals more features. In this case I'm now able to use the extra power being generated to manipulate the repellent field around your mouth."

"You tricky little."

"Hey! Would you rather I just drop the HUD?"

"No this is great actually, best of both worlds even."

"What's even cooler is I haven't actually disabled the field to your mouth, I just made it very thin, so as food passes through it is subjected to the static field itself killing all germs."

"Granted you're the genius scientist here, but wouldn't that also kill all nutrients as well?" I ask, crunching on another piece of bacon.

"First, as if bacon had any nutrients, and second not with a supercomputer deciding how much to charge each mouthful as it enters. It's literally just enough to make sure no germs get in. Dane wanted you safe, what can I say? Oh, and I have been monitoring the satellite system for saucers, ever since we left last night as you asked, it may take them a while to realize that the base is gone and send out a recon force, but I guarantee you will be the first to know," she reassures me.

"I'm starting to nag you at this point huh?"

"You really are."

"See how annoying it is?"

"I… just… whatever," she answers.

I take my time eating and drinking my coffee, actually grabbed a whole pot for myself, one of the perks of being a *General*.

Spend some time doodling plans on a sheet of paper, just to see if anything brilliant would come to me. Just about the time I'm ready to head up and check in on Bradley there's a knock on the door.

"Come in!" I yell, standing up figuring this wouldn't take long and then I could be on my way.

Flinging open the door with one hand it's the *Lt.,* "Bradley! Good to see you kid. What the hell are you doing up and around so fast? I was actually just getting ready to come check up on you again."

"Likewise John, on the 'good to see you part' anyways. Nurse Beckie told me you were concerned so I figured I should stop in, and make sure you knew I was okay," he responds.

"Well that's excellent, I was a little worried the way you hit your head, come in have a seat. I've been going over some things, and I'm interested to hear what you think." I reply, pulling out the chair on the other side of my desk so he can get into it easier.

"Really?" He asks enthusiastically, as I motion him over.

"Absolutely, I have it on good authority that you my friend are going to be a great *General* someday. So I figure I should pick your brain now before your ego gets too big."

He chuckles, "Well, yeah I guess if you're serious?"

"I couldn't be more serious kid, come on have a seat," I say motioning him in to a chair by my desk.

As he hobbles over on his one crutch, and sits down, I start to explain what I'm thinking; the talking George into nine or so of his people, Bradley being one of them, and two of the Dreadnaught tanks.

"That sounds brilliant John, actually I know exactly what we do if you can get the *General* to go for it," he replies while easing forward in his seat, as I take mine on the other side of the desk.

"Okay, what have you got for me?"

"Well our intel says that there is another major three way railroad switch, much like the one we already took out. It is in what was New Mexico, just on the other side of the Rocky Mountain range. You see that's why that substation we took out was so important. That was their major fan out after they passed the Rockies. So if we take our tanks down old Route sixty six skirting just south of the Rockies, to that substation in New Mexico and grab a train headed south into old Mexico. Well from what I've heard, it runs the whole way down to the tip of South America at this point."

"Now you're talkin' kid, and to sweeten the pot for old Georgey, we set up some more remotely detonated explosives at that substation and blow it once we're on the train headed South and just clear. That should block their attempts back to this side of the country, further forcing them to have to repair that switch before even getting to the one here in Nevada.

It could also work to our advantage sneaking aboard that train too, as they'll likely figure we were after the train as part of the attack, and just missed it. Hell if we time it right, they'll probably be too busy considering themselves lucky we missed them, and never even look for stowaways," I respond.

"Great! When do we move out?" He asks.

"Well that all depends, what did Nurse Beckie give you for a timeline on that ankle?" I ask.

"Well the doctor came in around zero-eight hundred and wanted to do some tests. You know as a civilian outfit they only get paid based on actually doing something. So he did his x-rays and told me no more than two weeks tops. But Nurse Becky said; you know once the Doc walked into the other room; she said that because of the lack of swelling, and how well I'd responded to treatment overnight, that it probably isn't anywhere *near* that bad so she was thinking really only a couple of days." He answers.

"Yeah, she seems to really have it together, I think it's her height," I say.

"Yeah, wait her height?"

"Never mind, why did the doctor think it would take so long?"

"He insisted that based on his x-ray, that there 'appears' to be a hairline fracture on my 'intermediate cuneiform', whatever that is. Apparently getting that cleared is really the only hold up, but when Nurse Beckie pulled me aside she said that it's probably nothing, they've been having problems with their x-ray machine for months, and on top of that as long as I'm not putting too much pressure on it a hairline fracture on that bone shouldn't keep me from doing what I need to do anyway," he answers.

"Ah, so even if it is injured what he really should have said is, no dead lifting weights, or no excessive walking, it sounds like," I say.

"Agreed," he replies, as I stand and make my way back around the desk to look at his foot.

"What do you think Dane?" I ask, immediately I can see all the bones of his feet.

"Nothing… there is nothing wrong with the bones at all. He will be totally fine in a few days, once the soft tissue pain has resided."

"From what I can see, Nurse Beckie is right on point. Your bones are all fine, no fractures of any kind, bone bruises, nothing. Once the rest of your inflammation is gone you'll be right as rain," I parrot back to him.

"Bet that x-ray vision really comes in handy. Hey you know we have a lot of women on base, you haven't?"

"No! Absolutely not! I'd like to believe I have a little more integrity than that thank you."

"Right, sorry." He says, looking ashamed.

"Bah don't feel so bad, I would have asked too. Anyway, I'm having lunch with George in a little while, so I'll let him know what we're thinking, and make no mistake *you* are my number two on this op, so we'll do what we need to do, in order to make sure that works with that ankle of yours.

First off though, I'm going to need your help in selecting eight to eighteen other team members, so the next step is going to be for you to take this piece of paper and start brain storming some names for me that would make a good team."

"I can do that."

"Excellent, remember though we want a team, so people that can work together well, we want a cohesive unit that we can count on. Oh, and I'd like at least two other demolition experts, also everyone needs to be top notch when it comes to repelling, and climbing rope."

"Sure, yeah I know who works together the best around here the best. So like twenty names, and you narrow it down from there?" he asks.

"That should do. The shorter the list the better though I'm really going to have to defer to you and George on this though, these are you're people and I don't really know many of them."

"I'll do it, but if you don't mind I'd like to head up to the mess and get some breakfast," he says.

"Of course! Don't let me hold you up, feed that brain of yours kid, we need you in top team selecting condition. Not to mention healing that ankle. In fact maybe you should put that ankle up in your rack when you get done too; it'll be good for the blood flow. Don't worry I'll come find you after I have lunch with the *General*, and we'll continue from there."

"Alright, see you in a while John," he says sounding excited as he grabs his crutch and hobbles out the door.

"Two more demolitions experts?" Dane questions.

"Yeah don't worry I didn't forget about you, I just want to make sure all our bases are covered. And if I need to drop a caldera on this bases head, I'm thinking charges placed in a triangular strategy of locations halfway down the inside of the shaft around the perimeter should cause the top to cave in, instead of out."

"I see, so three people set charges to get in and out quickly."

"Yeah, the faster we can place them, get out, and get down the mountain, the less chance they'll have of detection, before it's too late, and the less chance we'll have any of our people getting hurt."

"I must say that is a very well thought out plan for execution Johnny, least amount of work for the highest possible yield." Dane replies.

"Yeah well I wasn't in special forces and then the CIA, because I was bad at my job."

"No, you were there because your Granddad wanted you to be it sounds like."

"Which is you…? Apparently, and how the hell did you know about my dream?" I demand.

"From your dream analysis, obviously."

"Oh, obviously, what the hell was I thinking? Now you want to explain why you are analyzing my dreams?" I demand.

"Ah yes, I guess that wasn't clear. You see the longer you are in the suit, or more specifically the hood, the closer your neural network and my Artificial Neural Network (ANN) become in sync. That's part of the whole you think things and I can do them without you speaking deal.

This is a product of that neural cohesion that is formed due to a relative proximity matrix, and melds our *minds* to a point of clear telepathic communication. Eventually, whether you have the hood on or not I will know what you are thinking and vice versa, although it does take the human mind longer to make those connections, at least that's what the studies have shown. However given your own genetic history, there may be a difference in what would be considered the normal time frame where that is concerned," she answers.

"So you're telling me eventually my sister will be so implanted in my head, I won't be able to do anything or say anything without hearing your comments on it, even without wearing the suit?"

"That's correct," she replies.

"Well there goes my sex life."

"And what if someone else were to wear this suit, would that add their mental imprint?"

"Well theoretically yes, in a manner of speaking. However the suit is genetically encoded for you, so it would take a considerable amount of time and knowledge of my inner workings to make that happen," she replies

"Great. Now not only do I have to put up with your jabbering the whole trip, but I can never separate myself from you either?" I ask.

"Well it would be unwise at any juncture, considering the benefits that you gain by wearing the hood. So I get to watch your thoughts and dreams. That's a small price to pay for command over complete system functionality with a thought, wouldn't you say?" She asks.

"You know I hate when you answer a question with a question."

"Yes… I do Johnny, but really… who am I going to tell?"

"Oye, alright, this is getting us nowhere," I reply.

"I'm going to lay down for a few anyway, now that I'm not worried about *Lt.* Bradley anymore maybe I can get a few more hours of shuteye before lunch with George."

Around eleven-thirty, I receive a call from George letting me know he's headed to his private mess hall, and that I should meet him there.

"Anything yet?" I ask.

"No... No UFO's yet," Dane says, as I make my way down the corridor and up the elevator yawning.

Entering the private room off the main mess hall, I find George sitting with a bowl of potato soup, a staple when you're living underground, and the Nazi's kill anyone who's not growing crops for them. Of course with potatoes being the staple food that means plenty of juice for the Vodka stills.

George is flanked by two MPs, which is not actually normal for the *General*, usually he enjoys his privacy.

"Pull up a seat son!" George says.

Sitting down I notice his demeanor is not as outgoing as usual.

"Something wrong George?" I ask, sitting down to join him.

He snaps at the two guards, one comes over setting a hot steamy bowl of soup in front of me, with a glass of water. The other hands me a file folder. Opening the file folder I see a photo of a younger version of the ex-Vice President, and a dossier exposing everything that they have learned of her over the last few days.

"So our gal has been busy I see," I say.

"Ha. I wish that were the half of it, turn the page and keep reading," he replies.

On the next page I find what George is referring to. Not only does it appear that she did get a chance to transfer her gathered intel on all four subterranean bases, she was able to get the word to her handlers, which means the Nazi base that we have been working to tunnel under, likely knows we're coming. The Nazi's themselves would know about our base and its protection via holo-shield, which they probably even have the resonance frequency for (used properly this frequency allows matter to pass right through it), and even with their downed train station, I'm sure they have the means to make a serious air attack.

"I see, so *General* it looks like this intel came from our own mole in the Nazi operation?" I ask.

"That is correct," he replies.

"And do we know if she had transmitted this data before or after her incarceration?" I ask.

"All indications point to the data being transferred after," he replies.

"Well first sir if I may, you know my 'condition'; may we have the room sir?" I ask.

"Ah, yes of course John I wasn't thinking. Gentlemen outside the door will be fine; I have nothing to fear from *General* Steal," he orders.

They comply and step outside of the room.

"Thank you sir." I reply.

"No, no that was my fault, I forget about that holographic image sometimes," he says.

"Well, based on that time-line we can only assume that there must be at least one more mole on base, and possibly more. Which is I imagine why the MP's are following you around," I reply removing my head piece.

"That was our assessment as well John."

"Is the prisoner still in her cell at least?" I ask.

"She is for now, but if they know our location, shield frequencies, and everything else, I don't know how long that will last, or any of this war for that matter. It's going to take at least two weeks at this point before we can get an engineer in here just to update our shield frequencies."

"Not to worry general, I can reset the shield frequencies, as a matter of fact I'm going to do you one better. I'm going to set up a modulator that randomly changes those frequencies, and build remote control that only you and your chosen senior staff will have access to," I reply.

"Well John that would be much appreciated. I had no idea you had the ability to do such things," he responds.

"Normally I wouldn't George, but my suit does, and that's going to give us a strong edge here. However if they do know we're tunneling to them, they may already be planning something on their end, or working on their own tunnel system to us," I suggest.

"That's also something we've considered, and believe me we're trying to come up with contingency plans for all possible outcomes," he says.

"Alright well we need to take this one step at a time. We'll want a strategy to sniff out any other moles you may have, so I'm going to discuss that with 'the suit' and I'm sure maybe you, the *President* and other *Generals* may have some ideas there as well."

"That's a good idea, I can get them on a conference call," he states.

"And while you do that, I'm going to be making sure no one can kick in your front door. Then we should compare notes and we'll address the tunneling situation. As of right now I assume you've pulled your teams out and are waiting for a plan of action?" I say finishing my soup and popping my hood back on.

"Yes, and I have just ordered a squad of thirty infantry down there to stand guard and set up defensive blockades. I'd hate to have them coming at us from our own tunnel," he replies.

"Good call *General.* I'll be sending your printer the information for the modulator and any other changes that will need to be made once I take a look at the shield generator itself."

"That sounds good John, I swear if you weren't here right now, we'd all be up shit creek without a paddle."

"Don't worry George, we're going to solve this. Tell me, do the other three bases have systems similar to yours, shield wise?" I ask standing up.

"Well most are hodgepodged together but I would expect that they are all very similar in design, we've only ever had one system designer that knew how to build the damn things."

"Good, who was that? I may need to speak with them."

"Well, it was your sister Dane, back when I was a *Colonel* she gave us the plans, and our engineers followed them as best they could with the parts we had available. That's one of the reasons I knew to trust you so implicitly when you finally showed up. Because of her, we've remained safe all these years."

"Dane, I should have known. Alright this will be easy then, inform the other *Generals* I will be sending new schematics to them for the modulation add-ons, and remote controls very soon and of course they're going to need to get their best people on it right away."

"Will do John, and thank you son, you are a true hero in any time-line, and don't ever let anyone tell you different. I haven't forgotten about that little present you brought in last night either by the way. That was a serious victory for us too, knowing their technology before they do will give us a massive advantage," he says.

"Well, Thank you sir, and I have another op I'd like to get moving on, but we can discuss that once these fires are put out. I'll get back with you soon," I promise.

"Sounds good son, I'll be in my office informing the other Generals to be on alert and stand by for your instructions."

"Sounds good George, keep an eye on your office printer, I'll send the new specs there as soon as I have them updated. Then you can get them to the other base commanders," I say exiting the room and heading for the elevator.

Walking through the normal mess hall I see *Lt.* Bradley eating lunch, and scribbling notes on a sheet of paper.

"Hopefully he's putting together a good list for me," talking to myself again.

Walking by I lean over and update him on our meeting, "Hey Bradley, I've got something else going on with the *General* right now, and I didn't get a chance to bring up our op yet, so keep with the names and it sounds like you may get that full two weeks before we head out anyway. I'll let you know more as soon as I can bud."

He looks a little confused but answers, "Uh, yeah sure John. I'll keep at it…"

Getting on the elevator I run into *PFC* Young, who also seems to be heading up to the top.

"*PFC First Class* Young, I'll be damned. I haven't seen you since you and the *Lt.* walked me in, how have you been?" I ask.

"Well sir, thank you sir. Actually it's *Corporal* now sir!" He answers.

"My apologies, *Corporal* Young I've seen your name in several reports, I know you earned those stripes."

"Thank you sir, I did hear of your promotion as well sir, it seems you are really turning tides around here. I sure am glad you're on our side sir," he replies sounding nervous.

"Ah, relax *Corporal*; I'm not going to bite."

"Oh yes sir!" He responds, "I was actually involved in a few of your ops, but I'm always in the background somewhere. You know, team lead and all, and your ops are always on the larger scale."

"That's true they have been a little on the large side haven't they? Well it's good to hear, that means you're doing your job *Corporal*," I say as the elevator doors open.

"Well sir, this is my stop, I'm up for guard duty," he says.

"Good mine too actually; I'm working on the shield generator a bit, make sure everything's up to snuff. *General Patton* asked me to give it a once over before my next op."

"Very good sir, I will be in the guard station if you need me." He replies as he heads over to the current on duty guard to exchange notes and pass the clipboard.

As I make my way past the guard station, I can't help but notice the confusion from the current guard when *Corporal* Young shows up to relieve him.

"What do you mean I'm relieved? I've only been on duty for an hour and a half?" He asks.

"Sorry *PFC*, those are the orders I got, come up here and relieve the current guard. If you care that much take it up with the *Staff Sergeant*," *Corporal* Young says.

I continue on to a small out cove on the west wall, once in the cove I spot the panel I'm looking for, it's at the floor level, and has a two handle release mechanism. They are held in place by a spring loaded nut, simply turn each handle away from the other until both are in a horizontal position then pull out. Once pulling up on both these handles I am able to remove the piece of sheet metal which protects the shield generator.

"Alright Great Dane, what the hell did you do here?"

"Wow, seriously? You're still going to use that stupid nickname?" She complains.

"Hey I didn't name you, grandpa did apparently… which I guess means you named yourself. Why would you name yourself after a dog though?"

"Actually, Dane was your Grandfather's older brother who died in a horse riding accident, your grandfather was just five years old; some accounts say that your grandfather was responsible having spooked the horse, and apparently whether he was or wasn't, he never forgave himself," she states.

"Wow, so you're a clone of my grandfather, and named after his dead older brother? That explains so much…"

"So much what?" She demands.

"Well you know, your affinity for sports, women, heavy metal, and general tom boyish behavior."

"You said you never cared that I was gay," she says sounding offended.

"And I don't, there's nothing wrong with a woman loving another woman, or a man loving another man; it's never been my position to judge anyone, you know that. I'm just saying you being a clone and all that may have had a little influence along the way."

"It's possible I suppose, cloning is wrought with variables no one has been able to predict," she concedes.

"That's all I'm saying, and that when you took forever in the bathroom, it wasn't just to brush your hair."

"Hey!"

"Just out of curiosity do you think clones produce more methane than naturally born people?"

"That's really NOT funny!" She yells.

"Ah! Not so loud... Sheeeesh it was only a joke... You know, sorta."

"Well that makes you a jack ass sorta," she says.

"Fair enough. So scanning this panel and knowing the objective, what can we do?"

"It looks like not only can we easily modulate shield frequencies, but we can also improve the shield generated by this unit one hundred percent, and decrease its power use by nearly seventy two percent," she answers.

"Now that's what I like to hear, but how did Dane miss something like that?"

"This is definitely not my work, I would venture a guess that she simply didn't have the sophisticated scanning tools necessary to make the calculations needed for such an alignment. Plus from the way her letter described the accelerated aging, she probably wanted to leave as soon as possible to set things up for you. Well, after drawing and turning over the schematics of course," She replies.

"You do realize you're now referring to Dane and you in the first and third person right?"

"Wow, I suppose I am. This was actually expected however, the more of her memories I am able to integrate, coupled with your memories of her, the more I will become her. That was her original prerecorded message right?"

"Well yeah… but not all explained and fancied up like that it wasn't. Alright so good point then. First things first what do we need to modulate the frequencies?"

"Seeing as the shield itself is contained within a laser generated hologram, we will need to build an 'Electro-optic modulator' (EOM) in this case a 'Mach-Zehnder interferometer' which is a phase modulating EOM that can be used to modulate the amplitude as well. This will allow us to split the current beam into two paths, one for phase modulation which will then be recombined with the original signal," she replies.

"I said what do we need? Not spit out a bunch of technical garbage at me," I answer.

"Ah yes, sorry. We'll need to fabricate a box containing a 'half-silvered mirror' to separate the laser into two parts, two additional mirrors, one for the 'sample beam' and one for the 'reference beam', and then a second 'half-silvered mirror' to recombine the lasers into one contiguous beam. I am pulling up the schematics for your viewing now. If you would like to change the remote control for this unit I recommend we modify the current remote unit to use a different signal pattern with an encryption algorithm," she replies.

"Yeah… my thoughts exactly. Send all that to George's printer with a note attached to get his top guys on it right away, also include the process by which this gets attached and utilized on the shield units, and the remote control units to make this a secure affair."

"Done," Dane says.

"Very good, I'm closing this panel for now and we'll wait for George's guys to get done with the fabrication."

"Are you sure that's wise? These measurements and components need to be configured perfectly in order for this to work correctly," Dane replies.

"They need to be able to do it, and they need to be able to explain it to the other bases once it's done. Besides, I think it's time we interrogate our ex-*Vice President*."

"I understand, and what about the power use modifications?" She asks.

"Ah yeah, well what do we need for that then?" I ask.

"Toward the bottom of the holo-shield generation unit, on the right hand side you'll find a power distribution box with a single pole twenty amp fuse attached, that fuse is being taxed to capacity by this unit. So we want to replace this fuse with one that supports thirty amps and uses both available poles, forcing this unit to use the two hundred forty amp full circuit it was designed for instead of the single pole one hundred twenty amp half circuit. That will draw power evenly from the generators, and produce a lower strain on the system over all." Dane responds.

"So you're telling me this thing is using all that extra power because it's trying to yank it all through one small cable instead of an even distribution across two, forcing it to work harder and strain for power?"

"That's very close to the concept actually, yes. It's also going to increase the shield's output performance as well. Due to that lack of 'strain' you describe," she replies.

"Well one thing's for sure, they'll love that fix. It doesn't get any easier than switching out a fuse."

"Not too much, no." Dane confirms.

8 THE FINER POINTS OF MOLE HUNTING

Entering floor nineteen's detention area had all the feeling of a cold hard prison, nineteen floors underground of course. As I exit the elevator, there is a log book sitting on a podium in an alcove to my right, with a light above it and a drawer full of writing utensils. Examining the log book, both to see who's been signing in and out to speak with the ex-*Vice President* and to sign in myself, I find a name that takes me completely off guard.

"Do a handwriting analysis on that will you Dane?" I ask while signing in.

"I have it stored, but I currently have nothing like it on file Johnny, I will need a verified sample of their writing in order to make a comparison," she replies.

"Understood," I answer.

Proceeding down the corridor, I find a guard station in a larger alcove, as it was dug straight into the earth behind it. Next to the station is a locked solid steal door, with only a small barred window for general communication purposes.

It seems they keep one guard stationed outside and one inside to patrol the cells in case of emergency.

"Sir!" The on duty guard salutes.

"At ease, what's your name son?"

"*Specialist* Hayes sir!" He replies.

"Well *Specialist* Hayes, how many visitors has our executive prisoner had, any idea?"

"Not really sir no. The guestbook outside the elevator will be our most complete log," *Specialist* Hayes replies.

"So is there a camera over the guestbook? Any camera's in the halls, cells, etc…?"

"In the hallway just on the other side of this door there is one that faces down the entire cell corridor, and there is another on the other side facing back," *Specialist* Hayes states.

"None in the cells themselves or facing the cells?" I ask.

"No sir that would be a violation of prisoner privacy," the *Specialist* responds.

"Alright, thank you. May I?" I ask motioning to the door.

"Of course sir!" He salutes and pushes a button that sounds a buzzer and kicks the door open an inch.

I salute back, and enter the corridor, closing the door behind me.

"I'm going to need the footage from these cameras Dane," I say.

"Already working on it Johnny, I will begin processing them momentarily," she responds.

As I approach the ex-*Vice President*'s cell I feel a chill run down my spine. There she is, sitting on her cot, looking straight forward at me, as if to look through me. The blank stare on her face tells a story all its own.

"*Specialist* Hayes!" I yell.

Hearing the same buzz and door latch, *Specialist* Hayes from the outside station comes running up to me.

"Is there no one to patrol this hallway?" I demand.

"Yes sir, but he called out sick today, and we only have the one prisoner so I didn't think too much of it sir!" The *Specialist* answers.

"Look at her, notice anything... different?" I ask.

"Uh, well... she doesn't seem to be acknowledging us at all sir."

"When was the last time she ate or drank anything?"

"I fed her myself last night at nineteen-hundred sir!" The *Specialist* answers.

"And where was the other guard at that time?"

"The *Corporal* was at the outside station sir, we take turns patrolling the hall, and feeding the prisoner, and what not," He responds.

"And you collected an empty tray when she was done?"

"No sir, our shift change with the night guards is at twenty-hundred, so the night shift guards usually perform their rounds right away and collect trays and what not."

"So this full tray is from last night?"

"Oh, no sir! That's the one I brought for her this morning but she was still sleeping when I placed it there."

"Ok, so you were here until that transition yesterday then?"

"Uh, well almost sir, there was a disturbance call on fourteen, they ordered one of us be sent up to assist, and the *Corporal* ordered me to go. He said I could just knock off once the disturbance was contained, he'd hand over the duty to the night shift."

"Fourteen? So in the infirmary? What time was this 'disturbance'?"

"Right about nineteen-thirty sir, but that's the funny part. I got there and there wasn't anything going on, and I looked around a good fifteen minutes for anything that looked out of place or suspicious in any way. I spoke with Becka? Or Beckie? The on call nurse and she said that she hadn't reported anything."

"His story checks out Johnny, the telephone switchboard has a call logged to the Brig's phone at just prior to nineteen thirty." Dane interjects.

"Alright, so you deliver dinner, does she pick it up?" I ask

"Yes sir, she came right over thanked me and took her tray back over to where she's sitting now."

"Okay, and almost immediately after there's a call for an extra guard upstairs in the infirmary, which obviously the *Corporal* answers, because you were in here delivering dinner and patrolling the hallway. Have I got this right so far?" I ask

"Yes, sir," he answers.

"The *Corporal* then pages you on the intercom, and sends you to take care of the disturbance upstairs. Remaining here to hand over guard duty to the night crew at twenty-hundred, and today he's a no show for work?"

"That's correct sir!" He answers.

"Johnny your 'prisoner' is moving." Dane interrupts.

Looking over I see her lay down on her side and roll over to face the wall.

"My gut says a fairly advanced hologram, for this time-line anyway, what do your scans pickup?" I ask Dane.

The *Specialist* also sees her moving and looks at me, "Uh, sir? That's how she was laying when I dropped off the tray this morning."

Dane responds, "Definitely a hologram, and you're right for the technologies we've seen thus far this is an advanced one, maintaining the façade of a mountain face versus a moving breathing person is quite different indeed."

"It's a hologram *Specialist* like your mountain only more complicated, I know it's a bit more advanced than you're used to, but someone has released the ex-*Vice President* and left a pretty fancy piece of hardware in her place in order to give her a head start. I would bet your *Corporal* is now AWOL and in on this whole thing as well," I say.

"Let's not jump to any conclusions Johnny, anyone with the know how to produce this level of hologram may be able to pull off other similar feats we're yet unaware of in this time-line as well," Dane says.

"Point taken," I respond to Dane.

"But sir! I mean I guess he was acting differently, but I can't imagine the *Corporal* doing something like this. I mean he's been talking about trying to make *Sergeant* ever since his promotion to *Corporal*."

"Let me guess *Corporal* Young?"

"Well, yes sir," he answers looking confused.

"And what do you mean he was acting differently today? I saw him on the elevator up to the top for guard duty." I reply.

"Sir? No sir, this is his post, he hasn't been on the roster to go topside since the V.P's arrest," Hayes explains.

"Wait you're sure about this?" I question.

"Yes sir, without a doubt. Okay look, first he called me and said he was 'sick to his stomach', and the 'infirmary told him to stay in the rack, eat some crackers and get some rest today'. Then he showed up like twenty minutes later, and when he rolled in, he just smiled and said 'those were some damn good crackers'."

"And what time did he actually show up here, do you know?" I ask.

"It was pretty close to eleven-hundred, sir."

"What time did we see him on the elevator?" I ask Dane.

"We boarded the elevator at twelve-hundred-two hours precisely," Dane responds.

"So it was an hour and two minutes before we saw him then on the elevator," I reply to Dane.

"Yes Johnny."

"Okay, so once he was here how long before you went to lunch?" I ask the *Specialist*.

"Immediately sir, we work twelve's, so I always take the early lunch, and he takes the early dinner. So he dismissed me for lunch as soon as he got in," Hayes replies.

"So then you come back at twelve-hundred?"

"That's correct sir! Maybe five minutes early?" The *Specialist* replies.

"Alright, I'm going to look into it *Specialist*, and let *General* Patton know that we have an escape on our hands."

"We may also want to check on the EOM fabrication as well, that shield needs to be ready if Young, or someone posing as Young was able to get her out of here," Dane says.

"Agreed. If their operative is free there's nothing stopping them from unloading an arsenal right in on top of us," I respond to Dane.

I suddenly have a flash of the time lab just before I jumped in the portal, the cement walls with spider web cracks like stress fractures caused by a massive bombardment from above.

"For now just return to your post, I'm sure someone will call down with further instructions for you shortly," I inform *Specialist* Hayes.

"Yes, sir, but I have to follow protocol sir. I have to report this up the chain of command." He replies.

"Yes, I suppose you do. Go ahead, I'm sure George would rather hear it from me, but I don't want you to risk your position *Specialist*," I tell him.

Heading back toward the elevator it occurs to me that this all seems to be too well orchestrated to have been pulled off by a *Corporal* gunning for *Sergeant*, which likely means that he's had some extra training, or that things aren't what they seem.

As the elevator reaches the tenth floor I know George is going to be going out of his mind with this one. The Ex-*Vice President,* our only prisoner and possible source of intel on other moles, is missing and *Corporal* Young implicated in it.

Entering George's outer office I can hear him barking at the *Corporal* already.

"Guess he already knows... wonder why *Corporal* Young came to George's office," I say to myself.

"What the hell do you mean you didn't go up top and relieve *PFC* Anderson? It's got your name all over that report! Then according to this, you abandoned the post you weren't even supposed to be at!" He yells.

"Sir, I don't know what's going on sir. I woke up this morning and was extremely ill sir, so I called the infirmary they told me to rest, lay in bed and eat crackers sir! Then I called *Specialist* Hayes and let him know I wouldn't be in today sir. Why would I do that sir? Call in sick, only to go topside and pull duty for someone else and then on top of that leave it sir?" Young responds.

You could almost hear the cogs turning in George's head.

"Well that makes a certain amount of sense, don't you think?" I ask Dane.

"It does yes, and it also explains why the other guard looked so confused when he showed up topside. It also sounds as if the *General* is unaware of the breakout as of yet, and this is purely a disciplinary meeting about guard duty," she responds.

"Yeah I was just considering that as well. So we're thinking that they've either cloned our *Corporal*, or worse...?" I say.

"It would seem logical to assume that this Corporal's story checks out, although I should be able to interface with the base's telephone switching server and see if the calls were placed as this *Corporal* describes," Dane replies.

"See what you can find out," I reply heading into George's office.

As I open the door, the *General* looks up from where his head is resting in his hands to acknowledge my entry, and wave me in. The *Corporal* is sitting across from him looking white as a ghost, and the phone starts to ring.

"Well I guess we know what this call is..." I say to Dane.

The *General* looks at me, and then at the phone. "Do I want to answer that John?"

"Probably not sir, it's just bad news," I reply.

He lets out a deep sigh, and picks up the phone, "Yes?"

"He did what!?!?" He yells.

"Scan the *Corporal* for any anomalies, and compare it to our original scan of him at our first meeting in the post office basement," I instruct Dane.

"No never mind I've got him right here. No, I'll be fine, I've got *General* Steal here as well, and the *Corporal* looks white as a sheet. Just put the base on lockdown immediately, sound general quarters, and I want a full sweep done room by room. Use all our senior MP's only. Do it NOW!" He yells slamming down the phone.

"This is the actual *Corporal* Young, Johnny, and he has been poisoned, really he should be in the infirmary with an IV to help flush his system. Also the base switchboard server confirms his calls were placed as previously stated, but it appears that the call to the infirmary was rerouted somehow," Dane replies.

"Rerouted?" I ask.

"Yes, the switchboard reports it sent the call to the infirmary, but lists the answering extension as unknown," Dane replies.

"So someone intercepted the call covering their tracks, and further implicating the real *Corporal* Young. That's also how he knew to say that the crackers worked so well, because he was the one that answered the phone, and told the real *Corporal* to eat them," I respond to Dane.

"That is plausible Johnny."

"That means this 'someone else' was using technology these people haven't seen yet. So they could even be using a holographic system much like the one the Viper uses for me," I reply

"After analyzing the simplicity of the unit placed in the detention cell it is likely that is not the case. I believe your first instinct of a clone is probably more likely based on available data," Dane replies.

"*Corporal*, you had better be on the level with me right now, or so help me God. I will toss you down the deepest darkest hole I can find," he yells across the desk.

"Sir, if I may," I say.

"Go ahead John, you're the only damn person I can fully trust around here anyway," George replies.

"Well George, I've been doing some digging already, in fact I pointed out to *Specialist* Hayes that the real ex-*Vice President* was missing, at which time he was totally unaware. The calls the *Corporal* described to you did happen as he stated."

Interrupting me the General states, "Now hold on John, I've talked to the infirmary and they told me point blank they never received a call from *Corporal* Young this morning."

"I understand that sir. The call was actually intercepted, and because *Corporal* Young was there when I first started using the suit, and he knows a lot of what it can do, I don't have a problem saying this in front of him. I've had your switchboard server logs checked, and yes the *Corporal* did in fact place the calls he claims to have placed. The call to the infirmary however was re-routed and intercepted by someone else; someone that told him to eat crackers get some rest and he'd feel better.

"That's why this person was able to fool *Specialist* Hayes. When he showed up for duty on the prison floor disguised as the *Corporal* at eleven-hundred hours the first words out of his mouth were that the 'crackers worked', and dismissed *Specialist* Hayes for lunch. I'm paraphrasing of course, but you see where this is leading, and yes, *Specialist* Hayes is the source of this information by the way sir. He can confirm the call from the *Corporal* here in which the *Corporal* relayed his message from the 'infirmary' to eat crackers and relax," I pause a moment.

"Okay, so you're telling me that we're dealing with a technology that can intercept calls, and someone who looks just like *Corporal* Young?" He replies.

"I wish that were the half of it George. When I went to interrogate the prisoner after sending you the modulator specs, I found a hologram in her place. This is another technology that I don't believe was known to exist at least not in your time-line and certainly not by this time in my time-line, and the projector is definitely more advanced than the one you use for the mountain entrance." I state.

"So then how did they get her past security? I mean if the *Corporal* here is sick, and I'll admit he does look it. Someone topside relieved Anderson that looked just like him," He replies.

"The best theory at the moment is a clone sir. I realize this is another technology you've yet to see, but in my time-line it is recorded that the group that started all this mastered it, to the point of being able to transfer someone's consciousness nearly fifty years before the rest of the world figured out just the cloning bit.

Also sir if I may, I've analyzed the Corporal here, and he's not sick, he's been poisoned, he really should be in the infirmary with an IV running to help flush his system. In the condition he's in he didn't help anyone do anything today, and frankly I'm surprised you didn't have to wheel him in on a chair for this meeting sir."

George grabs the phone, and punches in the infirmary extension. "Who is this?" He demands.

"Okay Nurse I know who you are. Listen I have a poisoned *Corporal* in my office I need you to send a gurney, and get him looked after immediately," e states.

Turning back to *Corporal* Young, "I'm sorry I doubted you son, they're on the way right now, and we're going to get you the best care possible."

I interject at this point, "George you know as well as I, if they got their operatives out, it's only a matter of time before they start knocking on our front door with very big knockers, for lack of a better word. Can I ask the status on the modulator specs I sent down?"

"My understanding is that the design was so simplistic they felt like morons for not seeing it sooner. They finished it just before my meeting with the *Corporal* here, and are preparing to install it now," He replies.

"*General* please have them stand down. I'd like to do the install myself; I want to inspect the work. If it's done incorrectly it won't work, no harm no foul, unless the bombs are already in the air, but if they managed to infiltrate your science team or that other Corporal Young got to it, we could be looking at sabotage. Someone who knew what they were looking at could potentially create a feedback loop and blow the whole unit, and leave you completely defenseless," I state.

"Go!" he orders, as he grabs the phone to halt the instillation.

Running toward the elevator I see the gurney headed down the hall for *Corporal* Young with two orderlies. Taking up the entire hall way. I have no choice at this point, I have to jump I can't risk that shield generator being blown.

I have Dane use the built in projection system to show me walking into the men's room while simultaneously cloaking me. Leaping forward I put myself into a dive over the gurney and then tuck and roll on the other side.

Both orderlies hear the thud on the other side (apparently I'm out of practice). I catch them in the suits rear view turning around to see what the noise was, before they both kind of shrug and continue towards the *General's* office, being invisible has its perks.

Making it into the elevator before it closes, I quickly hit zero, and start tapping the close door button. Eventually the elevator starts to move up and I have Dane uncloak me.

Reaching topside I find the science team on the phone, obviously with George, while one is still trying to attach the modulator. I run at him and just before he has a chance to flip the breaker on, I pin him to the wall.

"Something wrong with waiting an extra two minutes to have your work checked herr Doctor?" I yell.

"How, how dare you! Unhand me immediately." He demands.

"Oh, I don't think so Doc. Not until you explain to me why it is when the commander of this base calls you up on the phone to wait a few damn minutes, you can't be bothered to do so," I explain.

"I am a very busy man, and the *General* is just being overly cautious," He replies while trying to push my arm away.

"I am the busiest man on this base, and when that *General* says 'jump' I jump. Perhaps some time in the brig will remind you of that," I say.

"Dane, you got some MP's on the way for this joker yet?" I ask.

"They are exiting the elevator now," Dane responds.

"Good timing," I reply.

"I thought you'd like that," Dane says.

Handing over the scientist to the MP's I notice a tattoo on the arm of the scientist. It's an 'S.S. Blood Group tattoo', "This is definitely a mole guys I want him treated as such. That tattoo is his blood type, so when you're done with him, if he needs a transfusion, well there it is, no testing necessary."

"Yes, Sir!" They both salute and echo.

I turn to the other scientists, "Anybody else have any tattoos I should know about?" I ask.

"No, No sir." They respond almost in unison.

One of the other scientists speaks up, "We were actually trying to stop him, that's why we called the *General* back to let him know that he wasn't stopping," He says.

"The one on the right has a girl's name tattooed on his right arm," Dane chimes in.

"Thanks, but I don't think that's incriminating," I respond.

"Alright boys, let's see what you've done here," I say removing the modulator module.

"Screw driver?" I ask.

One of them hands me a number two Philips head screw driver, and four screws later, I'm definitely looking at the circuitry that would have fried the holo-shield generator completely.

"Alright Dane, what do I do to make this thing work right?" I ask.

"Remove the three extra mirrors, I have highlighted on your HUD they would have redirected the laser disbursement back into the generator," she says.

I pull the three mirrors Dane has indicated, and put the unit back together. Examining the shield generator I see that they haven't changed out the fuse.

While setting the modulator aside I demand that one of them fetch me a thirty amp, two pole fuse. One goes to their tool chest they brought up and pulls a new one from the box.

"Dane, check and make sure we have nothing incoming before I switch this out."

"You're clear Johnny," she replies.

I flip the switch next to the old fuse off, shutting down the entire holo-shield. Then install the modulator and the new thirty amp fuse. Flipping the switch back to the on position, I watch as the improved laser holo-shield generator fires up, beaming the outside of the mountain to the rest of the world, and a beautiful self-modulating shield just inside it.

"Nice," I say. "Now you two, Bonnie and Clyde, get these specs to your friends around the other bases, also let them know that *NO* changes to this design will be tolerated, and will result in a full court-martial."

"Dane, call down to the *General* and let him know we do have some good news for him today. Also make sure that he knows about our new prisoner, and that the other commanders should require inspections on these units as they are completed. Hell it probably wouldn't hurt for you to print off schematics of a new upgraded model shield generator for them, and have them start working on those too, just in case," I say.

"Will do, Johnny…" Dane replies.

"One last thing…" I say, running toward the mountains giant exit.

"Johnny?" Dane sounds concerned.

"Let him know I'm going after the *Vice President*, and then show me satellite telemetry for a five mile radius along with any energy signatures in the last hour." I demand, passing through the holo-shield. Once on the other side I go invisible with a thought.

"Your information will begin displaying… now," she says, as a floating map overlay appears from left to right in the upper portion of my HUD.

At the bottom of each map is a time signature from the satellite itself. Which appear to only take snap shots every thirty minutes?

"Two, that's what you have for me to look at? TWO?!?" I demand.

"I can configure the satellite that maintains this orbit to take pictures more often if you like, but that may alert the enemy and only provide further proof of where area fifty one is," Dane responds.

"Wait… what's that little blip at the top of the first shot? Enhance and magnify," I say.

"That appears to be a jeep, Johnny."

"Alright, were there any pickups or anything that would send out a jeep from the base at that time?" I ask.

"No Johnny, that is either the escape or someone that was traveling in the area, and then turned around," she replies.

"Okay, which way is that heading, looks like West toward New Frankfurt?" I ask for confirmation.

"That is correct. That heading would take them straight into New Frankfurt." Dane replies.

I start to jog toward the jeep's last position, picking up speed with every stride. My HUD readout shows my speed as it increases thirty two, forty eight, fifty six, and then I get angry sixty seven, seventy nine.

"Johnny!" Dane sounds alarmed.

"WHAT?!?" I demand.

"The Viper was never tested at these speeds, I'm not sure what could happen if you keep pushing this," Dane explains.

"This suit is supposed to be near indestructible right?" I say now breathing much harder.

"Yes, but that is not my concern! The muscle contraction aid could destroy your heart at these levels!" Dane says.

"Yeah... or it could be... you just worrying... like an... old lady... again..." I respond. "Trust me... I know my body... if it starts to hurt I'll slow down... you just keep me on a trajectory... that doesn't include... hitting a tree."

New Frankfurt is now just over the horizon, and I begin to slow down, seventy, sixty five, fifty one, forty four.

"Alright I'm almost there can you estimate the speed of that jeep and see how far into the city they may have gotten?" I ask.

"Yeah, glad you slowed down... no sense denting a tank," Dane replies with her snarky condescending older sisterly tone.

"Wow, she really did do a brain dump on you, didn't she? Just answer the damn question AI," I demand.

"Estimating max speed they could be anywhere in New Frankfurt," Dane replies, still sounding irritated.

"AH, Damnit!" I yell, stopping just at the edge of town, still completely cloaked.

"Okay wait, let's think about this. Does New Frankfurt have its own satellite?" I ask.

"It actually has two, according to the logs I've examined, this is due to a strong resistance presence in the Northern portion," Dane responds.

"Ooh, this is good, and how often do they take photos?" I demand.

"It is staggered to every five minutes for the southern half, the Northern half actually has a live feed running." Dane responds.

"Okay, come on North side of town! Based on your max speed estimates, what was the fastest they could have made the Northern portion of New Frankfurt?" I ask.

"Seven and a half minutes ago, but why would they hide where they are likely to run into the resistance?" He asks.

"Because right now only military personnel know that she's a traitor and that Corporal Young is a clone, dumbass. They'll hide her from the Nazi's in their best spot, probably their base. So she'll hide out there till the Nazi's send in their next sweep, and then expose the resistance cell at the same time returning to her side with the intel we really don't want them to have." I say.

"Well... that actually makes sense," Dane says, a little less snarky.

"Of course it does, I didn't spend all that time in the Rangers picking my nose. Now show me the footage from nine minutes ago, and run it forward until you spot our Vice President being escorted off the street." I say.

"There, five miles north of the center of town, they escort her into a white building behind a local street vendor cart," Dane shows me the snap shots.

"Got it, let's get there fast before she blows this cell's entire operation." I say.

Now that my body has had a few minutes to catch up, my pulse has returned to normal, and so far I don't see any negative reactions to my rage run.

I begin to jog up Main Street at a mere forty miles an hour, reaching the center of town within only a few minutes. Turning north on Center Street, I pick up the pace to fifty miles per hour.

Five minutes later I'm looking at a street vendor, selling watermelons of all things. Being cloaked I easily slip behind the cart and study the wall for a secret latch.

"You got anything for me here Dane? Infrared scan, something to figure out how to open this thing?" I ask.

"Scanning… wow very intricate, there is a loose board that looks like an accent to your right. Two feet over your head is a nail that sticks out a centimeter. Pull that nail approximately five centimeters out, and it will release the door latch from the inside, thus opening the door," she replies.

"Alright, so I do that, when the street vendor notices hopefully he'll come over and check it out, opening the door wide enough for me to slip in and then reclosing it for me," I say.

"That could work…" Dane replies.

Pulling on the nail I hear a small pop on the other side of the wall, and the wall to the left of it slides open a little. Just loud enough to catch the street vendor's attention, startled he scans the street for surveillance and then looks over his shoulder to see who is coming out. After around two minutes he slowly backs up to the wall and quickly has a peak inside.

"No, one? Must not have latched well when they brought her in," he says, with that he opens the door almost a meter at which point I jump in, and he slams the door shut behind me.

"See, told you that would work," I say walking down the dimly lit staircase into a well-fortified bunker.

Entering the first chamber at the bottom of the stairs you can tell this is just the normal 'hideout' in case of emergency, and currently it is totally empty.

"Scan the room, there's another hidden door here for the actual base," I say to Dane.

"Scanning…" She reports.

To the right side in the rear view of my HUD I see a door outlined in red. Turning I begin to approach it looking for another latch or key hole.

"Thoughts?" I ask.

"Using infrared scans I can see wires running to this door from the inside. So it would appear that this door is triggered via internal switch. There is also a hidden camera imbedded in the wood directly above you," Dane reports.

"Oye… alright then," I say backing up a few feet.

With a thought I uncloak myself wearing the traditional *General's* uniform very much like George's field uniform. Stars on full display, and my United States patch in position. I walk back under the camera and beat on the door while looking up.

"Open up! Hell, I'm sure you've heard of me, I'm the one that took out the railroad station not far from here?" I say.

There's no response, the doors don't move, not even an acknowledgement.

"Nothing, you sure we're in the right place?" I ask Dane.

"This is definitely the place Johnny. Scanners have picked up a roomful of equipment, soldiers, and a clone approximately ten meters below us to your right." He answers.

"So what then, twenty meters or so under the intersection?" I ask.

"That is a close approximation yes."

"Good strategy." I have to admit.

"Listen guys, I'm sure the ex-*Vice President* and *Corporal* Young are telling you it's a bad idea to let me in, but I can assure you, that is not the case. Those two believe it or not are fugitives, from you actually. They are traitors, hell *Corporal* Young there isn't even human, he's a clone of a really good guy, they poisoned the real *Corporal,*" I state looking into the camera.

Still nothing.

"Alright well don't say I didn't warn you. My only option at this point is to short out your door, and take the prisoners into custody. I don't want to do that, I'm sure you'll have to replace all your wiring and the terminal on the other end as well, but it is a better solution than letting those two morons expose you the next time the Nazi's sweep this zone. So I apologize for this but, well, you know…" I say, drawing my BARB I adjust the setting to a broad band electric shock that would short out anything in its path.

Just as I aim it at the door a voice comes over their intercom.

"Hold fire! Hold fire! Please! We're opening the door now!"

With that the door begins to slide inward and then parts in the middle. The next stairwell leads down and to the right, and is solid steal the whole way down.

As I walk down the stairs Dane already starts to nag, "Be careful Johnny, this could be a trap."

"Would you relax already, so what if they believe her and it is actually a trap? I'm wearing you aren't I?" I reply. "Uh... suddenly I feel icky."

"Hey, you said it!" Dane replies.

Rounding the corner you can see a very large data center. Servers in the back, workstations set up with monitoring software and what looks to be cameras all over the country likely provided by different revolutionary cells.

"Hack it all... and figure out how the hell they're all linked," I say to Dane.

The *ex-Vice President* and Cloned *Colonel* Young are tied to chairs facing away from each other in the middle of the room.

"Impressive setup, people," I say to the room. "Who's in charge here?"

"That would be me!" I hear from a tall balding man in the corner. He looks to be in his mid to late forties and physically fit, although maybe a little too much of the Nazi ale in the stomach. He speaks with a thick Russian accent, and definitely looks to be a descendent of that region.

"Johnny, it looks like they are using an encrypted radio signal system that bounces off of several Nazi towers, also I have copied their entire network of which is all stolen modified Nazi hardware, just like the Military uses," Dane states.

"Excellent! Wonderful to meet you sir, I'm John and you are?" I ask.

"My name is Al," he says.

"Well look Al, I'm not here to step on any toes, I only want to help. I've been at a military base helping out for a few months now, and I'm sure you've heard of some of my help," I say confidently.

"Oh we know who you are John, but if you're looking for a pat on the back you're in the wrong place."

"No. No. No thanks necessary, making your lives easier is just doing my part," I say with a bit of sarcasm.

"Well that's good," He says. "We're not in the habit of rewarding people for doing the right thing around here."

"Heh… Understood sir." I say. "Well look really I'm here for these two schmucks, they escaped custody about two hours ago, well she did, this other jackass aided and abetted, and I would really like to return them to their nice comfy cells we have waiting for them."

"I see… and what do we get for our efforts in this capture?" he asks.

"So you don't reward for doing the right thing around here, but you expect it Al?" I ask.

"No, I wouldn't say that. I was thinking a little more we scratch your back you scratch ours," He replies.

"I see…" I pause a moment stroking my chin. "How about this Al, you let us walk out of here and I can promise you my next mission will be to;" I pause again to look over his broad shoulder at the two prisoners and then lean in to whisper, "take out the train station hub in New Mexico. My understanding is that will keep the Nazi's busy and out your hair," I say looking up at his bald head. "Uh so to speak, and out of this half of the country even, for quite some time. Give you a chance to bring all of New Frankfurt into the resistance, maybe even rename it. What do you think, Al?" I ask.

"Now that sounds like something I could live with." He replies.

"I had a feeling you'd like that. Now for the hard part, I see you have sewer access to get around the city undetected. Which one do I need to take these two down to get out on the east side without running into any opposition?" I ask.

He claps, and a taller lady runs over. "Lisa dear, show this nice gentlemen and his prisoners to the east bound city exit." He says.

"You got it my love," she responds.

"She'll take you as far as the last turn out to the eastern exit. After that you're on your own back to area fifty one."

I give him a wink, "Thank you sir, you are a true friend." I say.

I see a pen and paper on a nearby desk I write down a quick note handing it to him.

"This is my private encrypted communications radio signal." I say. "I've kept the same one since I was a kid, so if you ever need me for anything at all, please use that code. If I'm still in your time zone I'll be sure to connect with you," I say.

"What was that about?" Dane asks.

"I don't know, he reminded me of someone I used to know."

"Who?" She implores.

"Just a really good friend, so make sure you monitor that line of communication," I say.

"Interesting…" Dane says.

I shake Al's hand, walk up to the backs of the two chairs that the ex-*Vice President* and the clone are tied to, and rip the ropes off.

"Stay in front of me, and keep your mouths shut, you both know damn well I have no problem knocking you out and throwing you each over a shoulder."

We follow Lisa toward one of the underground base exits.

"Alright prepare yourselves. It gets pretty rank down here," she continues while slipping on her gas mask, and offering one to me.

"It's okay I've dealt with worse I'm sure."

Opening the door a fan system kicks on to keep the smell in the sewer system. She motions us through, I shove the *Corporal* into the ex-*Vice President* and we start down another set of stairs.

"Glad I don't have to smell this," I mention to Dane.

"Yeah, from the looks on those two's faces you won't have to worry about them calling for help," she responds.

We continue through the twisting system for what seems like forever, finally reaching the last turn. Lisa taps me on the shoulder and waves, pointing me down the corridor. There is definitely light at the end. I thank her and give the *Corporal* a good shove again into the ex-*Vice President* who finally stumbles and falls into the raw sewage.

"Ew… you're going to need some kind of shot after that. Now get up and move!" I say.

Exiting the sewer system, Al was true to his word not only were we on the east side of the city, but he had a jeep waiting there for me, keys in the ignition, water buckets to clean our shoes (I would imagine), and two pairs of shackles.

The prisoners both take a minute to catch their breath, and I grab a bucket of water and dump it over each of them. Before shackling them in the backseat of the jeep.

After fastening in my passengers, we head off down the road.

"Hey Dane, what are the chances you can cloak this whole jeep?" I ask.

"You know I can't do that," she responds.

"Yeah, yeah I know, wishful thinking. Well then how about using your satellite uplink and making sure that no pictures are snapped of us returning to base." I say.

"Already taken care of Johnny, that particular satellite has suddenly entered maintenance mode, and will be unreachable until it is finished in six hours," she responds.

"Now that is convenient." I remark.

"It is, yes," she replies.

"One last thing, radio the base and let them know we're coming in with a pair of stinky prisoners they've been looking for."

"Will do Johnny."

9 TRAITORS AND CLONES AND UFOS? OH MY?!

The following morning I wake to Dane screaming in my head.

"JOHNNY WE GOT THEM!" She yells.

"Okay first of all that was in my head, you don't have to yell, and second of all, got who?" I ask

"The base, I have an approximate location," she says.

"UFO's?" I ask.

"Yes, they finally sent out two, I'm not sure to where yet, but they were captured on a satellite over Peru leaving. Based on the timing, speed, and trajectory of the images and the craft it can only be one of five specific mountains," Dane replies.

"That's Great! Five mountains versus a whole damn range is a much easier hunt," I admit. "I guess that means it's time to get this show on the road."

After lunch I find myself sitting in George's office going over the details of the previous day.

"Son, I've said it before and I'll say it again, you are the best thing that has happened to this country since all this nonsense started."

"Well *General* I appreciate that, and based on that fact I think it's time we take the fight to them."

"The mission to South America?" He asks.

"Yes sir, I've finally been able to narrow down the search to five specific mountains, but I thought I'd even sweeten the pot a little bit for you." I say.

"Now this I gotta hear." He says.

"Well George, it just so happens that the fastest way to get down to Peru is a bullet train, and as it turns out we know of another major train hub they use. Which has just such a train route running out of it. This is the one that would take me and a small team down to the Andes' Mountains and into Peru, it also supplies a great deal of their operations in the northern part of this country and up into parts of Canada, as well as runs over and links up to the one we just blew to hell. I figured you'd appreciate it if I blew that one up too. You know since it's on the way and all." I suggest.

"Well, that would be a gift now wouldn't it?" He says.

"Sir, I'm a giver, I've always believed it was better to give than receive, my Grandmother taught me that."

George chuckles, and says, "It would help the war effort that's for sure."

"Well you see I kind of figured if we pull this one off, that would leave almost half the country out of the Nazi bullet train loop, and the amount of tech you've already scavenged, plus the amount of troops and other gear they'd leave stranded, that could be easily over powered and repurposed. You could mount yourself a proper war, once their main base of operations is destroyed, which would coincidentally be removing their most dangerous air support," I continue.

George grinning again says, "Son that is the best plan I've heard to date." Pausing a moment and looking more serious he asks, "Son, who can I send along to watch your back?"

"Well sir first I'd like to promote *First Lt.* Bradley to *Major*, I've used him on several operations now, and frankly looking at his personnel file he should have made *Captain* a year ago. He's smart as a whip, and a hell of a good soldier, and I truly believe he can handle the bump. Second I'd like to take him as my second in command. I've already had him roughing out a list for me of a cohesive unit the last few days, and I'm sure he's got something fairly comprehensive by now."

"Son, I trust your judgment, so done and done. You take whomever you like, but I would like a little help figuring out what to do about this other base we currently have up our collective asses before you leave, if you wouldn't mind that is." He replies.

"Actually sir I had a thought about that, while running around yesterday. I'm sure they've fully loaded the thing by now, since they're expecting our assault and have no idea that we know that they know, what we know… shit now I'm confused." I say.

George chuckles. "I think I'm following, go ahead son."

"Anyway you know they're planning for our attack, and they are likely plotting a way to get in here from their end at the same time." I say.

"Yeah, that's what worries me." He says

"Well look at it this way, your engineers have been down there digging for a month and have just now gotten under their base. They've had a day and a half maybe?" I ask.

"Okay, so what are you thinking?" George asks.

"It seems to me this base is more than you need really. So I propose we give up on taking theirs. Especially with it fully staffed. Hell they probably have the majority of their troops on this side of the Rockies in that thing at this point." I say.

"You make a good point, so how do you recommend we rectify this situation then." He asks.

"Well George, what kind of explosives do you have lying around?" I ask.

"Well there's the rest of the C-4 you brought in with the convoy, but that's not a whole lot at this point. We do have a pretty decent stockpile of TNT."

I laugh, "That's perfect, have your engineers start their dig upward, go fifteen meters as fast as possible. Then we package up a shaped charge of TNT to blow straight up at them. Set it on a remote detonator and then have the engineers put up five meters of concrete at the entry to that tunnel."

"So we blow it, and because of the massive amount of earth we've displaced, the whole base will just collapse down killing everyone inside, before they ever know what hit them."

"Then the lovely part is, you can drive around to the front of their base with a platoon, pick off whoever is left and doesn't want to surrender, and then scavenge till your heart's content. You'll make out like bandits."

"Sounds like a solid win all the way around. Thank you *General*!" He says with a grin on his face as he's picking up the phone.

"No, no, thank you *General*." I say with a smile. "Talk to you later George I'm going to go promote me a Major."

"Sounds good!" He says, as he tosses a little box at me on my way out the door.

Walking down the hall I open the box to find a pair of *Major*'s oak leaves contained inside. I open the door to the hallway of Officer's quarters and walk until I see *Lt.* Bradley's. Lucky for me, they all have plaques just outside the door with the Officer's name and rank on them, so it's easy enough to find.

Knocking on the door I hear the *Lt.* yell, "Come in!"

Entering the room he's lying in the bed with his foot elevated by a couple of pillows.

"Hey Bradley, how's that ankle treating you?" I ask.

"Not bad, hey I've got that list ready for you! It's on the desk by the door there." He points it out for me.

"Great, let me take a look here, Shaw, Jackson, Jenkins, Judge, Anderson, Carter, wow there's like twenty names here, all look good on paper. You make the final cut though. I've decided I want five plus you and I, *Major*." I say tossing the little box at him.

"Whoa, what?! John are you serious?" *Major* Bradley asks.

"Serious as a heart attack kid, I told George I'm promoting you, and that you should have been made *Captain* a year ago. He said if I think you deserve it, then he's sure you deserve it too. So, congratulations *Major* Bradley. Oh you're going to want to have them change that on your plaque outside the door here too. I'd hate for people to roll up in here calling you *First Lt.* when clearly you're above that now," I say with a smile.

He laughs, "Thank you John, this is amazing."

"That's right, you just remember who takes care of you, and pick me the five best people off that list. You're my second, so I expect you to act like one now," I say

"You got it sir!" He says.

"Oh enough with the 'sir' shit, really?!" I groan.

He smiles, "You got it John."

"Alright then, take a bit to relax and revel in the promotion and all, then meet me for dinner. Let's say eighteen-thirty, and have your five meet us there too. You can pull them from whatever duty they're on. Just make sure they have replacements in place before heading out, also we're doing dinner in conference hall seven."

"Will do! See you then John."

Heading back down to my room I realize it's only thirteen-hundred.

"Alright well what's next on the agenda Dane?" I ask.

"Uh, well I hate to say it, but I think I just found where your UFO's are headed," she says.

"That doesn't sound good. Where are they now?" I ask.

"Currently they are on a heading that will put them directly overhead in a matter of minutes." He says.

"Are you kidding me? I've been trying to get this mission rolling for damn near a month now, and they're sending their damn UFO's here now!?" I ask

"That would seem to be the case, yes Johnny."

I run down the hall and ping the elevator. Waiting for it takes forever.

"Where the hell is it?" I demand as the doors finally open.

Punching zero I realize at this rate the UFO's are going to be all over us before I can even get up top. Suddenly it happens, the entire elevator and even the base itself shakes.

"DANE?!? What's that satellite telling you?" I demand.

"I have switched the camera to live feed they are in fact firing on us, however their beam technology does not seem to hold a candle to the shield we have put in place.

They would actually have a better chance at blowing the mountain apart behind us than the shield," she says.

"Great how long till they figure that out?!" I ask.

"Currently they are trying a concentrated burst on the shield to see if they can punch through?" She answers.

The doors finally slide open, and I can see what is going on from right underneath the shield.

"What do we need to do to that generator to cover the mountain?" I ask.

"It's not possible, they need a second," Dane insists.

"God damn it, there has to be something!" I demand.

"Wait, they're stopping," she says.

"Yeah well that could mean they're going to shoot at the other side. Now think damn it!" I say

"Oh, got it. They're just hanging there probably figuring out their next attack, we can turn the shield modulation array into a concentrator." Dane says.

"I must have missed that day at geek academy, what will that do?" I ask.

"In short we run a line off of the shield to a dish which would allow you to focus the shields power for a few blasts, we could shoot them down." Dane answers.

"But our shields would be down to do this? Doesn't that mean they'll land on us?! That's not a good plan Dane!" I say.

"If we have one of the men standing by the generator to switch it back as soon as you fire there's a chance that the shield will reinitialize by the time the ships fall, or they fire again, whichever occurs first." Dane says.

"I really, REALLY don't like this plan Dane." I say.

"That's all I got Johnny. It's the only option," she replies.

"You're telling me my BARB can't do anything to help here?" I ask.

"Well, based on their hull plating... No, it would be an extreme long shot."

"You do understand I'm a marksman with anything right?"

"Understood, just can't channel enough energy through the BARB at these power levels to do what we need to do," she confirms.

"Holy crap... I can't believe we're going to do this." I answer.

By now there are more and more people getting off the elevator to see what's going on.

"You!" I say yelling at the guard station. "Bring me a ten meter length of the longest thickest insulated copper wire you have."

"Yes sir!" the guard yells as he runs for a maintenance cupboard in the back of the huge room.

"Okay Dane, where do I get this 'dish'?" I ask.

"Well here's the fun part you are the 'dish', with all that voltage hitting you directly in this suit you should be able to put your hands together and focus the beam like a bolt of lightning. I am currently rewriting all the safety protocols to allow this to work." Dane says.

"Oh that's reassuring... Wait safety protocols? You mean I could die doing this?" I ask.

"There is a remote possibility," she says.

"How remote? Five percent? Ten?" I ask.

"Sixtyish give or take?" She answers.

"SIXTYISH?!?! Give or take what forty?!" I demand

"Uh, well close to that," she answers.

By this time the guard is running up with an enormous length of copper line.

"Alright have him plug that into the external port on the shield generator, and wait to flip the switch by it."

"Oh for cry'n out loud," I say running to the shield generator.

Ripping open the panel I show the guard the external port and the switch accompanying it. I plug in his end of the cable, and give him explicit instructions to not flip the switch until I say, and keep it on until I get two shots off. Then shut it down immediately.

Running back to my position on the opposite side of the massive room, my hair is already standing on end.

"This better work or I'm going to kill you Dane." I say

"If this doesn't work we'll both be fried technically," she answers.

"Well good then, at least you'll get what's coming to you. So what do I need to do here?" I ask.

"Take the cable, hold it in your hands like you're clapping and point it at the first UFO, once that shot fires point it at the second. Then tell the guard to flip the switch back off," she says.

"Hey, what are the chances any feedback could be redirected to the 'Relativistic Prototype' instead of trying to disperse it across the suit?" I ask.

"Huh… that may actually work. And our chances of survival go up incredibly," she replies.

"I thought you were supposed to be the brains of this outfit?" I ask.

"Oh, very funny, now quiet I'm reconfiguring…" She says.

"You can't 'shooosh' me! I'm… ME!" I reply.

"Ready, and it looks like they're building a charge between them if we're going to do this it has to be NOW!" Dane says.

"NOW!!!" I yell to the Guard.

The shield drops from the entire staging area, and we are all completely exposed. The saucers are still charging their main cannons for a simultaneous burst of energy. I aim the point on the first saucer where the cannon meets the rest of the ship. It's a direct hit the RP's power levels shoot up to sixty percent, I aim at the same spot on the second saucer.

"We can jump now!" Dane yells.

"I'm not leaving these people to die." I say.

"I figured you were going to say that... firing!" She says.

The second is another direct hit, the RP's power levels jump to one hundred twelve percent.

"Now!!!" I yell again to the Guard, as the first saucer starts to spin out of control quickly followed by the second, both now descending slowly and uncontrollably.

The power keeps streaming and the ships are starting to come down faster. Looking over I see that the Guard is lying down, and looks like he's taken a massive shock.

I run full speed to the generator and flip the switch back to normal operation. The shield engages just in time to cut one of the UFO's front sections off, it falls to the floor in front of me, while the rest of the two ships fall in a heap just outside the shield and then detonate, leaving a large crater.

Checking on the Guard, a *Second Lt.* Rhoads, he was dead blackened beyond recognition.

"He obviously took a massive arc from the generator when the power was first switched over." Dane says.

"That's bull shit Dane! You didn't tell me this guy's life was in danger too. I could have flipped the switch and then sprinted into position!" I yell.

"I honestly couldn't have known Johnny, the *General* himself told you this system was a hodgepodge of parts put together as best they could."

"DAMNIT!" I yell, while walking over to check on the third of the ship that ended up inside the shield.

"Why didn't this thing blow too?" I ask.

"Based upon the way those ships detonated, it would appear that was a failsafe to keep their technologies secret, this portion of the ship must have been severed from the failsafe mechanism when it sent the signal." Dane surmises.

"Outstanding, at least we get a peek inside their ship. That should make *Second Lt.* Rhoads feel much better." I say disgusted by the loss of life.

"Johnny, this would be a very stressful situation for anyone. Without considering that you've already lost all resemblance of your normal life. It may be a good idea to go sit down with George or *Major* Bradley. Get some perspective, and let them clean this up."

"Thank you Dane… but I can deal with this, Rangers don't walk away from responsibility. Besides, this is apparently what I was *made* for remember?" I reply bitterly, approaching the giant piece of UFO now lying in the main entry bay.

I walk along the edge of the holo-shield gliding my hand across the shields electromagnetic barrier, a process that would generally throw anyone else fifty feet across the room, but the Viper keeps me insulated, and the static field it generates almost makes it feel like running my hand through a gentle waterfall.

As I come to the very edge of this giant piece of circular ship, sitting only millimeters from the shield itself, I can actually hear people yelling at each other in German.

"Are you kidding me? I got survivors?" I ask Dane.

"It does sound like it," she agrees.

"Translator?" I ask.

"Ah yes, sorry." Dane answers.

"Why are we still alive?!" Prisoner number one demands.

"You're asking me?! I thought these things were supposed to be indestructible." Prisoner number two answers.

Then I hear a gravely, much darker voice. You can almost hear him sneer when he answers the other two. This can only be the ships commander.

"No… they are not indestructible, they are apparently very destructible, so much so that they decided to equip them with automatic self-destruct devices if enough damage was done to them. Now shut up and let me think." He answers.

Hearing this exchange I grab the edge of the ship at the shield and swing it open like a giant door.

The ship itself has three decks each of which were approximately ten feet tall, with a spiral staircase that looks to have wrapped around the central core which is likely where the engine was, and the self-destruct device.

Since this one was cut just to the side of its core, I can still see the remnants of the elaborate winding staircase, wrought iron steps and bars, with a dark red wood railing.

The three men I've been listening to argue are on the middle floor trying to get to the armory, but having no luck, as it was cut off as well, and the handle is now fused shut.

"You idiots have names or shall I call you 'dead man walking, one, two, and three'?" I ask.

The one sounding like the leader from their previous exchange steps forward and says "No, no names for you. Only rank and serial number."

"Ah good, I'll make up my own then. Get your ass down here Boris." I say. "You too, Natasha and Squirrel." I command.

They look at me and refuse to comply.

"You're going to have to make us you rebellious piece of shit!" Boris yells back.

"Sounds good to me." I reply with a grin.

Now due to the saucer like shape of this craft it's tapered along the top and bottom. Meaning it's wider in the center and quickly goes down from its ten feet per floor to what appears to be seven feet per floor along the outside. That being the case, as they each go for their side arms I stomp on the bottom of the ship with such force that it bounces, tipping the whole thing toward me. Thus throwing them all off balance and falling out of the ship to crash on the cement floor.

"Now lie down on your stomachs and put your hands behind your head," I demand with my BARB drawn.

The two underlings comply right away. Their boss on the other hand reaches for his gun again.

"You just don't get it, do you Boris?" I ask stepping on his forearm as he is still trying to fight through the pain and pull his pistol on me.

"You American scum will die for this. You are worse than a rat infestation," He argues.

"Yeah yeah, save it for the interrogation Boris."

With that I bend over and grab his gun, tossing it over to the edge of the room.

"Now, put your hands behind your head, or I'm going to knock your dumbass out... your call Boris," I say to him.

He finally complies. Moving to Natasha and Squirrel I take their side arms and toss them over by Boris's. It's about this time the elevator finally opens and a large group of MPs come rushing out.

A few stand back and initiate a crowd control on all the civilians, and other base personnel that had come up earlier. The others come over to my aid.

"I got it guys," I say.

"Sir?! We heard there was a possible massive incursion sir?" One of the MPs questions.

"Possible yes, successful, not a damn chance, I knocked both birds out of the sky, and captured almost half of one. Not to mention Boris, Natasha and Squirrel here," I say.

"You do realize that Boris and Natasha were Russian characters, and Squirrel was their enemy?" Dane asks.

"Yeah well do you have a German equivalent?" I ask.

"Well, I do have the complete collection of all German cartoons created until the twenty fourth century, but no, no one as notable as that series," Dane concedes.

I look over to the MPs who are now discovering the guard Second Lt. Rhoads by the shield generator. I get so angry I kick Boris who then yelps in pain.

"That was for the guard you assholes fried," I state.

Dane points out, "You know you did just break two ribs right?"

"Anything punctured?" I ask.

"Nothing…" She admits.

"Call it an enhanced interrogation tactic, I believe that's what they called torture in our time-line around this time wasn't it?" I ask.

"You would be correct actually, but you didn't actually ask him anything."

"Good point," I admit.

Leaning over I say to Boris, "Now, give me the exact coordinates of your base in the Andes' mountain range, and don't think that lying will help you. I already have it narrowed down to one of a few mountains. The only thing you're going to do is end up with a few more broken ribs if you answer incorrectly," I demand.

"But, but they'll kill me!" He whines.

"They already did remember? You're ours now," I clarify.

"Oh, uh… but we have inside people." He admits.

"Good we needed some help verifying that we have caught all of those now too. I'll tell you what, you cooperate and I'll give you the nicest cell we have, it's basically a suite, three squares a day, and no one can touch you there, hell there's even natural sunlight florescent bulbs in there so you don't even feel like you're underground. You'll have complete privacy from other inmates, you and your friends here, we'll keep you all on the dead list. Otherwise, I really don't have a reason not to bust a few more ribs, and that goes for you two as well Natasha and Squirrel. Oh and then of course just parade you around the base until one of your other plants notices you and either lets command know, or takes care of the problem themselves," I say.

"Fine, but we totally disappear in this 'suite' and get complete amnesty," Boris says.

"Amnesty meaning if the United States ever establishes itself as an independent and free nation again, you three go free?" I verify.

"That's the deal, take it or leave it." he replies.

"Well I suppose when that day comes you won't want to go back to the Nazi's anyway, they'll kill you themselves for treason." I say.

"Yeah sure what the hell, I can talk George into that. Coordinates?" I ask

"16.294°S 71.409°W You happy now?!?" Boris says.

"Dane, are we happy now?" I ask.

"Ah, yes we are most definitely happy now. That was actually not one of the five I had extrapolated, but it was on a secondary list if the others didn't pan out," Dane replies.

"It's a good start," I say. "But if you're going to be handed citizenship at the end of all this. I'm going to need a complete list of spies you have in our organization, that's all bases, cities, resistance fighters, etc… I would hate to see you walk right by one on the way to your lovely home, or just out on the street one day. Only to have a former associate recognize, and kill you, we protect our citizens.

I mean after receiving all your special treatment and all, you've obviously been cooperating on a pretty high level right? So death is the most obvious choice for them, although they may torture you first? Huh, that's a tough call too I guess, maybe spend some time trying to find out what exactly you gave up for your freedoms. I mean you can see how that would look bad for you guys right?" I state.

"Okay, okay!" he says.

By now the General, Major Bradley, and several other Brass are exiting the elevator.

"Better talk quick here come some of the brass now, if you have another high level plant Boris now's the time to speak up." I say.

"*Major* Andrews is one of ours," he says reluctantly.

"Interesting, play dead and he won't find out you made it." I say, they all relax on the floor.

"*General!* A moment please," I shout, before the group reaches my position I start running toward them, by the time I reach them we are too far to tell whether the recovered bodies are dead or alive.

Andrews isn't actually with this group but I figure if Boris gives up more information later it might not hurt to keep him and the other two off the books, maybe even honor the total agreement if they turn out to be truly valuable assets.

George approaches, "John looks like you saved our bacon again son."

"Well, almost sir," I say looking at the fried Second Lt.

"Hey now, you saved a base full of nearly ten thousand people here, don't let this get you down son. You've lost people under your command before I'm sure?" He says.

"Yes sir I have, and unfortunately it never gets any easier. Anyway we can talk about that later over a glass of Scotch?"

"No, unfortunately it never does, of course son." He responds.

"Right now I have some pretty reliable intel that *Major* Andrews is a spy George," I say.

"Well he's on the next elevator up, he wanted to see what happened here for himself," He replies.

"That makes sense George, he wants to make sure there were no survivors he needs to worry about," I say pointing over my shoulder at Boris, Natasha, and Squirrel.

"That does make sense John I'll go meet him on the elevator with some MPs and take him down to my office for a meeting, we'll wait for you there." George says.

"Sounds good sir, thank you." I say.

"No, no thank you son, we stand in your debt again." He says looking around in amazement.

Walking back to my prisoners I say, "You hear that from over here, kids? You were only seconds away from being spotted." I point out to the new prisoners.

I whistle at the MPs still examining the shield generator situation, motioning for them to send three over.

Running over they salute. "Yes sir!?"

"I need you guys to cuff these three and take them down to nineteen put them all in the suite for now, and station two of you outside the door until we get this situation worked out," the guards immediately pull out some handcuffs, pull their arms behind their backs and restrain them properly.

"We've got them now Sir!" they salute again.

"For now?" Boris demands.

"Yeah for now, until you guys start providing me with a list of names, and become truly cooperative I have no reason to honor anything. Hell let's not forget I haven't even had a chance to really verify your coordinates, or Major Andrews yet." I say, as he grumbles.

"Thank you sir." Natasha says.

As they drag them to their feet I wave and smile, "See you in a little while kids!"

The other two grumble, as they're all being lead to the elevator.

"That may be your link to all the intel you need right there," Dane chimes in, as I watch the MPs escort them to the elevator.

"Yeah, you could be right," I say.

As they're reaching the elevator I yell, "Oh and don't let our current 'detainees' see these three, these three are ghosts, got it?" I order.

"Yes sir!" One yells, as the other two nod.

"Ok Dane, I need you to do a complete scan of this entire section of ship. I want measurements full spec sheets, and particularly any exploitable weaknesses we can use in the future. Got it?" I ask.

"Scanning now Johnny, but I will need you to climb up floor by floor so I can get everything," she responds.

"Of course you will…" I say. "Let me know when you're ready for number two."

Thirty seconds or so pass.

"Now we can go to the second floor," Dane says.

I jump up and stand in the middle of the second floor, another thirty seconds or so.

"Perfect, now the third?" She requests.

With a light hop I grab the bottom of the third floor and fling myself up onto the deck. This appears to be where the actual command center is. Navigation, helm controls, scanners, weapons, the works.

"Definitely make sure you get every detail up here," I say.

"I always do Johnny."

This scan seems to take a bit longer.

Finally she says, "Now we just need the top, and then a walk around the outside, it would also help if you could then push it up on the split side and allow a full scan of the under carriage."

"Yeah I think I'm going to let their engineers take it before I go flipping it around anymore. Ideally the scans you took during the fight should have caught everything on the bottom anyway." I respond.

"You are correct I did take very thorough readings, the underside is likely unnecessary at this point, but it never hurts to double check readings," she says.

"Alright." I say jumping and grabbing the top of the craft and pulling myself up onto the roof. "Do your scan and let's go talk to George."

A few seconds later, "Done…" is all she says.

"You still want me to walk around the outside?" I ask.

"Yes, that would be the last step for now."

I slowly walk around the front of the craft laying there as an almost half circle.

"That will do it, Johnny," she finally says.

"Great." I say heading over to the shield generator, where they are just raising the gurney brought up for the *Second Lieutenant's* body.

"May I have a moment?" I ask the EMTs.

"Uh. Yeah why not." They all step off to the side to give me some space, even the engineer who was looking at the shield generator.

"Look… I know I didn't know you personally, but I don't like to see anyone lose their life under my command. You were a brave SOB, running over here to help with one of my hair brained plans. You did what had to be done with no thought of your own personal safety. Just like most of the United States Soldiers before you, and most of them since, you carried yourself with honor, dedication and conviction, and you exemplified what being a soldier is all about. Protecting your fellow soldiers, and protecting those that can't protect themselves. I salute you, and if there is an afterlife I hope you end up where ever you were hoping for." I salute him, and walk towards the elevators, motioning the EMTs, engineers, and everyone else to go back about their business.

"That was very moving Johnny," Dane says as I enter the elevator.

"It was very personal, the *General* was right I have lost men before," I admit.

"And you will no doubt lose men again before all this is over," Dane confides.

"Thanks for your confidence." I say, now distant and preoccupied.

The elevator doors open on ten, and I exit heading straight for George's office. The two MPs are standing guard outside.

"Why are you out here?" I demand.

"The *General* ordered us out sir. He said that he and the *Major* had some things to discuss," One of the MPs answers.

"Outstanding," I say opening the door, praying that George is still alive, and that he isn't actually one of the Nazi spies.

Entering the room I find George sitting in his great big chair with *Major* Andrews cuffed to the chair across the desk from him.

"I bet that's a load off your mind," Dane interjects.

"Yeah, speaking of minds, stay out of mine, will you."

"George, how are you and *Major* Andrews getting along here?" I ask.

"Oh. We're having a lovely chat John, please sit down and join us. Andrews was just about to tell us when, were, and how they got to him," George says.

"That does sound interesting, please continue," I say sitting down a few feet from Andrews.

Andrews looks at me, and then back at George and says, "You two can go to hell, I have nothing to say to either of you. I am no traitor."

"Oh, so you've always been a Nazi hand maiden then?" I ask, George just smiles.

"Kiss my ass time traveler!" He says. You can immediately see in his face he already realized he screwed up.

"Well now, George I'm sure you didn't mention that I'm from another time-zone. Where do you suppose he learned that little tidbit of intel?" I say smiling myself.

"Um…" He's stuck thinking.

"Yeah, that's what I thought," I say.

"Good catch John." The General congratulates me, as I turn my whole chair to face Andrews.

"How the hell did you know I'm not from your time-line?" I demand.

"Call it intuition." He says.

My HUD readout displays …LIE…

"I'll call it bullshit, if you don't mind," I retort.

"You'll like this General," I say looking at George.

Redirecting my attention back at Andrews I ask, "Whose mind was used in the cloned copy of *Corporal* Young?"

"Oh that's *Corporal* Young's mind, hell you'll find that out from questioning him," he replies.

The HUD readout displays …TRUE…

"Great, so what did you do to his mind to make him release the ex-*Vice President,* and help her escape?" I ask.

"That's a bit above my pay grade chief."

The HUD readout again displays …TRUE…

"Alright, let's try something I know that you are well informed on Andrews. Tell me about the base in Peru?" I demand.

"Ha! What base in Peru?" He plays stupid.

The HUD readout displays …LIE…

"Well from the way your pulse just increased and you began to perspire when I mentioned it, I'm going to assume you're full of shit, how about a real answer now?" I demand.

"Go to hell time traveler."

"Tell you what, you just tell me if I'm getting warm, then you can claim that you didn't admit anything?" I say.

"I'm sticking with go to hell," He says.

"Alright I guess I'll just have to drop a nuke on 16.294°S 71.409°W, and see what happens then." I smile.

"Nuke? What's that?" He asks.

"Well you see in my time-line, we have this bomb that could level a city, and cause so much radiation that it will kill anyone or any organism that tries to live there for the next sixty to one hundred years, depending on clean up procedures. It actually burns so hot that it will immediately turn sand into glass. It's kind of cool. You mean you guy's never figured this out?" I ask.

"Uh. No, we have no such weapon," He admits.

The HUD reads …TRUE…

"Well guess what Andrews, if that's even your real name. I have all that technology stored in my photographic memory, and when I drop that warhead in that caldera everyone and everything inside will be vaporized. Hell the volcano will probably erupt from the heat and pressure. Oh and did I mention that in my time-line other countries figured out how to do this, but the United States was the only country ever crazy enough to use them, and we did it twice," a look of horror covers his face.

"You must be lying," he argues.

"Try me…" I say.

"If you have such a weapon then why not use it and end this now?" he asks.

"Because I don't like to see innocent people die, and that's always what happens with a weapon like this. Women, children, school teachers, everyone, it's indiscriminate. I'd rather use a scalpel to remove a cancer than a hand grenade," I concede. "But you force my hand, and I will be forced to make sure this ends with the complete annihilation of the Nazi forces, and not just your leaders."

He looks like a trapped animal at this point, finally backed into a corner that forces him to think of the greater good.

"Alright, those are the correct coordinates, but please use your scalpel. I have family there, and I would prefer that they not be killed," He admits.

The HUD reads …TRUE…

"Guards!" I yell.

They burst in, "Sirs?"

George says, "Take this idiot to a private holding cell with no light, and walk him right by the ex-*Vice President*'s cell. I want her to see him brought down."

"Sir, Yes Sir!" They salute, and then begin un-cuffing the Major from his chair, re-cuffing him behind his back and begin escorting him out of the office.

"Nice touch George," I say.

"I thought it might add a little something to it," He admits.

"Oh I agree, let her lose some faith maybe she'll get a little closer to talking herself," I concur, as the guards drag him from the room closing the door behind them.

"So, about that Scotch?" I ask.

"Of course John, can I get you some ice?"

"No, thank you, just the Scotch would be great."

"How are you doing son?" He asks.

"Better… I got to say something to the young man and wish him my best in whatever he goes on to now," I concede, as he hands me a glass.

"Yeah, that always helps ease the conscience a little. You don't blame yourself do you?" He asks, sipping his Scotch.

"I guess in a way, but I had to be where I was to make sure the shots got fired," I admit.

"The shield wasn't going to hold them out eh?" He asks.

"Oh yeah, the shield would have repelled them for years actually, the worry was that they would realize that, and then could have moved to the other side and started shooting the actual mountain, that they would have brought down on our heads," I say.

"I see. So what do we do now that they know we're here?" he asks.

"The plans for the generator I gave you? Make three of them. One to replace your current one, one to aim in the opposite direction and cover the backside of the mountain, and one spare."

"And that will hold them out for years?" he questions.

"According to my numbers, using the generators that I supplied plans for, they would hold up to ten of those ships under constant bombardment for a minimum of ten years, seven months, and twenty two days," Dane chimes in.

"According to Dane it would hold up to ten of those ships for nearly eleven years," I inform him.

"Well I guess that needs to be priority one around here, since they know where we are now."

"Yeah, I would make sure that gets done ASAP, but with my little lightning show I probably gave them a little something to think about, before they send out another attack," I suggest.

"I know it would make me think twice," George admits.

"Well, I'm going to have to leave that portion to your engineers I'm afraid, in order to get this done, we're looking to ship out day after tomorrow sir," I say.

"Sounds like you've found your team then?" he asks.

"Actually, I let Bradley handle the whole thing for me. We're meeting at eighteen-hundred for dinner this evening to go over the plan, let everyone know this is strictly a volunteer operation, and make sure we don't need to replace anyone."

"Good, that's going to be one hell of a mission son, if I was twenty years younger, I'd be begging to get on that team," he admits.

"Bah, if you were twenty years younger you'd be running the team sir."

He chuckles, "You're probably right. I would have been."

"One last thing sir, and you're not going to like it, but I haven't had a chance to talk to you about it yet, with everything going on," I say.

"Spit it out son. What's on your mind?" he asks, looking more serious.

"I'm going to need one of those initial dreadnaught class tanks we captured, in order to slip in to their train station undetected, and get loaded on the southbound train," I say.

"Ha! Is that all? I was worried you were planning to take all of them," He admits.

"No, I had originally thought to take two, but our team is small enough, and I don't think we'll be able to get the other on the train. Not to mention I would never want to leave you without the ability to do what you need to do on your end."

"Of course not John and I know that. Just wasn't privy to your plans is all," he responds.

"So I take it this is good with you then?" I ask, just for clarification.

"Well as I figure it, you brought them in, if you want to take them out then who am I to stand in your way."

"Thank you sir, it's much appreciated and it will make destroying their base much, much easier," I admit.

"Just bring me back a souvenir would ya?" He asks.

I laugh, "You already into my escape plan sir?" I ask.

"No, John I just know the way you operate by now," he gives me a wink and a smile.

"Understood sir."

"Johnny it's nearly eighteen-hundred hours, time to meet your team," Dane jumps in.

"Well sir, I won't take up any more of your time, it's almost time for me to meet the team as it is."

"Sounds good John, enjoy your dinner."

Leaving his office I head over to the elevator and down to level eleven.

Once arriving I see most of my 'team' sitting in a corner off by themselves awaiting my arrival. First I head over to the chow line and grab this evening's special potato soup and a lovely flat bread.

Joining the table everyone stands and salutes, "Oh please guys sit, sit. I don't run things that way. Do I get the respect yes, do you follow my orders of course, every team needs a solid leader, but I want a team that can think for itself too, work together, and accomplish goals based upon the whole team not just me. I won't be around forever, and Bradley here will be stepping into my shoes at some point. So I need to make sure that this group can take care of itself and become a top notch Special Forces beacon of hope for the United States military." I explain.

They all smile and nod in agreement.

"Johnny you know with your current power levels we can leave whenever you are ready and fix all of this," Dane says.

"Not if the multi-universe theory holds, I'm just leaving these guys holding the bag," I say.

"Well, I guess I see your point," she admits.

Sitting down I ask, "So it looks like we have an empty chair? Who are we missing?"

"PFC Lee, Sir. He radioed ahead and said he would be right here," Bradley responds.

"Well he's got another five minutes technically," I admit. "So tell me, who are my demo experts here?"

A smaller framed man with a thick mustache and beard, dark brown hair, and a southern drawl speaks up, "Well I suppose I would be one sir."

"Nice to meet you, what's your name soldier?" I ask.

"*Second Lt.* Brett Berry, sir."

"Okay *Second Lt.* Berry, and what kind of explosives have you worked with in the past?" I ask.

"Well just the normal military type I suppose, C-4, some TNT, oh and of course gun powder," he answers.

"And you are skilled at selecting strategic locations for maximum collateral damage and, say, building implosion?" I ask.

"Oh yes sir, I can pick out the highest stressed area of any wall or supporting structure."

"Excellent." I say

"And who's the other?" I ask?

The soldier next to him speaks up at this point. You can see he's much cockier. Tall, muscular and speaks with a heavy Russian accent. "I am 'other'." he says.

"Okay, is your family Russian originally?" I ask.

"Yes, is that problem?" He asks.

"No, not in the least. I've worked with many Russian operatives in the past, and have always been impressed by their training regiments, and discipline in the field." I respond.

"Ah yes, we like to train, perfection is always goal," He says.

"And what is your name soldier?" I ask.

"*Sergeant* Anthony Khabalov sir, but you may call me 'The Russian' everyone else does."

"Is that your preference?" I ask.

"Eh, it fits, and I am only one on base," He says, obviously not bothered by it.

"Okay Russian, and can you also find the stress point on any structure?" I ask.

"Ha! You bet, I can bring down mountain, base, hotel, women's undergarments, you name it. I find your spot." He says, causing the rest of the table to laugh.

About this time a smaller framed Caucasian man approaches with a German accent. He takes the remaining seat at the table. "Sorry I am late sir, my current duties kept me longer than expected," he says.

"PFC Chad Lee is it?" I ask.

"Yes sir." He responds.

"Okay, we're all just getting acquainted here, so what is it that you specialize in *PFC* Lee?" I ask.

"Well, I guess you would call it espionage?" *PFC* Lee replies.

"So then breaking in, intelligence gathering, spy stuff basically?" I ask.

"Basically, yes that's the gist of it I imitate different accents, and am very quick on my feet," He continues, in a modern American accent.

"Sounds like good choices so far *Major* Bradley," I smile. "Who are our other two teammates here?" I ask the Major.

"Well sir, we have here *First Lt.* Faye Stills who is our hand to hand expert as well as one of the bases highest rated snipers. She and *Specialist* Mac Simms, to your right, who is currently the highest rated marksmen on the base, have worked together on many ops, and are a very good fit for long distance cover fire. I also figured with *First Lt.* Stills' hand to hand expertise, she makes perfect sense as a second for *Specialist* Simms as she can defend against anyone attempting to overtake their position."

Both Stills, and Simms nod and smile.

"Alright, Stills, Simms pleasure to meet you both," I say.

"Likewise sir," they say almost in unison.

"Yeah I guess they have worked together before," I comment.

"They will be a huge asset to this team sir," *Major* Bradley comments.

"I can see that *Major*, it looks like you've done your homework, and an excellent job putting this crew together. Now, before I tell you all what it is you're signing up for, I want to be perfectly clear. This is a volunteer mission, you do not have to go, and no one will think any less of you if you get up and walk away right now. But know that if you stay, and listen to the mission brief, you're going on the mission or to the brig until we return. I can't have any chance of this operation being mentioned to the wrong person while we're gone or compromised in any way shape or form. 'We' meaning this team, are quite simply going to change the entire tide of this war. So if you want out now's the time to say something."

Major Bradley speaks up, "I have already discussed the importance of the mission, and that we are leaving the country for parts only known by you sir. I've also expressed the importance this mission will play in the war, and everyone has agreed that they are in for the long haul concerning this mission, sir."

"Is that true?" I ask scanning around the table. Everyone is enthusiastically nodding in agreement.

"Alright then, originally I wanted to ship out the day after tomorrow, but since we all seem to be on the same page, thanks to *Major* Bradley's wonderful team building skills I see no reason to wait. We ship out tomorrow at zero-eight-hundred, the sooner we get this done, the sooner this war will be headed in the right direction," I announce.

"To our resounding success and kicking some evil Nazi ass!" Stills' raises a glass.

Everyone echo's "To our success!" and slams their glasses together.

"Major, a word please," I state, motioning him away from the group.

"Of course sir!" he replies following me across the room.

As he joins me just out of the table's earshot, I ask. "So Stills, you don't think there will be any problems with her and the other guys?"

"Oh, you mean because of The Russian's comment? No sir she's proven around here that she can not only take care of herself but generally everyone around her as well," Bradley says.

"Okay then, I just thought I'd ask. I know I made this your call, but I wouldn't be a good leader if I didn't make sure everything was going to run like a well-oiled machine."

"Understood John, I wouldn't expect any less," he replies.

"Good job kid. You're definitely going to be 'that' *General* someday," I say.

Walking back to the table the group has all finished their soup, and are polishing off the last of their Vodka.

"Alright, guys I'm not going to be long winded about this, I think I've seen most of you on a few of the other ops that I've run, since being here.

That said you probably all know I set objectives, and a strategy for getting to that objective, once there I tend to play things by ear, sometimes even a little loose.

I learned in the Rangers it's a lot easier to make adjustments in the field when you don't have hard and fast orders to adhere to. So I want you all to understand that same thing.

From this moment on we are a team. We have each other's backs no matter what, the team comes before everything else, and because of that everything else will simply fall into place, because the team works to make it happen that way," I say, the new team all stands and raises what's left of their glasses waiting for my toast.

"Nicely put Johnny," Dane says.

"Thanks I've been rehearsing it in my head for days now."

"Actually I would have heard that. You spoke genuinely from the heart," she replies.

"Alright, alright, no need to get sappy," I say.

My toast, "To OUR team. May we always keep one another safe, strong, and ready to take on whatever the Nazi empire throws at us."

"Here, Here!" Everyone slams their glass on the table and polishes off the rest of their glass.

"You're all dismissed, get some shut eye and pack lightly. We'll need to be very versatile. I'll see you all in the morning at the loading bay. There you'll all be briefed on the first part of the op."

263

They all begin to separate out from the table and head for the door.

"Oh… and Lee, don't be late again," I say.

"Understood General, zero-nine-hundred right?" He says in an Australian accent, smiling.

"Zero-eight-hundred smartass," I reply, he just winks at me, and they all file out to their respective bunks.

"I don't know about you, but I like that one Johnny," Dane says.

"Of course you do, he's giving me a hard time. What's not to love?" I reply, arms crossed, watching them exit.

Bradley approaches "Well, what do you really think boss?" He asks candidly.

I chuckle, "Lee's a little rough around the edges, but I've met his kind before, and they usually are. That said, I think you did a good job putting together a team. Unfortunately this is one of those situations where only time will tell if people really step into, and embrace their rolls or not."

"That make's sense, and you're right of course, Lee's got a bit of an attitude, and that's actually the reason he's still a *PFC*, but I tell you boss. With the mission briefings I got my hands on and the things he's apparently pulled off. Well let's just say that's why he's a *PFC* and hasn't been court-martialed," Bradley responds.

"Good call then, I probably would have made the same choice in your position. When betting on people, always bet on someone with something to prove, not the one who's already proven it, at least in that line of work. They're always willing to go the extra mile to sell the con, getting your team in the door, and making the op work."

Bradley smiles, "Glad you approve John."

"Hell I had faith in you from the moment we met, kid. Anyone who gets up with a fractured rib, and runs five miles is either stupid or dedicated, and I could tell with you it was the mission, which shows dedication in spades. Now get out of here, I'll see you in the morning," I reply.

"See you in the morning, John." He responds, walking out the door.

"Dane, print a letter to the good *General's* office letting him know we're shipping out a day earlier than expected, and that I'll meet him for breakfast to go over the details. Also print him a list of the team members we're planning on taking," I say.

"Done…" Dane replies.

10 MOVE'EM OUT

Zero-six-thirty the next morning, I meet the *General* for breakfast.

"John! How are you this morning, ready to move out?" George asks.

"Yeah, looks like Major Bradley did a fine job putting a team together for me."

"I saw that, you're taking a few of my best people," he responds in between bites.

"I was wondering how you'd feel about Simms and Stills."

"Well I can't say I'm overly ecstatic about it; if I'm being totally honest, but I do know the importance of your operation, and you've certainly done so much for us already. So I'll deal with it. Just do me a favor and get Lee shot will you? That man's been nothing but trouble since the day he transferred in, you'll save me some trouble, and probably court-martial proceedings," He says with a chuckle.

I smile, "I don't know George I see potential there. If I can straighten him out for you, I think he could be one hell of an asset in the future."

"Well good, either straighten him out then, or get him shot, because frankly all the disciplinary action on him is driving me up a wall. I'm going to bleed to death from the multitude of paper cuts it takes just in filing his paperwork." He says with a smirk.

We both know he's really just saying this to avoid the elephant in the room, we're both going to miss our talks, our comradery; he knows as well as I that I'll likely not be returning from this mission one way or another. And I know I've been the only true friend he's had in quite some time, maybe ever. Finishing off our potato grits, it's getting near time for me to head up and check on the equipment we'll be taking along.

"Alright George I'm headed up to get the Dreadnaught's prepped and ready to go, then prep my team. I'll see you in a few weeks. I'm sure you'll hear of our exploits in New Mexico in the next few days though." I say.

"Sounds good son, and God speed." George replies, standing and giving me a proper salute; probably the only one I've seen from him since arriving. I of course respond in kind and shake the man's hand. He's become a good friend, to me as well, almost like the military mentor I never had, with maybe the exception of John Steal who disappeared on me all those years ago.

"One way or another George, it's been my honor to serve with you sir." I say, turning toward the exit.

Glancing back he has that fatherly concerned look to him, heading out of the officer's mess, and entering the main mess hall, I catch a glimpse of my team grabbing their breakfast together at a table in the back, all except for Lee, of course. They all look up and smile at me, I smile and nod to acknowledge them, and keep heading toward the elevator.

Upon entering the elevator I run into *Sergeant* Young exiting, obviously on his way to breakfast.

"Morning *Sgt.*?" I say.

"Good morning sir!" he replies snapping to attention.

"I trust you'll behave, and do your best not to get cloned anymore in my absence."

"I'll do my best sir!" he says with a smile.

"No one can ask more *Sgt.*" I say, entering the elevator.

Heading up top is a somber feeling, like the calm before the biggest storm of your life. I could literally almost smell the ozone in the air, like the lightning was on its way, and it knew exactly where to find me.

Exiting the elevator the guard on duty is obviously expecting me and gives me a salute. I give him a quick salute and continue over to the guard station where he waits by the machine elevator switch panel.

These switches control a series of massive lifts that raise and lower the Tanks and other vehicles on base into the mission prep area from the repair and maintenance bays below.

Ideally once a vehicle has been requisitioned; it will be inspected for mechanical issues, re-fueled, and re-stocked with mission critical supplies. For this mission, the four cases of C-4 I requested in the tank, along with a complete arsenal of shells and ammunition for the tank itself.

The control panel at the guard station has elevator two lit up indicating it is ready for activation. Pushing the two button I watch as sections of the floor open, and the tank rises up into view.

"This tank is really going to give me an edge. It's too bad we're going to lose it in New Mexico, but you gotta do what you gotta do, right?" I say to myself.

"So you're really going through with that plan are you?" Dane asks.

"Didn't I tell you to stay out of my head?" I ask.

"You did, but you should know by now that is literally impossible. Besides you just said you were going to lose it in New Mexico; with the amount you talk to yourself who needs to be inside your head? You just say it all sooner or later," she replies.

"Yeah that is the plan. Now get over it." I insist.

Around this time the main elevator doors open again. Looking to see who it is I notice the time is now almost zero-eight-hundred. I'll be damned here is my team all smiles, still minus *PFC* Lee.

"Interesting first day so far," Dane announces.

Just as I'm about to get irritated enough to call down to the MPs and have them go drag his lazy ass up here, even though it's really just now zero-eight-hundred. I hear a noise from behind me; it's the tank hatch opening.

"Man these things are kick ass and they're cozy too!" *PFC* Lee says standing in the now opened hatch.

"Well, I'll be damned," I say turning around.

"Was it something I said…? Sir?" he asks.

"No *Private*, you just surprised me is all."

"Ha! You thought I was going to be late again didn't you?" he says with a grin.

"The thought had crossed my mind."

"It's okay, I understand. I'm sure you looked into my record by now, and *General* Patton probably doesn't have too many nice things to say about me either come to think of it," he admits.

"Actually, the *General* said I should make sure you get shot," I confirm.

"Ouch, that's a little harsh," he says.

"Well just so you know, I did tell him that I saw some potential in you, and that if you could live up to that you'd be one hell of an asset to this team and in the end to this Country."

"Wow, well thank you sir. Most people wouldn't stick their neck out for me around here."

"The *Major* here vouched for you, and that's all I needed," I admit nodding at Bradley as he walks up. "And I do see a spark there that if used properly could really aid in this and future missions. Just don't make him or me a liar," I caution.

"I promise I won't let you down sir, and I never make a promise period. So that should tell you something," he replies.

"Good to hear *Private*. Now fall in and let's get through this briefing," I say.

The team gets together with their gear.

As we're already standing near the guard station I tell the on duty officer to "take a fifteen minute coffee break would ya? This won't take long, but it is classified."

"Aye sir!" he responds heading for the elevator.

Once he enters and the doors swing closed behind him, I order everyone to take a knee and begin my briefing. "Alright, so obviously there is a Dreadnaught class tank that we confiscated being used here. Unfortunately these babies top out around sixty two miles per hour. So we're going to be in it for a while." I pause, gauging the reaction to the sore butt syndrome to follow.

"That's right we're going to fabulous NEW MEXICO!" I say, Bradley chuckles, they all just kind of look at each other.

"What? Nothing really? I worked on that delivery for like five minutes last night," I say.

I get the obligatory "Sorry, sir." From almost everyone, Lee of course goes with, "But New Mexico sucks!"

"Alright in all seriousness, the first part of the mission is to prepare for a remote detonation of the bullet train switching station in New Mexico, which I'm told is just on the other of the Rockies? Once the C-4 is in place we will be boarding a bullet train that stops at the station just east of the switch. This train will take us down into South America, the idea of course is to blow the C-4 just after the train makes it through the switch, making it look like the train was the target and it was just missed," I say.

"Wow… that's actually a clever strategy," Lee says.

"Thank you; I pride myself on my ability to make you feel comfortable," I smirk.

"Right, uh sorry sir," he shrugs.

"Obviously while planting the C-4 we're going to want to take out a few men quietly and relieve them of their uniforms, so as to not draw any attention to ourselves once we get on the train. I'm hoping with the added distraction of the switching station blowing up behind them, the Nazi's on that train will be counting themselves lucky they weren't hit, and therefore avoid looking too hard at anyone on the train itself," I finish.

Lee raises his hand, "Question sir?"

"Go ahead *Private*."

"Why do we need the tank for this op? Couldn't we just take a jeep or something, make sure the base has the extra firepower if it needs it?" He asks.

"Wow… That's actually a good question *Private*. The real reason for the tank boils down to misdirection.

What we want is the Nazi forces protecting the train HUB to believe that it is our only target, so it must look like we committed enough resources to take out this location, or at the very least put in enough effort to really mess the place up.

Additionally the tank has the added benefit of giving the Nazis something to shoot at while we're busy setting the charges. That said I'll be operating the tank by remote control, the more they worry about it, the less of a chance they have of seeing what we're up to.

Also, I made a promise to *General* Patton that this would not blow back on him. Which means we are going to take great care in making this attack look like there's a new internal Nazi power struggle beginning, that way our friends in the resistance and the actual United States bases are free from reprisal. Allowing them time to bolster the resistance and really put the west in a much better position. Ideally we're going to have the Nazi's chasing their own tails for a while.

Now for the C-4; we will separate into three groups, each group will consist of one explosives expert, and one other specialist, and each group will be responsible for dispersing one case of C-4 around the switching station itself. Group one will start on the north side, that's Stills and The Russian. Group two is Berry and Bradley you'll take the south and you'll both meet in the middle. Lee and, I will take the control office, and then we'll all hoof it to the train station. Where we will maintain our groups and ideally avoid looking suspicious, then board our southbound train.

The extra case of C-4 we brought along, will also be distributed evenly to everyone. That case however will need to be concealed and carried with us to South America. Remember we're operating in teams of two here, so as we board the train that will remain the case. Cover your partner's ass, and be as inconspicuous as possible." I say.

"Well said," Dane applauds.

"Thanks… and stop sneering I can hear it through your audio voice replicators. I'm not sure who's going to be the bigger problem at this point, you or *PFC* Lee," I say.

"I'm offended at that thought Johnny."

"You're right of course it's obviously PFC Lee, you're just his cheer leader. 'Ra ra sis cum ba', and all that," I mock.

"You all are just staring at me with blank faces. Well except PFC Lee who looks like he may have just wet himself. Are there any questions? Comments? Concerns? Anything I should be aware of now?" I ask.

"No sir!" they reply in unison.

"Just a lot to take in all at once, sir," *Second Lt.* Berry says.

"Don't worry Brett, you were all handpicked for this operation for a reason, we have every confidence that you will do your jobs and come home as heroes," I reply.

"Yes sir!" he says sounding more confident.

"That's more like it," I say, continuing, "Alright, I want the rest of you to grab your gear and load up. Major you've got the driver's seat."

I hear *First Lt.* Stills whispering to her partner Simms as they grab their gear "Wow. He already knows our names ranks and specialties without thinking about it."

Simms replies, "You do know there's a rumor running around the base that the guy is some kind of robot from the future right?"

"Oh shut up, don't be jealous," she tells him.

"No, no, that's really what I heard," Simms replies.

I have to just smile, jumping up to the hatch on my tank.

"You do realize that if they are in an actual relationship it could compromise the mission, right Johnny." Dane asks.

"Yeah, I do. That's why I'm having them do this exercise. It's called team molding." I answer.

"You just made that up," she replies.

"Yeah tell that to my Army Ranger trainer, and while you're working on that I'm going to need you to setup a random maneuvering and firing pattern for the tank once this op begins." I answer.

About this time the elevator doors open and its *General* Patton along with the MP I put on a fifteen minute break. By this time the rest of the team was inside the tank, and I was climbing in myself.

The MP takes his post, and George comes up to the tank and motions for me to step down.

Walking with him away from the tank and earshot I ask, "George, what's going on?"

"I just got word John. We've got a lot of air reinforcements coming in fast. If you're going to get out of here you need to do it now," he says.

"Well we knew that was a possibility sir, and we're on our way out as soon as I'm in," I reply.

"Good, good. And you're sure that these new shields are going to hold?" he asks turning to head back toward the tank.

"Absolutely George, don't worry about a thing. The way I have those shields configured, you could hold off a constant attack for a week at today's technology levels. But we're going to blow that train switch in fourteen hours max. They'll be gone before the end of the day sir."

"Good to hear son," he says shaking my hand again.

"I'll send you a post card sir," I say hopping back up to the tank hatch.

He chuckles, "You do that."

Closing the hatch I tell *Major* Bradley, "Alright *Major* we're good to go, let's put the pedal down, the *General* says we've got helo's coming in hot."

"Pulling out now sir!" he responds.

Forced to take back roads and really no roads at times, it takes us nearly an hour before we actually reach route sixty six.

Turning onto the highway we get an immediate transmission, the Nazi's have set up a nearby checkpoint, probably after the convoy heist.

A German officer demanding we identify ourselves, and explain what we're doing before they open fire! Dane handles the translation for me.

Lee looks at me and says, "He said…" I cut him off.

"Yeah I know what he said, just tell him we're on a top secret mission involving the verification of the hidden rebel base in the area, and now we are to report back to our commander," I say.

Lee transmits my message over the radio.

To which they respond, "Then you know procedure we need your ID Code, and you must halt until cleared, otherwise we must fire."

"Okay, stop the tank," I order which the Major does right away.

"Dane, I need codes."

"Working on it," she replies.

"I say again, I need your travel codes or we will open fire. You have one minute to comply." The voice says.

"Just a minute, please, we are pulling the codes now. We were told all check points would be expecting us!" I reply with Danes translation.

"You got the codes yet? And why are you making me sound like Colonel Klink? That's just wrong."

"Very well, due to the nature of your mission, and the fact that you have stopped, you have two minutes," The voice responds.

Lee turns to me, "What should we do sir? You want me to try one of their old codes?"

"No, just give me a second."

Two codes finally appear on my HUD.

"Thank you," I say to Dane.

"Alright Lee transmit these, first code: sierra golf one bravo echo sierra tango [stop] Second code: sierra hotel oscar whiskey echo victor echo romeo [stop]," I say, and Lee complies, while looking at me like I'm nuts.

"Apologies for the delay Colonel Klink, we were not expecting you. Your codes have been verified, please give my regards to New Freiburg."

"Tell him not to worry I like strict protocols to be followed strictly, but I will have the head of the moron that did not radio our passing ahead. Good day," I say to Lee, which he translates back in German.

"Understood Colonel, I will radio ahead personally and have you cleared all the way through to New Freiburg. Good day!"

"Alright Major Bradley let's move out," I say.

"Well that's clear sailing now kids. Sit back and enjoy the bumpy ride," I say.

"Colonel Klink?! Are you kidding me?" I chastise Dane.

"What? I had to upload a back story, along with proper approvals, and authorization codes. It was the first name that popped into mind," she defends.

"Great who did you tell them I had with me Sgt. Schultz?"

"No, just your team, although I did add his name to the team roster if they were to check. That may be who they thought Lee was," she answers sounding very proud of her work.

11 THE BAIT AND SWITCH

Pulling into New Freiburg it's almost midnight. The city itself is obviously a huge industrial manufacturing center for the Nazi empire. There are many factories most of which are already shutdown for the night, the switching station is situated between several of them.

We approach the switching station and park the tank right out in plain sight, so when the fireworks start they know exactly where to direct their attention.

"Okay, so you all know your assignments. Since these factories are closer than had been anticipated, let's get some of that C-4 in a few of them to the North and South, preferably on or near something combustible. We have the opportunity to give them a real show, and burn down some of their war machine while we take out the switching station."

"Yes sir!" they all sound off excitedly.

"Good, just remember each team should save a block to attach to the actual railroad switching as well, and each person should have two extra blocks hidden on their person somewhere to take to South America.

Also, there are going to be several guards on patrol, you'll need to be alert and take them out quiet and clean, then change clothes. Once all your charges are placed we'll rendezvous at the South Bound Platform. We'll use two walkie clicks from each team to signal that they're on their way to the platform. Any questions?"

"Sir? I don't have an assignment," says Specialist Simms.

"Ah yes, take your silenced rifle and get someplace high, keep an eye on teams one and two, if there is anyone they don't see take them out quick before they can radio it in."

"Yes Sir!" he confirms.

"That means I'll need one of you to grab a uniform for Simms. Simms if you run into someone on your way to the perch, just follow the same protocol when you have the uniform that way the others stop looking."

"Understood sir," Simms replies.

"Other than that, there should be total radio silence, unless one of you hits major trouble, then I want to know about it. Everyone should be on channel two by the way, the Germans are using frequency nine here," I say after confirming with Dane.

With another, "Yes sir!" I instruct my teams to grab their gear and head to their assigned locations. Grabbing their gear and exiting the hatch of our respective tank the entire team is cautious not to make any noise.

Quietly approaching the central office behind *PFC* Lee I draw my BARB and change with a thought into an officer's uniform, the BARB now looks like nineteen oh eight German Luger. Seeing a patrol this is our chance to grab Lee a uniform.

"Stop!" I call to them in German.

Lee turns around looking mortified. Then seeing me he instantly puts his hands up.

The two man patrol stops and shines their flash lights in our eyes.

I order them to put their lights down, as I am escorting my prisoner to the central office for transport and interrogation.

They immediately comply and salute due to my *General's* rank insignia. I fire off a round with the BARB and electrocute them both.

"Go ahead and get your uniform Private."

"You know I'm starting to buy that rumor," He says.

"The one about me being a robot from the future?" I ask.

He nods, not taking his widened eyes off me.

"I like that one. We'll go with that for now," I whisper.

He still seemed to be stunned but quickly trades clothes with the guard closest to his size.

"Look if it makes you feel any better I'm actually trying to chase down another time traveler who screwed up the entire time-line. Now suck it up, and let's get to work," I order.

"Yes sir!" he whispers.

We continue toward the switching station control office. As we approach *PFC* Lee is seen by another guard walking outside away from the control office having a cigarette. Lee quickly approaches the guard who happens to turn around to face him at the last moment before Lee can grab him. The guard yells "Halt!" obviously not recognizing Lee as belonging in that area, and reaches for an alarm radio transmitter on the wall. Before I even have a chance to react Lee has jumped up wrapped his leg around the guard's neck taking him to the ground and breaking it on impact.

"One uniform down, eh future man?" He whispers to me, with a quick thumbs up.

"Good job, now toss it here, and drag him around the corner before you get seen again," I whisper back.

"Apparently you were right, there is some skill there," Dane says.

"They trained us to spot our potential threats well in the Rangers and the CIA," I admit.

Progressing forward everyone in the team is able to take out their first target without another round fired, supplying the whole team with uniforms.

It looks like there are only a few people left inside the switching station office. So Lee and I are going in for a little surprise inspection, forcing all attention on us. While the rest of the teams' plant their C-4 on the railroad itself.

As Lee and I enter the *switch* station Lee screams, "Achtung!"

Everyone drops what they are doing and turns toward the door, I goose step in taking a hard turn toward everyone in the room, and all attention off the front of the building.

"General!" Everyone does the one hand in the air Nazi salute.

As I speak Dane translates it to German for me on the fly. "Relax idiots. I'm here for a quick inspection."

Facing out the windows I can see my team running around dropping bricks of C-4 in strategic locations.

"But sir we had our monthly review by *General* Bauer last week!" a Lt. insists, as he finishes telling me this I see my team run off toward the south bound train station.

"What?!" I ask, in my most demanding tone.

"Sir it is true!" he insists.

I turn to Lee, "Schnitzel radio headquarters and verify this." I order, the others in the room snicker.

He looks irritated as he grabs his radio calling for HQ.

Since Dane is the biggest and strongest receiver around I have her answer the radio request. "Ah, yes there was a mix up with the paper work; they have already been inspected this month," Dane broadcasts back.

With that I roll my eyes, do a solid goose stomp turn and walk right back out of the office, with Lee apologizing and following right behind me, although looking in the upper left quadrant of my HUD for rearview, I catch him faking a sneeze and planting a small block of C-4 under a desk right by the front door.

We begin walking toward the train station ourselves.

"That went well I think," I comment.

"Schnitzel? Really?" *PFC* Lee asks sounding offended.

"I can't help it. You look like a Schnitzel to me. Plus, I'm kind of hungry, we haven't eaten all day. I hope there's food service on this train. What do you think Herr Schnitzel?"

"Wow... and I thought I was the smartass of the group. Did you catch all the snickers at me?"

I laugh, "Yeah that was worth it on all on its own, and trust me kid, you're not the smartass of the group, but you're welcome to challenge me for the title any time you like."

"Huh. I may take you up on that *General*," He says.

"You did do a good job with the sneezing C-4 plant though."

"You caught that?" He asks sounding surprised.

"There's not much I don't Schnitzel."

He just glares at me as we walk.

Approaching the station dock to wait for the train I have Dane do a quick crowd scan to verify that all teammates are accounted for and paired off.

"Everyone is accounted for Johnny, Specialist Simms is our odd man out," she reports.

"Alright where's he at? We'll make ours a team of three," I say.

"He's ten paces to your left and two forward, and don't you mean four?" she says.

"Yeah, I suppose you count. This time..." I reply.

"Why thank you, you're too kind," she says.

"Alright Schnitzel we're going to go grab Simms I believe he's over here," I say to *PFC* Lee in *German*.

He nods, and follows me as I head toward *Specialist* Simms's position.

Brushing up against a member of each team as we pass; I whisper to let them know we'll be getting off on the first exit in Peru and rendezvousing behind the train station there.

Approaching Simms I tap him on the shoulder solidly with two fingers, I may be getting into this German *General* thing a little too much, but I can't risk my cover.

Looking startled he turns swiftly and then smiles seeing that it's just me and PFC Lee.

He does the Nazi salute and bows to me.

I look over to PFC Lee and say in German, "You could learn a lot from this man."

"Yes sir!" He answers, by this time the train is pulling up.

We quickly board and grab one of the small suites for the three of us. I have *PFC* Lee close the door and sit across from the *Specialist* and me.

As the train begins to move forward, I have Dane on standby to fire the tank's cannons and then detonate the C-4.

Just as the engine clears the turn at the switch station. I have Dane start the Tank firing its main cannon on the switching stations offices, as we round the turn ourselves I can feel the train speeding up, and we all see soldiers running out firing their automatic weapons and lobbing grenades at the tank. At that point I have Dane use the fifty caliber machine gun to mow down some of the soldiers, there's no way to know that the tank is empty at this point.

Since the Dreadnaught class of tank has an auto reload feature on the main cannon I have Dane fire a second shot from the closer of the two tanks just to the front of the engine compartment, exploding only twenty meters or so from our position.

Waiting for the last train car to pass I have Dane transmit the detonator frequency, for the C-4 to the South side destroying the South route train station, a good portion of track we had just been on, and the factory that was just on the other side of the tracks begins to blow out from underneath, crumbling down toward the tracks to bury them in rubble, the fire escaping forward toward the train to the point that we could feel the heat from the blast.

"Nice, buried the remaining track in rubble, that'll make it a bigger cleanup operation, before they can even start on the repair and rebuilding," I comment.

As more soldiers poor out I have Dane transmit the detonator frequency for the C-4 to the North of the main facility. The entire factory behind lights up like giant a volcano, exploding like a fireball straight up into the atmosphere.

"Guess they got one of those in the right spot too eh?" I say.

Both Simms, and Lee just nod in amazement.

One of the soldiers gets off a shot with a rocket launcher, hitting the tank near the main fuel tank exploit, blowing the whole thing into the air. As it hits the ground Dane blows the last C-4 on the central facility itself.

Only seconds later there is a huge explosion from behind us, and the train comes slamming to a halt.

"I guess it's time for me to go take control of the situation and get this train moving again. Be right back don't let anyone take my seat Schnitzel, and if anyone asks about Simms', he's mute due to a recent operation, but you can vouch for him." I say closing the door behind me.

Walking toward the front of the train entering the engine compartment I find the engineer desperately trying to radio the switching station to find out what he should do.

With Dane continuing my German escapade I demand, "What are you doing idiot?!"

"Sir!?" he turns and salutes.

"There was an attack just behind and in front of us and you stop to give them another chance to hit us?! Go you idiot, Go NOW!" I demand.

"Heil," He says, and begins to slide the acceleration switch forward building up speed.

"I will find out what has happened, and who is targeting us on my private communications array. You drive," I say.

"Yes sir!" he answers.

"Idiot!" I yell heading back out of the engine room.

Entering the cabin I find Simms' and *PFC* Lee opening a bottle of Champagne.

"What the hell is this?" I ask.

"Apparently when you tell the train conductor that your commanding officer had just gone and saved all of our lives this is what you get," *PFC* Lee answers.

"Huh, well what the hell, when's the food get here?" I say.

"Oh yeah, he's bringing you a plate of Schnitzel too," he answers.

"Now you're learning kid," I reply, he just smiles.

"Are you messing with me? Because Schnitzel is no joking matter, and I'd hate to have to throw you off this train, especially since we're now moving at almost three hundred fifty kilometers per hour," I say.

Simms chuckles, "No, he's actually serious this time. I understood enough German to know that he told the conductor if he really wanted to thank you, to come up with a plate of Schnitzel for you. The conductor said he'd get on it right away."

"Well, alright then. Who knows Lee, you keep this up and there may be a promotion in it for you before this op. is over."

Watching the trees go by heading south is kind of surreal for me. Not just because these are trees that wouldn't normally exist in this part of the country, but by the twenty second century, a hundred years in the future in my time-line, the earth's ozone layer had been so depleted by fossil fuels that they had only just realized in the United States that bullet trains could move just as fast as an airplane with almost zero carbon footprint. I suppose that's what you get stuck with when living in an oligarchy though.

They say the fracking is really what put the nail in the coffin for all these species of trees, and with that much Methane gas being released into the atmosphere everyday who could argue with that? Seriously though when you're able to light your water on fire, there's a god damn problem. No wonder the 'Zyndraph' waited so long to let us know they were out there, they figured we were just as nuts as the 'Doo-Rinda'.

As I sit there pondering how different the world is; the door slides open and to my delight it's actually the conductor with three plates loaded with Schnitzel and steak smothered in capers and gravy.

I nod, and thank the conductor.

"No, no, thank you sir. We were obviously in great danger back there, and all I want is to get back to my family. So thank you for making that happen. I am grateful to be able to see my three sons again," he says.

"No, please we were all in danger. I was just doing what any good Officer would have," I reply.

"I thank you anyways Herr *General*, please enjoy your food!" he says, as he exits the suite.

"Not bad Lee, now pull the shade on the door and lock it," I say.

He looks at me quizzically but does as instructed. As he sits back down I disengage my strategic repellent field, revealing my real face.

"Wow…" Lee says, as I take a big bite of steak.

"What?" I ask trying some of the schnitzel.

"Nothing sir… I just figured you'd be uglier I guess," he says.

"Ha ha… And what the hell is that supposed to mean?" I ask.

"Well you know, you can look like anyone with that thing, I kind of figured you'd have picked someone much better looking than yourself is all," he replies.

"Oh… so you think there are people better looking than me?" I ask choking down another bite of steak.

"Um… no sir you are the most handsome man I know sir!" He says with a stupid grin on his face.

"You should probably be careful with comments like that though," I say.

"Why? You said I was free to go after 'your' title anytime," he argues.

"Oh that's true, you can. I just meant you should probably be careful with comments like that, you know looking the way that you do. You know Pot… Kettle… I'm sure you get the idea, or maybe you don't?" I reply.

Simms just smiles and enjoys his steak.

After finishing our meals we stack our plates outside the door and close it.

"Next stop Peru," I say yawning.

"Yes sir," *PFC* Lee says, while Simms looks like he's lapsed into a food coma.

"I think I'm going to grab some shut eye too," I say.

"Sounds good sir, I'll keep watch," Lee says.

"It's okay *Private*; my suit's AI will let me know if anything happens that we need to know about. You should get some rest too, I'm going to need you frosty when we get there," I respond.

"Well hell sir. That thing takes all the work out of work," he says.

"Yeah it's not too bad," I say, yawning and closing my eyes.

Roughly four hours later Dane wakes me with her usual, "Pssst, come on Johny, wake up."

"Are we there yet?" I ask still half asleep.

"Ten minutes," she says.

"Alright, thanks," I say opening my eyes.

Simms and Lee are still out cold. Kicking Simms's foot he wakes up and looks over at me.

"`Bout that time Sir?" he asks.

"Yes it is."

"You want to wake sleeping beauty or shall I?" he asks.

"No, no I got it," I say.

Simms smiles, "I figured you'd say that."

SMACK! Right across the face, Lee just about hits the ceiling. "What the fuck?!" he yells.

"Oh sorry, I don't know my own strength sometimes," I say.

"Yeah, right," He says sitting up and rubbing his face.

"No seriously, ask Bradley, when you see him. The first time we met I cracked one of his ribs and had no idea how it happened."

Lee just continues to rub his jaw, as the train finally comes to a stop.

"Zero-fifteen, pretty damn close to on time," I comment.

"Yeah, let's get this show on the road," Simms says.

"I agree, come on Lee pick up your jaw and let's go."

"Yeah, yeah," he says standing to follow us out.

Exiting the train, it looks as if Dane's intel on the area is accurate. This is a very small town with only a few houses, a gas station, what looks like it would be a police station, and one big road that just leads off into the mountains, which means it's likely they just use this stop as a means to bring in supplies out to the base. All except the 'would be' police station have their lights out completely.

We also seemed to luck out, in this hemisphere it's only a quarter moon, and by this time it's almost down, so very little ambient light at all. This all makes sneaking behind the small train station, which happens to be the only real source of light in the area a non-issue.

Rounding the corner we run into the rest of the team.
"Russian, Boomy, Bradley, Stills, good to see you all, any troubles on the train?" I ask.

"No, sir. Nothing I couldn't handle," answers Stills.

"Meaning?" I ask.

"Oh, some Nazi officer scum bag thought I was his little fräulein or something like that. I played along till he led me into a suite, and then knocked him out from behind. He'd been drinking heavily so I doubt he'll remember the impact," she answers.

Looking at Khabalov, "Didn't I order you to stay with her?" I ask.

"Uh… yes sir." He says.

"And?" I ask.

"He was not interested in me sir," he answers.

"Jesus… I'm surrounded by comedians," I say.

"As you sow, so shall you reap?" PFC Lee jumps in.

"That was not your queue," I state, pointing at his face, which he was still rubbing.

"Alright, so next step we need to get vehicles that can get us out to the base and of course head out while it's still dark. My intel says it's a pretty long drive so preferably we want them with full gas tanks, and maybe even a couple of spare cans of fuel. So fan out and keep in radio contact. Frequency two as before, when you find an item, report back," I order.

"Yes sir," they all answer.

Within fifteen minutes the Russian radio's back, "I have two VW Kübelwagen in front of police station. You want?"

"That'll work any guards we need to worry about?" I ask.

"No sir. They are in parking lot, no lights, just need key," he responds.

"Sir, Lee and Stills here, we have three full spare gas tanks," Stills reports.

"Great, let's have everyone meet over with the Russian and check these 'things' out then, the sooner we get to the base the better," I say.

"Roger that," the whole team replies.

Approaching the parking lot I have my enhanced infrared vision on and see that Lee and Stills have already made it to Khabalov. I also see the light at the 'police station' door mysteriously flicker out, and a group of six soldiers exit dressed all in black with night vision and automatic weapons closing on their position fast.

With a thought I go full cloak and make a dash for the closest soldier quickly snapping his neck I jump for the second sweeping his leg, he lets out a slight yelp as he falls, I snap his neck on his way down. This one everyone hears even my people, who are now all on guard trying to make out shadows in the dark.

"That you sir?" Stills calls out in a whisper.

The other four soldiers pause looking around realizing they're not the only hunters in this situation as they see their two comrades on the ground. They go back to back, two facing Khabalov, Lee, and stills two facing back toward me.

Another benefit of the Viper suit, no heat signature so to their infrared style night vision, I'm virtually undetectable.

Walking up to make my next victim, the soldier in front of me falls from a bullet wound, entering from the left temple and proceeding straight through.

"Simms that you?" I ask.

"Yes sir. I heard your other guy yelp and got into a decent position," he responds.

"Nice shot," I say, while snapping the neck of the one he was back to back with.

"Thank you sir. I take it you're the one down there I can't see, bending peoples necks in all kinds of unnatural positions?" he asks.

"I like to think of it as willful medical malpractice," I reply.

"Whatever you say sir; the other two are on top of our people now, yelling for them to put down their gas cans and weapons."

"Alright Simms, you take the one on the right I got the one on the left," I say, standing in front of the one on the left.

"Roger," He says, and the one on right suddenly goes limp.

The last one is freaking out at this point looking all around, trying to duck behind the Russian. Grabbing him by the head I whip him around and twist, it's all over.

"Wow…" Stills' says inhaling deeply.

I go visible, "You alright?" I ask.

"Yeah, yeah fine. I just uh, well I guess as alright as you can be with bullets whizzing by your head and you doing your thing," she says.

"You're okay Stills, area's clear now," I say.

"Thank you sir," she says.

"Hey what about us? May be the Russian needs a little comforting too eh?" Lee says, putting his hand on Khabalov's shoulder, who crosses his arms and just smiles.

"Everyone come on over to the parking lot, Khabalov got the vehicles, and Stills got us the extra fuel, we're ready to move," I broadcast.

"Seriously am I invisible now?" Lee asks.

"No, far as I know I'm the only one that can pull off that trick," I say.

"Oh great… rub it in. Probably bullet proof too," he says.

I don't say anything.

"Wait, are you bull shitting me right now?" he asks.

I just smile.

"What the hell do you need a team for?" he asks, as the rest of the team shows up.

"I get lonely, now load up," I order.

"But we still have no keys," Khabalov points out.

Walking up *Major* Bradley tosses me two sets of keys, "Those what you're looking for?"

"Where you find those?" Khabalov asks.

"Someone left them on a hook just inside the 'police station' I figured since they were all dead out here, I'd step in and take a look around for them," Bradley says with a smile.

"And that's why he's second in command," I say, looking over at Lee again.

Once the extra fuel is loaded and everyone is ready we head out on the massive road headed due west.

"Alright Dane, what's this route look like?" I ask.

Bringing up a map in my HUD she shows me a red line that leads west ninety three kilometers, and then south another twelve kilometers with the last two circling around each other repeatedly until stopping at near center.

"The second part of your trip, after the big turn is all incline taking you up into the Andes', and as I'm sure you noticed the final two kilometers are around the caldera itself, that will take you to the top," she says.

"Yeah, and I'm guessing they're not going to let us just drive up that road either. I'm sure they'll have a gate right before we get on that two mile wrap around."

"That is a likely security scenario Johnny."

"Alright, we'll cross that bridge when we get to it."

"It may not be a bridge Johnny."

"Seriously… you too? Damn, Lee was right I'm definitely reaping it today," I grumble.

"Alright team, we stay on this heading for another ninety kilometers then make a left. Kick back and enjoy the ride."

12 INFILTRATIONS IS A GAME BEST PLAYED IN THE DARK...

Driving at the topped out speed of sixty two kilometers per hour for the last hour and forty or so minutes, we were able to make our turn south without incident and continue on toward the mountain.

"Just passing kilometer eleven, Johnny. And radar scans show a guard station up ahead," Dane lets me know.

"Alright, radio the team and have everyone pull over for a meeting," I reply.

Coming to a stop along this desolate road in the middle of nowhere we all hop out. Everyone gathers around for a quick meeting.

"Alright kids, so we've got just under a klik to go and it appears we'll be running into a guard station," I explain.

"Okay so what's the plan? Play it like the train station Herr *General?*" Lee asks with a smile.

"The information I have on getting into this installation from their satellite system says that they require a special magnetic access pass to get through. I can mimic the magnetic field, but the ID to broadcast is another story, they are all randomized and transmitted upon request of a specific handset ID,." Dane says.

"Wouldn't they have to have a database of those IDs to transmit to then somewhere?" I ask.

"Yes, but not on any network I have made it into as of yet, which really means that it is likely they transmit the signal directly from this installation, as it is the only one to my knowledge I have not been able to infiltrate, their security is highly adaptive, even for tech of our time this would be beyond what we would consider state of the art," Dane suggests.

"No that's not going to work here Lee; my intel says they have a magnetic ID strip entrance on an alternating random ID generator tied to specific devices," I relay to the team.

"Oh, that's going to be an issue. What the hell does that mean?" he asks.

"It means that the front door is not an option."

"Alright, what about going around the check point all together then?" Lee asks.

"There seems to be a service road that runs along the gate, the turn off is approximately half a kilometer from here. It will allow you to get close enough to the fence to cut through, although it is an electric fence so you will likely need to close the circuit as you cut," Dane suggests.

"The BARB on a lower level laser setting can cut and fuse at the same time right? Like a laser scalpel?" I ask.

"Yes, level one actually should do what you request, but you must make your cuts very slowly so that the fence is fused, completing the circuit before removing your entry point," Dane replies.

"Understood."

Answering Lee, "Actually, that's exactly what we're going to do, but there is an electric fence," I say.

"Of course there's an electric fence, there's always an electric fence," Lee says.

"I got it covered Lee; don't worry your pretty little head about it *Private*. I'll take the lead at this point so everyone pile in a Kubelwhatsit and we'll be there shortly, then the fun starts. Remember we're less than a klik away from that checkpoint now, so lights out. Bradley I'll have you driving the other Kubelthingy, just follow me as close as possible," I say.

"Yes sir!" he says.

Just as Dane said, half a kilometer up there is a service road turn off. Slowing down we turn to the left, making sure the Major is still behind me I slow to a speed of around ten kilometers per hour. The idea at this point is to conserve energy for the climb, and keep engine noise to a minimum for any guards that may be in earshot.

It takes almost another kilometer before the road takes us close enough to the fence to make our move. I come to a stop examining the fence and the road on the other side, which appears to be completely dark. It is possible that the checkpoint was just that, only a checkpoint and the real security is up top.

"Dane, what are the chances that if I make this hole big enough to fit the Kubeltelecope through we can drive up to the top without being spotted?" I ask.

"My scans suggest this is a good strategy, although you will want to abandon your transportation approximately one half kilometer from the summit, as there is a guard station there, and what appears to be a massive elevator to take you down into the caldera itself. Also it is of note that the caldera of this Volcano is closed off at the top and solid. So this base is in an air pocket beneath."

"How do they get the UFO's out then?" I ask.

"There appears to be a massive Hanger door on the South side of the mountain that is in between the winding road layers. This is likely why I could not find it by normal Satellite imagery, as I was looking for an open caldera with which to launch these units from," Dane replies.

"Those clever, sneaky, bastards," I say.

"Indeed… Johnny," she responds.

Boomy whispers on the radio, "What are we waiting for boss?"

"Nothing you all wait in the Kubelschnitzel and be ready to roll,." I whisper back, jumping out and moving over to the electrified fence.

"Yes sir." He whispers back.

Drawing my BARB I set it to level one, another handy thing I can do with my mind now, and begin slowly cutting the fence, watching it fuse its own ends in front of me. Within ten minutes I have cut a hole big enough to drive through, and we're on our way.

As we round the corners I watch above for this UFO launch bay. They must have gone out of their way to blend it into the rock face of the mountain completely, because from the bottom it is not visible at all which means from the top I'm sure they made it equally difficult. Of course it doesn't help that at this altitude we have now entered the snow line.

Finally nearing the summit I kill the engine, and order Bradley to do the same. As we stop everyone jumps out weapons drawn and ready for action.

"Alright, first things first I want to plant this C-4 where it's going to do the most good. Russian, Boomy the top of this volcano is solid it's several meters thick with only a slight depression so we're heading out there to deposit this stuff in a manner that will bring the whole thing down on their heads."

"Boomy?" Berry asks.

"Yeah everyone needs a call sign, and well you're kind of short and stout," I say.

"I still don't get it," He says.

"You know like a dwarf, Happy, Dopey, Sleepy, Boomy?" I say.

"Uh…" He says.

"It's from a French fairy tale from the seventeenth century I believe," Stills says.

"I like her more and more, I thought I was the only one that knew that," Dane says.

"Yeah well, you're married and not even corporeal."

"That's enough of that, I'm married not dead. Well... shit I'm sorry," she replies.

"Look never mind, it doesn't matter. Just go out there and find me a nice week spot to plant your C-4," I snap at Boomy.

"Okay sir, are we doing this in a triangular pattern then?" he asks timidly.

"I knew Bradley picked you for a reason Boomy. That's exactly the plan. You got that Russian?" I ask still trying to shake off the comments about my dead sister, from my dead sister.

"He's already gone Johnny, looks like he's planting his C-4 to the northeast," Dane replies also timidly.

"Ah Russian's got northeast, Boomy you take west, and I'll take southeast," I say.

"Got it sir!" Boomy says, running over the crest in the Russian's footprints.

I follow and breakoff to the southeast with Dane using penetrating radar to select the weakest point. As I set my charge it occurs that these explosives aren't going to do a hell of a lot of good unless we can ensure that all their force is directed downward.

"What can we do about this?" I demand Dane.

"Scanning the area and considering possibilities," she responds.

"Seriously? I've got you at full power, let's go damnit," I reply.

"The plating on the bottom of your Kübelwagen was meant to withstand heavy mine explosion. Cutting off pieces and shaping them with your BARB should allow you to cover the C-4 and direct a larger portion of the explosive impact directly into the week points selected," she responds.

"About god damn time," I say running back to the rest of the team.

As I run I radio Boomy and Russian, "Hey guys we're going to need something to make these blasts directional, so meet me back at the wagons, I have an idea." I say.

"Not here, mine's all set," radios back Boomy.

"How so?" I ask.

"I found a lovely thermal vent to stuff mine into."

"Thermal vent? That's like a little cave right?" I ask, approaching the rest of the team.

"Uh… yes actually." he replies.

"Just checking," I say.

"You're going to give him a complex Johnny, please stop making your team pay for my slipup. I really didn't mean to hurt you, it's just the more of her memories I process the more I feel like her," Dane says.

"Okay I need everyone out of one of the Kubelprizes," I announce to Stills, Bradley, Simms, and Lee.

"What's up boss?" asks Stills.

Looking at her in the snow with her red nose, I take a deep breath and explain that I'm going to need to roll it over and remove some armor plating from the bottom.

Everyone migrates to the wagon closer to the summit while I lift the rear one onto its side as my team watches in disbelief.

"I've been lifting weights," I say.

"Go weights…" Stills responds looking more than a bit impressed.

Winking at her, I draw my BARB and increase the laser power to four. I begin cutting off two large pieces of sheet metal, each at least five centimeters thick.

"I don't think with this thickness any shaping is required Dane. Not with a big enough piece," I suggest.

"You are correct, a two by two meter square with that thickness will be heavy enough to make sure your blast is directed down as intended," Dane replies, just as the Russian appears over the crest.

"You have heavy metal for me?" He asks, in that thick Russian accent.

"I do, can you handle it?" I ask, knowing he's easily the most built of all of us.

"I think I can sir," He musters as he attempts to pick up a piece.

"Johnny these pieces are several hundred pounds each, he is going to hurt himself without the suit," Dane says.

"Alright, don't worry about it. I'll put those in place, the rest of you go scout the elevator and see what kind of resistance we're looking at," I order.

"Uh sir?" Simms says.

"Yeah what's on your mind Eyes?" I ask.

"Well if your explosion works aren't we done? Base destroyed? We win?" he asks.

"Not entirely. I was hoping to give George a present before I had to leave," I reply, finishing my final cut on the second piece of steal.

"Ah, and may I ask what it is we're risking our lives for then sir," he asks.

"Well, one because I order you to and two because I think George would really like to have you guys back, as well as a complete intact UFO, you know before I destroy what could be all of them. That okay with you Specialist?" I ask.

"Uh… Yes sir, sorry sir," he replies.

"Don't worry about it; I like my people to use their heads, and eyes."

"Ah thank you sir," he replies running up to the others who have already started to walk up toward the summit.

Radioing them I let them know I'll catch up as soon as the two pieces of sheet metal are placed.

With that I grab both, and run towards my C-4 location.

"Uh, Johnny I know you're probably not going to listen but even with the Viper this is highly dangerous to your own muscle tissue."

"I understand, thanks for the concern."

Reaching my C-4 load, after ten minutes of strenuous hauling and red alerts going off all over my HUD, I make sure to place the sheet metal so that the C-4 is in the exact middle. I then head for the Russian's site, with the last piece of steal.

With one less piece I am out of the red but I can feel the ache in my muscles already, I definitely pushed them too hard. It takes another eight minutes or so to get to the Russian's C-4.

As I approach my radio crackles to life, "*General* Steal is it? We've been expecting you for some time," an unfamiliar voice with a heavy German accent says.

Reaching the Russian's site I place the steal appropriately.

"Dane, analysis, who is that and where are they transmitting from?" I demand.

"Tracing… It's coming from the summit, its being broadcast from a tower toward where you just sent your team. Most likely at the elevator entrance or very nearby."

"Great, so they're probably underground. Who is IT!?" I demand.

"*General* I have your 'team' of miscreants here. You may want to answer before my trigger finger gets, how do you say? 'Itchy' and you lose one of them," the voice says.

"Johnny, based on his first transmission we must assume that they were expecting us due to another mole, or our time-line destroying friend."

"I'm here… What is it you want?" I radio back sounding more pissed off than ever.

"Ah, *General* Steal, good to finally hear your voice I almost had to shoot this wonderful specimen of a fräulein."

"Has to be a mole who else would know I'm going by Steal or that I'm a *General* in this time-line?" I say to Dane.

"Possibly, unless he's already tortured them enough to give him that information," Dane responds.

"That's a possibility I didn't want to consider, thanks."

"You have my attention… what should I call you? You know beside Nazi asshole…" I radio back.

"Now, now such name calling is uncivilized, you may call me Doctor Edison the fifth," he responds.

"Yeah, I thought killing around four billion people was uncivilized. Our definitions must be a little different wouldn't you say Mr. Edison, with a German accent?" I say.

"Johnny, if this is Thomas Edison I would surmise that the fifth means the number of times he's been cloned."

"Yeah I figured that part out myself, thanks."

"I never had any allegiance to anyone but myself. Considering who controls the world why wouldn't I have a German accent? And it's Doctor." He asks.

"Alright Mr. Edison, and what is it you want from me?" I ask.

"You're complete and utter surrender, boy," he says.

"Whoa, whoa now, first of all I don't know that you even have my team. So far all I know is that you know I have an attractive female on it."

"And what do you suggest then, hmmmm? Shall I personally waltz them out the front door so you can see them, and take a shot at me?"

"Yeah, that'll work, and while you're at it, can you bring me one of those fancy UFO's you've been working on down there?" I retort, cloaking with a thought.

"It was a joke herr Steal"

"Oh, I got it Asshole. You're going to have to provide proof of life first though, before I consider anything like surrendering myself though. Let me talk to them... and I mean all of them. For all I know you may

311

have them, you may not, you may have already killed them," I respond, while running towards the summit at full speed.

"I see, well I think we can prove that to your satisfaction." Edison replies, as I reach the elevator there are two guards outside both dead.

"*General! General* it's Stills, I'm sorry sir they grabbed us nearing the elevator," she says.

"It's okay Stills, it looks like you got at least two of them, is everyone okay?" I ask.

"Yes sir, they haven't touched us yet, they've locked us in a room by ourselves so far, but there are Eyes everywhere," she responds.

"It's okay Stills, Squawk seven and I'm going to get you out of there," I say.

"I think that should do it don't you Herr Steal?" Edison cuts her off.

"Oh not hardly Asshole, that was only one of my team. How do I know you didn't force her to say that under duress? Or that she's not the mole for that matter?"

"General? Its Lee sir, I'm sorry sir they came out of nowhere!" Lee gets out before being cut off.

"There that's all the proof you're getting herr Steal."

"Alright, Asshole and what will my surrender do for my team, are you going to let them go free?" I ask, examining the bodies a little closer.

"Johnny based on temperature these guards were killed after Edison started transmitting. They were also killed by one bullet."

"Yeah she said Eyes is free. See why it's important for people to have call signs?"

"Oh! Wow, you really learned a lot in your training." Dane says.

"You know for a super computer you can be really dumb. Change to channel seven, and continue to monitor two for Edison," I say.

"How about this they'll potentially live a little longer, until they prove to be of no more use to me that is," Edison says.

"That also means I told him that they missed at least one and that they've already killed their two guards they left up here. I used that opportunity to have 'Eyes' switch to channel seven, and made it sound like his call sign was 'Squawk'."

"So these doors should open very soon with reinforcements," Dane says.

"Now you're getting it, they're sending us an elevator," I answer Dane.

"No deal Edison, my team goes free if you want me," I say, backing away.

"Ha! That's never going to happen, Herr Steal."

"Eyes you on seven now?" I ask.

"Yes sir," He replies

"Good man, I take it you're in a good position?" I ask.

"Aye, sir."

"Good I expect this door to open up with a platoon coming out any moment now, don't worry about hitting me, and just take out however many you can."

"Yes sir," he replies, as the doors begin to slide open.

Eyes takes down the first two that march out of the elevator with a single shot. The second two I drop to one knee and punch in the gut, grabbing them around the tops of their heads and rolling backwards, their necks snap as they hit the ground.

The final two struggle to close the door, but I've already rolled back forward into the elevator. Punching one in the lumbar area of the spine I kick the other one in the head as he turns to look. I then make myself visible, and smash the first ones head into the wall of the elevator so hard he dies on impact. The second I disarm and cuff with his own cuffs.

"Alright Eyes, elevator is secure come on in."

"On my way sir," he replies.

Meanwhile Edison is yelling for a status report from the team that he sent up to kill us, over their radio's.

"What's your name?" I demand of my new prisoner. Who refuses to talk.

"You want to end up like your five buddies here?" I ask him.

"It's Adolf sir!" he responds in German.

"Wow, how ironic," I say to myself, as Eyes enters the elevator car.

"Okay Dane, now that you have his voice. I want you to radio a status report to Edison, they've captured the other two and are on their way back down."

"Done, Johnny. He says he will meet you at the elevator."

"Sounds good to me!" I say to Dane, knocking out Adolf with a quick jab to the neck.

"Eyes," I say pointing up at the elevators maintenance hatch. He nods, and I reach down to give him a leg up, and then go invisible, as he enters and closes the hatch.

"Okay Eyes, Edison's supposed to meet us at the bottom of this thing. Once he realizes that he's just got an elevator of two dead soldiers and not getting what he expected I'm going to follow him back to our people. I need you to stay up there ready to pop that hatch and cover our exit if need be," I say.

"Understood, sir."

Finally after what seems like five minutes the elevator doors open to at least twelve soldiers ready to fire. Edison steps out from behind them once he sees the state of the elevator car.

"Well, it seems he's better than I expected. I think it's time to kill a hostage and up the stakes." He says, turning to walk toward what appears to be a huge complex. The size of this cavern itself is enormous you could easily fit a large city in here, with plenty of head room.

13 SIGHT SEEING

Exiting the elevator, from what I can see, they have it set up so that electrical generation, water purification, and waste disposal are all on the bottom floor where the elevator stops. Just outside of the elevator I follow Edison and his men as they board a giant escalator that goes up at least two stories. When we exit we are on what appears to be a detention level. There is a large open center to this complex allowing you to see all the way up to the top of this massive cavern.

I continue to follow as they board a second escalator that goes up to a level which appears to be housing, and then one final escalator that takes us up to the actual laboratory level.

This is where he heads for a door, he turns and tells his men to wait outside and has one of them hand him their pistol.

"This is it; he's going to shoot one," I say, running to slide into the door before it closes. Sliding in, I brush against his fingers on the door.

Inside the room he walks up to a two way mirror and looks down on my team. Then he picks up a radio and contacts me.

"You realize of course I have to kill at least one of your people now Herr Steal."

"You could just surrender now," I answer.

"Ha. I am standing here trying to decide which of your team to execute and you think I should surrender? You are truly a fool Herr Steal."

"You know I think you said the same thing to my Grand-dad a few times." I reply.

"Wha?" is all he gets out before I grab his gun and stick it in his mouth, uncloaking with a thought.

"Guess who, Asshole," I say nice and quiet.

"Bu… bu…" he gets out. I slide the gun out of his mouth just a bit so he can talk.

"Call for help and they won't be transporting your consciousness anywhere except off of the wall and into a waste basket," I tell him.

"How can you be here? I was told you were dead," he says obviously shaken to see me.

"You know, time travel… it's a bitch sometimes."

He yells for his guards, they all start to run in. I drop his gun and pull my BARB turning to put him in front of me.

As they line up in parallel telling me to drop the weapon, with a thought I change the setting to lightning and then crank the power of the BARB up to eleven and fire a ball of plasma straight down the center. Electricity shooting out killing each one as it passes them.

Mentally switching it back to particle beam I set it at three, and point it back at Edison's head. Siren's begin to sound throughout the secret base.

"No, please?!" he begs.

"You have executed countless billions, why is it I should spare you?" I demand.

"This oughta be good for a laugh," Dane says.

"I... I... can change!"

"You know it seems to me you've already had five clone generations to do that. By the way at this setting, it will actually vaporize your brain," I say, pulling the trigger. The laser bores right through his head and into the concrete wall behind him.

Dropping him, I radio down to Eyes still in the elevator shaft, "Hey Simms, I've taken out Edison and all his guards, but those sirens likely mean there's a lot more about to make an appearance. We're sticking with the original plan. See if you can get your butt up here and we're taking a UFO out. I'll have the whole team in a few seconds."

"Sounds good, sir. Some directions would be helpful though, now that I see this place, it's freaking huge!" he responds.

"Yeah sorry, up three escalators and second door on the right, we'll meet you outside once you make it up the stairs though."

"On my way sir!" he replies, as I open a door to my left leading down into the team's holding cell.

"Hey did you guys miss me or what?" I ask.

"*YES?!?!*" They all yell.

"What, you were expecting Thomas Edison?" I say.

They all just look at me.

"What too soon?" I ask.

"Never mind, let's grab Eyes and get the hell out of here with a UFO!" I say.

Stills runs up and hugs me, "Thank you sir!"

"Whoa, you're welcome," I say.

"Oh, I'm so sorry sir, I uh forgot myself!"

"I didn't say you had to stop, you just surprised me is all," I say giving her a wink.

"Oh..." She says blushing, the rest of the team tries to look on as if not to have noticed.

"Now that's what I call a thank you," Dane says.

"Hey I saw her first, and you're not even corporeal!" I respond

"Where's Bradley?" I ask.

"Um... sir." Stills says with tears in her eyes.

"You better let me, Stills," Lee says.

"Wait, what's going on? Did that bastard kill him?" I demand.

"No sir. I'm sure he's running around here somewhere," Lee answers.

"What, is that supposed to mean!?" I reply.

"He was a mole sir, that's how Edison knew who you were. That's how he knew a lot of things that he shouldn't have known," Lee says.

"A lot of things?" I say in complete shock.

"Yes sir, like you being from the future, and the suits cloaking capabilities sir. He knew all about it."

"No wait that doesn't make any sense, if he'd have known about the suit he'd have known I was in the room when I brushed against him running in."

"Sir..." Stills says, still tearing up.

"Wait, just a second," I say.

"Dane did Bradley ever know the suit was bullet proof?" I ask.

"No Johnny, the last time it was mentioned he was in that 'police station' getting the keys. Which coincidentally I recorded a radio spike from the building at that time, which I attributed to faulty equipment, but it could have been a signal of some kind I suppose."

"Which also means, he probably never knew or realized it was sound proof either, and I that half the time I was talking to you."

"It is possible, that's why the suit was made this way, or at least one reason, however you also must consider that the knowledge he has comes from the future as well," Dane answers.

Now addressing the team, "Oye… I just checked my… brain; it looks like as much as I hate to admit it, he fooled me. When Edison was radioing me threatening to shoot one of you, he was listening for my radio, trying to pin down my location in the room."

"He fooled us all," The Russian says, putting his hand on my shoulder.

"Alright you know what, let's just get the hell out of here. This looks like a really boring room, we'll see if we can find us an exciting UFO, and hopefully we'll run into *Major* Bradley along the way, and he'll have some sort of explanation," I say, fighting back my own feelings of betrayal.

"YES SIR!" they all say.

As we walk out the door we see Eyes one level down and to the left locked in a fire fight trying to get up the last escalator. "You guys are all unarmed so stay back a minute, I'll take care of this."

"Eyes you look like you could use a little help." I radio.

"Wouldn't be a bad idea sir, I'm seeing a group coming up the escalators on the other side. There's at least thirty running up, and I'm running low on bullets."

"Got it," I say.

Watching from the upper deck I can see them coming at him.

"Alright I need you down, don't give them anything to shoot at." I radio.

"Yes sir!" he replies.

With a thought the BARB goes back to the electrical setting level eleven.

"Time for another ball of plasma I think Dane."

"You need to be careful with those Johnny, they use a large amount of power, too many more and you won't be able to jump," she says.

"Understood," I say, looking down from the upper deck I see *Major* Bradley leading the charge.

"Speak of the devil," I comment.

"Uh, Sir? That looks like *Major* Bradley? Leading the attack coming at me?" Eyes radios.

"*MAJOR!!*" I YELL:

He stops dead in his tracks looking up at me, the rest of the crowd keeps moving, and I fire a ball of plasma right into the middle of the crowd, and watch as the lightning streaks out all along the sides as it spins toward the group, killing every soldier it connects with.

"Okay Eyes up that escalator now!" I radio.

"Aye sir!" he says running up.

He approaches the group, "See that wasn't so bad." I say, obviously affected by the latest series of events.

"Uh, yes sir. Just like we planned right?" He says.

"Yeah, just like we planned…" I repeat trying to deal with what has happened.

The team just looks at me in shock.

"Alright, enough sulking around here, let's go get that UFO. I've got a time line to fix," I say, obviously now upset. Heading for the last escalator I take point with eyes pulling up the rear until we reach the top.

Exiting the escalator we see a field of UFOs. This level is literally at least twenty kilometers long and nothing but UFOs as far as we can see.

"Wow…" Says PFC Lee. "You have a preference *General?*"

"There must be a couple hundred… there's got to be enough here for a full scale invasion." I say.

Dane chimes in, "Twenty point five kilometers long by fifteen point two kilometers wide, allowing for point two kilometers for the sides and the skylight is three hundred seven point five cubic kilometers with a size of roughly thirty six point five seven cubic meters per UFO and an average distance of nineteen point eight one meters in between. That would be approximately four hundred twenty five UFOs."

"Great thanks, that's much better," I reply.

"Well to be fair we don't know what lies at the other end of this complex, they actually could have decks of these things and elevators," Dane responds.

"You never know when to shut up do you?" I ask.

"Uh… Oh, apparently not, I'm sorry Johnny."

"Yeah… it's alright you still don't have the emotional detection that the real Dane did. I get it."

"So boss?" Lee asks, still waiting for an answer.

"Well by my calculations, our caldera collapse isn't going to do much against this complex or the number of UFOs they already have. The sheer volume of earth that either they removed, or the volcano left open for them was not something I could have planned for. So we need a plan to blow this base, any suggestions?" I ask.

"What about like a self-destruct sequence on the UFOs themselves? You said they all had them right?" Lee asks.

"True, but you're not seeing the bigger picture here *Private*. There are God knows how many of these damn things in here it would take days to set the self-destruct on all of them. Even if we set one and manage to get them to cascade, they still have the facility to build more," I say.

"Where this place get power?" asks the Russian.

"I believe it's all geothermal," I reply.

"Huh… I know not what to do with that," responds the Russian.

"That is correct Johnny, from what I have been able to ascertain from a few systems I have managed to crack. This is all based on an old design of your Grandfathers again, probably stolen by Marconi."

"Alright, so how do we use that?" I ask.

"Well water is trapped in a massive closed circuit pipe like a huge oval that runs down near the magma to boil and turn it to steam, as it turns to steam it is forced up the other side of the oval. Once that steam reaches the top it spins a turbine creating electricity, it then condenses and basically rains back down the other side of the pipe again constantly repeating the cycle. It's perfectly clean, sustainable energy," Dane says.

"Wait... that's it! Russian you're a genius!" I say.

"What I say?" he asks, as I begin to examine the UFOs around us. The others just look at him and shrug.

"Good job," Lee says slapping him on the arm.

"Wait I said it all," Dane replies, as I board the nearest UFO.

"Yeah but he asked the right question."

"I see, so what is this plan?" she asks.

"You chose now to stop reading my mind?" I ask, while the rest of the team follows me up the ramp.

"Oh... OH, you're going to blow the volcano?!" she replies.

"Now you got it. Why do you have a better plan to take out this base?" I ask.

"Well… no actually, but how do you intend to do that? This is obviously a very stable magma chamber. As of our own time-line, in the twenty fourth century this volcano has not erupted since ancient times," Dane says, I continue to look around the ship.

"Okay, so basic volcano principle then says that there's a vent that keeps all the toxic gases and other pressures from building up then correct?" I ask.

"Well, yes, that is very likely, but that could be miles out at sea though," Dane answers.

"Yeah well I'm betting it was originally the small crevasse that Boomy found for his C-4, and that Marconi and his myriad of scientists came up with an alternate man made system."

"That's actually not a bad working theory!" Dane replies.

"You know, you don't have to sound so surprised, every time I come up with a brilliant idea," I answer, with the team still standing by the entrance. I begin making my second round of the ship.

"Uh… should we be doing anything sir?" Stills asks.

"Yeah, sorry guys, I'm too used to working alone. Look to your right, you'll find the armory. You and Simms grab a couple of rifles and cover that entrance for me. Boomy and Russian just arm up, and any explosives you see are always handy."

"Yes sir!" they respond.

"And me?" Lee asks.

"Uh, just grab some weapons… and try not to get shot." I respond still examining the ship.

"Okay then."

"What are we looking for here Johnny?" Dane asks.

"A way to access their internal detonation device, I'm sure it's got a panel to open or something. You can't leave these things without service entries."

"There is a panel to your right on the floor that appears to have a fairly large energy signature under it, with a hinge on one side," she replies.

"Now you're talk'n," I say walking over to it.

Removing my toolkit from its pouch I find a laser dye. Now a laser dye is a wonderful device if you don't have a screw driver that will fit your particular screw. It's all the size of a laser pointer, but with the press of a button it opens a tripod with magnetic feet, to be mounted directly over the screw you need to remove. The laser itself can be controlled by a dial on the top for laser width, and slider on the side for depth. Thus allowing you to customize it to any tap and dye set you may require, it also has an auto-detect feature that is near flawless, but I've always preferred the manual setting.

After disintegrating the screws on the four corners of the access panel, and putting my toolkit away, I use the finger holes on the opposite side of the hinge and carefully lift it open.

"Bingo!" I say aloud.

"Sir?" Lee asks.

"Bingo… it's a game? With random numbers and balls?" I say, as he still looks confused raising an eyebrow at me.

"Also an expression, as in I found what I was looking for."

"Oh… that glowy thing?" He asks.

"Yes, that glowy thing, supplies the power for this whole ship. A plasma based power core, this is technology far beyond what they should be capable of." I say.

"That helps to explain the readings I was taking outside of the ship's hull," Dane says.

"What readings?"

"The metal, it is of very similar composite to that of the Viper suit, and the Relativistic Prototype," she answers.

"So these are new models then? You didn't mention that about the one we filleted."

"That's correct this is definitely a newer model than that one, it had a simple stainless steel aluminum alloy hull. This one is likely even capable of space flight with that hull coupled with that drive core," Dane replies.

"Oh that's just wonderful," I state.

"What, is this what we need?" Lee asks.

"Yeah this is what we need alright," I say, carefully removing the crystal surrounded blue plasma drive core from its chamber. As it pops out like an oversized glowing antique fuse; the lights and the entire UFO go out.

"Okay so what's the plan boss?" Eyes yells back over his shoulder.

"The plan is for us to migrate to the next ship over at the moment."

"Aye sir," Stills and Simms respond, hopping to their feet from a flat lying snipers position. They move down the ramp in pairs attempting to cover every angle.

"I don't understand, they should be swarming us by now," I say to Dane. As we run up the ramp into the next ship.

"Perhaps they are just guarding the exits. Not expecting you to be able to take one of their ships?" Dane posits.

"Possibly," I say, heading over to the flight controls.

"Stills, Simms, same deal keep that ramp covered. Boomy, Russian, behind them. *Private* Lee, please tell me you know how to fly," I say, as Stills and Simms lay down on opposite sides of the door to the ramp, and both look over their shoulders not believing what they just heard.

Lee walks up behind me looking at the controls. "Uh... don't worry boss I got this?" He says scratching his head.

"You don't have a clue do you?" I ask.

"Not a one sir. Sorry."

"Don't worry this thing looks like a child could fly it. Luckily you qualify."

"Gee thanks, I think?"

The controls are laid out in a triangular shape, and look like something out of an old video game as opposed to real flight equipment.

"Okay look, just have a seat and I'll go over this with you." Lee quickly sits down and I continue, "This blue stick is up and down. The red one is right, left, forward and backward, and the yellow stick at the top just adjusts the pitch, just leave that one alone. The red button in the middle is 'all stop'. You with me so far?" I ask.

"Uh... up, down, right, left, forward, backward, stop. Yeah got it," He replies. "Yeah that seems easy enough."

"Okay good, that's all I need you to be familiar with for now," I reply, walking over to their armory I find they have ear pieces for radios and even Kevlar vests.

"Stills, Russian front and center," I say.

They both run over to me, "Sir!"

"I want you to take these vests, make sure everyone puts one on, also take these ear pieces and set them all to channel twelve, and pass those out as well," I say.

"Yes sir!" they reply, while I continue to search the armory.

"Here we go, programmable remote detonator. What frequency is that C-4 at up top?" I ask Dane.

"Twenty seven point eight hertz," she replies, and I set the detonator accordingly.

"Okay, now that we're all on the same page it's time to get this done," I say.

331

14 THE GREAT ESCAPE

"I want Simms to keep this door covered, this is our boat now, *Private* Lee you back him up where needed. Boomy, Russian, and Stills, I want you running to all the ships around here preferably without getting spotted and grabbing as many of those vests, earpieces, and gun clips as you can. I want this boat loaded to the brim by the time I return," I say.

"Yes sir," they all reply.

"Lee I want you ready to take off at a moment's notice. With every one of you on board got it?" I ask, handing him my reprogramed detonator.

"Roger that sir," he says.

"Good, now when I give the order you press that button, and the roof will blow, once all the slag hits which I've looked and we're well outside that radius, that's when I want you to get underneath the hole," I say.

"Wait, what?" Stills asks.

Ignoring her I continue, "Okay, now here's where it gets dicey. I have to go handle the complete destruction of this base. So I need you all to be clear here. When I give that signal, every one of you needs to be getting back on board this ship. Once everyone is back on board I want you to have this boat floating right over the middle of the base under the hole."

Grabbing Lee by both arms and looking him dead in the eye. "I'm counting on you Lee, after blowing the roof be under that hole. If you don't think you can do it now's the time to speak up!" I order.

"No I got it sir, but what about you?" Lee asks looking very concerned.

"Obviously, I may not make it back kids, but that's what we all signed on for remember? Now promise me when you're under the hole keep the door open for me until you see the magma coming. One sprinkle of molten rock and this tub is done. I'll do my best to be here by then. If I'm not though, you hit this button and you get your asses out of here and back to the mountain."

"Okay but…" Lee starts.

"No 'buts' *Corporal*. Follow your orders these people's lives are now in your hands. You see magma I want this team up and out the top of this mountain and headed due north. Take it to George, that's it. GOT IT?" I demand.

"Yes, sir… we got it. Wait *Corporal?*" Lee says.

"Yeah added responsibility, field promotion if you do it right. If you don't, well it could be the shortest field promotion in history."

"Dane where's the tracking device in this boat?" I ask.

"Starboard side under the 'Do not touch' panel Cap'n," She replies.

"Oh for crying out loud you're processing her early twenties?"

"Aye… RRR"

"Don't let it interfere with the mission," I order.

"No, sir Cap'n."

"Why did she have to get so into Role Playing Games in college?" I ask out loud.

Quickly moving to the panel Dane indicated I find it to be a simple latch to open. Once opened the transmitter portion of the circuitry lights up on my HUD, and I carefully disconnect the ribbon cable running to it.

Turning back to my team, "Alright, tracking device is disabled, everyone has their orders I expect them to be followed to the letter. I'll see you shortly. Eyes, remember, no one on or off this boat once you see magma," I say, heading down the ramp.

"Roger that sir," they all agree.

"Good now keep each other safe, and get this boat stocked until I return!" Are my last words as I step off the ramp.

"Alright, Dane scanners up, where's this gas vent?" I ask.

"Well from what I can tell of the complex it doesn't run this far up matey, so it be down through the belly of the beast," she replies.

"Yeah, great! So bottom level then? Just give me an 'aye' for yes and an 'rrr' for no," I say obviously irritated.

"Aye, Cap'n!"

"At least that makes some sense, that is where we saw all the power generation, and utility type equipment," I say, walking over to the edge of the top floor.

"That be the safest bet Johnny, reviewing my charts I spy a rather large pipe I noted that I couldn't account for." Which a map to is now displayed on my HUD and then minimizes to the side.

I walk off the edge, and think static as I fall. A half bubble of static electricity erupts from the bottom of the suit as I near the bottom and gently lands me on the rock bottom.

"I didn't know you had learned to use the suit to that degree yet Johnny," Dane states sounding almost normal.

"Yeah, I've figured out a few things that I thought might come in handy," I reply, heading into the utility area, all conversations with Dane now occur within my head.

There are several turbine style enclosed generators lined up, with all of the pipe works that Dane had described for thermal power generation.

"I have it Matey!" Dane says.

"The gas exhaust?" I ask.

"Yes, it is straight ahead and fifteen paces to yar left," she replies while highlighting it on the map.

As I begin walking toward it the HUD goes red. "Dane?"

"It appears you were just hit with some sort of advanced weaponry cap'n!" She replies as the HUD returns to normal.

"Is it dangerous?" I ask ducking back in between two of the generators.

"Quite. It is most likely from our own time-line, and if it is what I believe it is. This is the one weapon that the Viper suit does not offer complete protection against, it's basically a rifle styled BARB with an oversized power cell, savvy?" Dane replies.

"Excellent, so what's that mean, one more hit and I'm toast?" I ask.

"It would have to be a direct and a sustained hit cap'n. However Dane be smart and did build in some aid for it," she replies.

"Okay, the Relativistic Prototype, the energy can be converted and stored, like the electricity?" I ask, poking my head out to look around and find where the blast came from.

"Aye, and your power levels took a significant hit earlier when ye be firing off plasma balls. They were drained to eighty seven percent, just one hit from that there cannon and ye be back at one hundred percent. The RP be capable of storing the one hundred percent long term, with an overflow of two hundred percent cap'n.

Anything over one hundred dissipates quickly however," she says.

"So don't let him hold the thing on me past two hundred percent," I ask, still scanning.

"Aye to be sure, but it has never been tested at that high a power rating, there be theories that you would burn to a crisp inside the suit at no more than one hundred fifty percent," she replies, as a shot wizzes by my head.

Ducking back for a moment I reply, "Well that's good to know, I guess. Being cooked alive isn't high on my priority list."

"Johnny that shot came from approximately thirteen meters southeast of here," she says, lighting up a red square on my HUD with distance vectors and an overlay of objects in between.

"Is that an oil drum just to the left of it?" I ask.

"Aye, it does appear to be petroleum based."

I draw my BARB, setting it to particle beam level eight. Rolling forward I fire hitting the drum and a stream of fiery oil shoots towards where the shot came from. Someone screams.

"Direct hit Cap'n!!" Dane yells.

"I hate you so much right now," I remark.

"Ye know now that you're talking to me in your head, ye technically be talking to yourself again," Dane says.

"Yeah well, I'm okay with it now, shut up and let me concentrate," I reply.

"What's the matter John?" a voice calls out.

"Isn't that Bradley's voice?" I ask.

"It does sound like he, a bit Cap'n, analysis confirmed."

"That you Bradley?" I yell.

"Well that's the name you know me by, but it's not my real name John," he yells back.

"Is it Shit Head?" I yell.

"Ha ha. That's quite the wit you have there John, I bet you're wishing you would have let me stay in that infirmary now aren't you?"

"Well if you're not going to tell me your name, I get to pick one right? And yeah I can't say the thought hadn't crossed my mind." I yell peaking over the pipe I had rolled behind to see if Dane can pin down where he's yelling from.

"You go ahead John, you wouldn't know me even if I did tell you. I have to admit though I am surprised you managed to grab a Viper suit, and get it through before the time portal closed behind me," he replies.

"Whoa, that be…" Dane starts.

"Yeah I get that," I interrupt, "but killing him now only stops further damage it doesn't repair the time-line I've got to kill this schmuck at his original arrival in 1939!" I reply to Dane.

"Okay how about Riefenstahl? Eh? You like that one?" I yell, still watching, as Dane calibrates for the acoustics of the room.

"Oh, very good John, but that was just an alias," he yells back, as I think to make myself invisible.

"Johnny, he be to your right behind a generator, still at approximately thirteen meters, I suggest level eleven on ye BARB, the plasma ball will burn strait through the generator, and hit him," Dane says.

"Good keep track of him I want to get as much information as I can before I kill the little bastard first though."

"Oh, aye good plan," Dane replies.

Redirecting my attention back to Bradley, "Yeah, I figured that out numb nuts. Just like being my friend. Except you don't even look like a Riefenstahl," I yell.

"Aw John did I hurt your feelings?" He yells back.

"I'm not even going to dignify that with a response. So what was the plan anyway, go back in time blow half the planet to the moon? Doesn't sound like you thought that one through does it?"

"Ah yes the comet incident. Well you see John I'm not the only one with power over this planet, and that was a catastrophic accident."

"So your dad Marconi made that call did he?" I yell.

"Ha, something like that. Your knowledge of the situation here is actually impressive," he yells.

"Johnny he moved up from the other generator, I think he be trying to flank ya."

"Yeah I see it on the HUD, it's okay let him come."

"Hey John, what did you think of the friend I left for you in New Frankfurt?" he yells.

"Oddly enough he had a lot more intel than you did. Why is that?" I yell back.

"Ironically, I was supposed to bring him in so he could supply me with any new information he had remembered once he was in the brig, you know before his expiration date, but you cracked my ribs and screwed that all up."

"Gee, I'm sorry to hear that Shit Head," I yell, watching him move up another generator. "So, how do you suppose he got so much information that you failed at?" I yell.

"Ha, that's the problem with blending clones sometimes they can access the memories of one of the 'clonies', and sometimes they access the others, only gaining access to the other donor's genetic memories late in their life cycle, or if a traumatic event occurs like coming face to face with the donor. Unfortunately your DNA was so weak, it seems that he didn't remember anything from your side until he actually saw you. Then it seems after talking with you long enough he literally became you, he actually tried to attack ME! I had to knock him out before he killed me in that hole."

"Ha, so much for weak DNA, eh? Sounds like my weak DNA beat out whoever you mixed it with in the end, it also sounds like you need a better intelligence gathering system!" I yell, watching him move to the last generator before mine.

"I don't know this one's worked pretty well for centuries now, and we always learn from our mistakes," he replies, now rounding the last generator.

As he spins around to the generator next to me I'm already trained on him and ready to fire when he turns to get the drop on me.

"So you really think you can beat us Johnny boy?" he yells.

"I'm pretty sure I get to beat you multiple times actually, you should take note. This is the start of a very humiliating and repetitive defeat for you *Major*."

"Johnny, John, John, you know it really is rude to call names, and throw around insults like that. Besides don't you think I'd remember if you had beaten me before?" he says spinning out from behind the generator to make his shot.

As he does I mentally change my BARB to the particle beam at level six, and fire at his rifle. Unbeknownst to me instead of being invisible like I had thought, Dane had me appear as a pirate complete with peg leg, and his shot hit me square in the chest. Forcing my aim to only graze his right arm.

He continued to roll to the next generator which was only slightly to my right, and I can see him holding his arm.

"Power levels at one hundred forty five percent." Dane announces, now sounding like her old self.

I hear Bradley / Riefenstahl laughing around the corner.

Quickly rolling backwards I duck behind a generator myself. "Okay, Dane anything you want to share with the rest of the class? Like maybe the reason that asshole just hit me square in the chest while I'm supposed to be invisible? And while you're figuring that one out, why don't you explain to me why he doesn't remember me beating him before if it's in his past?" I demand.

Just as I finish asking the questions Bradley while still laughing through the pain, yells, "Nice outfit John, I didn't realize Halloween came so late this year."

"What did you do!?" I demand of Dane again.

"It's entirely possible that when you thought of being invisible, I processed that as Pirate Captain with peg leg," she finally replies.

"Are you kidding me!?" I scream "This asshole has a real good chance to kill me now because you're processing memories?! I thought you were incapable of hurting me?"

"Well technically he hurt you, I just didn't make you invisible," she argues.

"Great, tell that to my French fried corpse in a minute." I say, while watching him apply something to his arm with my advanced view.

"How's that arm Shit Head?" I yell.

"About as good as your Viper suit I would imagine," He replies.

"What's he talking about?" I ask Dane.

"Well the shot he made may have temporarily screwed up some power relays, which I am actively trying to route around. Luckily he doesn't know about your A.I. as the Viper was never supposed to have one, and your clone never had the opportunity, or desire it would seem to tell him."

"Great what does that mean for me right now!?" I demand, not noticing she's finally stopped with the pirate speak.

"It means that you are currently cloaked, but that you are periodically uncloaking for a split second here and there."

"Great, just get it fixed," I tell her.

"Yeah, that was a nice shot, I'll give you that. I didn't expect to have to use any special features on a schmuck like you. So I figured, what the hell a pirate I shall be," I yell to Bradley.

"Underestimating your opponent, that's a fatal flaw Johnny boy."

"Yeah so is having a temperamental suit apparently," I say to myself.

"Hey! It's not my fault her memories are so enrapturing and overwhelming," Dane replies.

"Is it fixed yet?" I reply not even acknowledging her excuses.

"Almost," she says as I watch him move up to the other side of generator that I'm up against. He's now only eight feet away from me.

"So you ready to surrender yet, I have George holding your cell, and you know how he hates waiting?"

"Oh, definitely. You do know another shot like the last one will bake you alive in that suit right? Or did you forget I actually know the specs of that unit and where it was at in development?" he replies, slowly creeping around the side of the generator.

"I know that's one THEORY!" I yell "Can I take that as a maybe on the surrender then?"

"He is right it's definitely hotter in here," I tell Dane.

"All environmental and system control systems coming back online now," she says.

Upon hearing this I roll to the next generator to get a better angle on Riefenstahl. He must have caught the last glimmer before my invisibility went fully online and we both fire at the same time, this time he's firing off of hearing mostly, and hits me in the left shoulder. Thanks to my perfect marksmanship scores, I catch him right between the eyes, and he's over. At least in this time.

"Johnny that shot could cause a critical overload. He managed to hit right where I just rerouted through," Dane announces.

"Then reroute through the other side. Quickly!" I insist.

"I am attempting to do so, but by my calculations this will be close."

Looking at the man I once called friend, his body starts to dematerialize and disappear in front of my eyes.

"Where the hell did he go?!" I demand.

"Unknown, scans are now showing no life signs in the immediate area," Dane replies.

"Alright, where's this vent then Dane? Let's finish this and get the hell out of here before I blow up," I say.

Dane highlights the pipeline on my HUD.

"Okay, uncloak me, drop shields, and shut down every unnecessary system and get it fixed," I order.

Making my way to the portion where the pipe actually goes down to the magma pocket I remove the plasma core from my satchel.

There is a vent opening here that looks like it would be for pressure release and maintenance, a large valve wheel next to its' right side is used to open it. It does look like the plasma core will fit through one of the vent slots though if I can manage to get it all the way open. I quickly slip the core back into my satchel and attempt to open the valve, but it doesn't budge. I quickly look around for a bar or a handle of some type to get extra leverage on the wheel.

My suit is getting hotter by the second, and I'm running up and down the rows of generators looking for something anything to give me the leverage I need. When suddenly I feel myself start to feint heat exhaustion, I know it well having served at the North Pole during the last major war of the twenty third century.

As I start to fall to the floor, my pulse is racing and it feels like I'm going to throw up.

Suddenly I feel it, Viper system reboot. My body quickly starts to cool. "Alright Lee, blow the roof," I order.

"Roger that. It's coming down sir." He responds.

"Good, now everyone get your asses on board and get that boat in the air," I order.

I slowly stumble back to my feet, and manage to make it back to the wheel. "Come on Dane... let's go... any second now," talking to myself again.

The HUD starts to power on, it slowly fades in. "Dane? Are we up?" I ask desperate to finish this before any guards appear.

"Almost... Done!" She announces

Full HUD, power level indicators, RP indicators, strength enhancement, and cloaking system online.

"Great now let's turn this damn wheel," I say.

Grabbing it with both hands and twisting with all my might I can feel the Viper's aid enhancing my movement, the wheel is actually starting to buckle, and distort its shape as I turn it. Red lights begin flashing on my HUD telling me the load is too great for the Viper's sleeves. Ignoring all the warnings I feel the suit begin to tear at the left shoulder where it had been hit, but finally the vent starts to crack open, the wheel begins to move more freely and soon the vent is wide open.

"Got it. Time to drop this plasma core and get the hell outta dodge."

"Is everyone on board?" I ask before dropping the core.

"We're running up the ramp now sir Stills replies.

"Great timing Stills. Strap yourselves in, this could be a bumpy ride, and if all goes well I'll see you in a few, be ready on that 'up' lever Lee," I order.

"Roger that sir!" he replies.

I drop the core into the vent and then use the Vipers strength to actually pinch the top of the pipe mostly shut, just to build up a little extra pressure. Running back toward the escalators the guards are streaming out now.

"There must have been an alarm when you opened the gas exhaust line," Dane says.

"Gee you think?" I reply through gritted teeth, jumping up to the second level. The static zapping my exposed shoulder skin as it spider webs across the opened portion. The suit has activated its self-healing or repair cycle.

All the guards on the escalator turn and start tripping on each other trying to get back up to me. There is another group running straight at me though and one grabs my arm, and then goes limp, hard to tell if it was from the massive electrical shock, or the sniper bullet passing right through his head. The group slows, and tries to surround me.

"I said strap yourselves in, and that's an order," I radio.

"What's that sir, your last transmission broke up a little," Stills radios back, as two more soldiers go limp.

"Ah… we're going to have a talk about taking orders you two," I say.

"Roger that sir," Stills and Simms say as two more fall to the ground.

The entire mountain shakes.

"Johnny my readings indicate the plasma core just hit bottom, the chain reaction is beginning," Dane says, as everyone tumbles to the ground. There is a huge upward draft so intense that it blows the entire instillation upward. The ship rises as I'm flying through the air.

"Uh, sir that's not me?" Lee Radios.

"It's probably a failsafe to keep you from hitting bottom," I suggest, still flying and flailing through the air with no way to stabilize myself. I finally land flat on my back knocking the wind out of me and I feel an intense pain shoot through my left side, but I'm now on the upper deck.

Coughing my way to a sitting position I wheeze out, "status report?!"

"Sir there's lava and the door it's closing on its own!" *Corporal* Lee radios.

"It's true sir, he's not touching a damn thing!" Stills says.

I jump to my feet holding my left side the HUD has a readout of my entire body showing two broken ribs, "Alright, just try to stabilize it where I said," I say still wheezing.

"Here goes nothing!" I announce, starting at a slow run holding my side, and quickly picking up speed toward a giant piece of rock that had dropped from up top.

Lava is coming up all around the instillation and the base itself is starting to sink melting as I run. I jump onto the rock and make a massive vertical leap straight up, which is calculated by Dane's A.I. to put me right into the rapidly closing door.

As my feet leave the rock I immediately feel another huge updraft from the volcano, flipping me end over end and carrying me right up past the ship.

"I missed it! Get out now, that's an ORDER!" I shout over the coms.

"Johnny! You're going to land... on top," she says, as I crash onto the top with a massive thud on my left side, again.

I scream, as the pain explodes through my body. I start to slide down, unable to stop myself while scrambling to grab and stick to anything on the hull before flying off the side. I just manage to grab the top of the door as it closes on my fingers.

"GO GO GO! I'm ON!" I order.

Lee hits the blue stick and we start rising like a rocket.

"John it's too late my sensors show it's about to go critical it's going to blow NOW!" Dane yells, instantly she gives me a morphine injection straight to the carotid artery.

Another huge updraft, I look down over my shoulder and see Dane's right, the lava's launching to engulf us there's no way we're going to make it.

My eyes start to blur from the morphine, and thinking this is the end I see my life, and everything I missed flash before my eyes. Apparently one of these thoughts activated the Relativistic prototype and we're gone.

Coming to I hear some unintelligible words in the distance, a language I've never heard before. Even after being stationed all across the globe. What's odder is that Dane's translation software isn't making any sense of it. I also hear a grinding sound, but can't distinguish where it's coming from, as this room echoes almost endlessly.

"That was so fast. What year did you jump to? I can't get a reading off of anything!" Dane asks.

I catch the power level on my HUD, the Relativistic Prototype is at thirty two percent.

I drowsily answer, "I don't… I don't know… I just thought of my life and what I had missed… I know you hit me with a shot of happy juice, but why is everything gold?" I ask, looking around still heavily medicated, and in a great deal of pain.

"I'm not sure Johnny, but it is real gold and it's thick. That's what is interfering with my readings I can't penetrate it," she replies.

"I guess that means we're not in Kansas anymore."

"We were in Peru near the Bolivian border Johnny, I'm doing a full workup on your vitals now."

"It's an expression Toto…" I weakly get out while observing some strange oblong shadows on the wall before slipping into unconsciousness again.

ABOUT THE AUTHOR

Husband, Father, Musician, Student, and Dreamer.

Proof

Made in the USA
Charleston, SC
09 November 2013